PRAISE FOR THE NOAH WOLF SERIES

Over 2 Million Copies Sold.
Over 120,000 Five Star Reviews.

"Soon to be a critically acclaimed masterpiece."

AMAZON REVIEW

"This series has replaced Vince Flynn's Mitch Rapp as my favorite read."

AMAZON REVIEW

"No remorse. No guilt. No inner conflict. The perfect assassin."

AMAZON REVIEW

"I would highly recommend it to everyone that likes Lee Child, Brad Thor, David Baldacci, etc."

AMAZON REVIEW

IN THE GRIP OF DARKNESS
A NOAH WOLF THRILLER

DAVID ARCHER

VINCE VOGEL

RIGHTHOUSE

ISBN-13: 978-1-63696-406-5

ISBN-10: 1-63696-406-0

Cover design by: Damonza

Printed in the United States of America

www.righthouse.com

www.instagram.com/righthousebooks

www.facebook.com/righthousebooks

twitter.com/righthousebooks

NOAH WOLF THRILLERS

Code Name Camelot (Book 1)
Lone Wolf (Book 2)
In Sheep's Clothing (Book 3)
Hit for Hire (Book 4)
The Wolf's Bite (Book 5)
Black Sheep (Book 6)
Balance of Power (Book 7)
Time to Hunt (Book 8)
Red Square (Book 9)
Highest Order (Book 10)
Edge of Anarchy (Book 11)
Unknown Evil (Book 12)
Black Harvest (Book 13)
World Order (Book 14)
Caged Animal (Book 15)
Deep Allegiance (Book 16)
Pack Leader (Book 17)
High Treason (Book 18)
A Wolf Among Men (Book 19)
Rogue Intelligence (Book 20)

PROLOGUE

Dr. Anthony Palmer eased his car onto the winding road that led home, the landscape bathed in the golden light of the setting sun. The tall trees bordering the road appeared to lean down on him, adding to the foreboding tension of the phone call.

His colleague Dr. Jonathan Taylor's voice crackled over the car's speakerphone. "Tony, I just don't get it. The protein strands should have bound with the subjects. Why didn't they?"

Palmer's grip on the steering wheel tightened as he navigated a sharp turn. "Our analysis must be wrong," he said.

"No. I went over the numbers at least five times. They should have bound at seventeen-point-four centigrade. The test should have been a success. Why wasn't it?"

Palmer sighed. "Look, we'll go over it all on Monday," he said. "It's my weekend off. My mind always works better when I'm not concentrating directly on the problem."

Jonathan's voice took on a more ominous tone. "You know they're not going to put up with this for long."

Palmer almost groaned, frustration creeping into his voice. "Put up with what?"

"Failure, Tony."

"We're not failing. We're getting closer each time."

"But they want results. We need to give them results."

"And we will."

"How can you be so cool about it?"

"Because I believe we'll get there in the end."

"But we're not getting there, Tony. Not since we had that breakthrough in mapping *Nematocerebrus dominatus*'s genome. That was eight months ago. We should be into the integration phase. Incubation at least."

"We will be. We will," Palmer assured him, turning onto his street.

There was a pause, filled with the low hum of the car's engine. Then Jonathan's voice returned, more anxious than before. "You know they've threatened me, right?"

Palmer rolled his eyes, though his heart rate quickened slightly.

"Told me to speed things up or they'll get someone else in," Jonathan went on. "Take the research off us. You know what that means, right? It means they'll kill us both, Tony. Kill our families."

"We're the only ones who know what to do. Anyone else would take at least a decade to catch up going through our research. And only I know where *Nematocerebrus dominatus* is found. Only I know the location."

"You think they won't find out? They are all-seeing.

Remember Tony? The all-seeing, all-knowing Council. We're in too deep to sing a different hymn now."

Palmer exhaled sharply as he pulled into his driveway, the garage door opening automatically. "So what?"

"So what? So we need to show them something by the end of the month. So please, Tony. Take this seriously. We need to find out what is going wrong with the experiments."

Palmer parked the car inside the garage, the engine ticking as it cooled. "OK, John. We'll look into it on Monday. I think once we get up the numbers, we should be able to find the anomaly. It's probably in the equipment."

"That's what I was thinking."

"We'll get there. Trust me," Palmer said, his voice firm.

"I hope so," Jonathan replied.

The call ended after that, both men wishing the other a good weekend and agreeing that they'd reconvene on Monday.

Palmer sat in his garage for a moment, the weight of the conversation settling heavily over him. Finally, he opened the car door, and his wheelchair automatically folded out. He transferred himself into it, then wheeled up the ramp into his house. The moment he crossed the threshold, the sterile atmosphere of his workday was replaced by the warmth and coziness of home. Instantly, like a topography of the soul, the personal touches—family photos on the walls, a vase of fresh flowers on the table, the comforting smell of a home-cooked meal—all of these things brought Dr. Palmer out of his depressive work mood.

"Welcome home, Tony! How was your day?" Emily, his wife, greeted him as he wheeled into the hallway.

"Long, but it's good to be home," Palmer replied, his

eyes softening as he spotted his teenage daughter, Sophie. "I hear someone got an A on their essay?"

Sophie beamed with pride. "Yes, I did. It was on Steinbeck's *Grapes of Wrath*."

"That's my girl," Palmer said, reaching out to hug her. He felt a swell of pride and love, momentarily pushing away the dark clouds of his work.

Emily smiled warmly at the scene. "I'm making brisket for dinner."

"How long until it's ready?" Palmer asked, already knowing the answer but enjoying the normalcy of the conversation.

"About half an hour," Emily replied.

"Then I need to just check downstairs."

"Don't work too hard, Tony. You need to relax too."

"I know, I know. I'll be quick," Palmer reassured her, giving her a comforting smile.

He wheeled himself to the stairlift at the end of the hallway and transferred into it. As he descended, the cozy atmosphere of the home gave way to the clinical feel of his basement.

At the bottom of the steps, Dr. Palmer climbed into another wheelchair stationed there. He then moved toward the back of the basement, where an unassuming wine shelf lined the wall. Glancing over his shoulder to ensure he was alone, he pressed a button on his wristwatch. The shelving unit slid aside, revealing a hidden doorway.

Beyond that was a laboratory, a clandestine space that even the Council knew nothing about. Palmer wheeled himself inside, the familiar scent of disinfectant and the soft hum of machinery greeting him. He made his way to the incubation units, where eight successful test subjects were held.

Having checked on each of them, he moved to the far end of the lab where Atlas, his first and most successful binding, was kept. The sight of Atlas filled Palmer with a mix of pride and determination. This was his true work, his real legacy.

A glass container the size of a shoebox held a piece of cow brain. Something writhed within it, burrowing into the tissue. The sight was unsettling, yet mesmerizing.

"Hello, Atlas," he whispered into the box. "How is it to have the whole world upon your shoulders?"

Soon, he would find a suitable human subject to ingest it. Then it would only be a matter of time.

Dr. Palmer knew full well why today's test at the Council lab had failed. It had failed because he had tampered with the pressure gauge on the containment unit, ensuring that the protein strands would not bind.

Why sabotage his own work? Easy. Because he had been performing his own research, ensuring that only he would control the final outcome.

As he stared into the container, a distant voice broke through his thoughts. "Tony, dinner's ready!" Emily called from upstairs.

"Coming!" Palmer responded, ensuring that everything in the lab was secure before heading back to the stairlift.

Entering the warm, inviting atmosphere of the main house, Palmer once again felt a fleeting sense of normalcy. Dinner was ready, and for a brief moment, he could set aside the weight of his double life. He wheeled into the dining room, where Emily and Sophie were setting the table.

"Everything OK in the basement?" Emily asked, her eyes filled with curiosity and a little concern.

"Yes," Palmer replied with a reassuring smile. "Just tying up a few loose ends."

As he joined his family for dinner, the secret of his true work remained hidden, locked away beneath the surface. For now, he was Anthony Palmer, husband and father. But deep down, he knew that his greatest work was yet to come.

They settled into their chairs, passing dishes around and making light conversation. The scent of Emily's brisket filled the air, mingling with the faint hint of candle wax.

"How was work, Tony?" Emily asked, her eyes searching his for any sign of the day's toll.

"Busy, as always," Palmer replied, forcing a smile. "But productive."

Sophie, eager to share her own day, jumped in. "Dad, did you know Steinbeck wasn't just a writer, he was a journalist, interested in highlighting the struggles of migrant workers and bringing public attention to their suffering?"

Palmer's smile turned genuine. "Yes. Steinbeck, like all great writers, focused on the struggles of his people. His depiction of the Dust Bowl is so vivid. Did you enjoy writing the essay?"

Sophie nodded enthusiastically. "Yes, I love how he captures their hardships. It's sad but so powerful."

"The people will always suffer when they see themselves as separate, when one group exploits another for profit. When the wealthy use their control of production and property to manipulate those who have nothing but need."

"You mean like the banks foreclosing on farms and California farmers exploiting the migrants by underpaying them?"

"Exactly that," her father confirmed.

Emily reached out, covering Palmer's hand with her own. "I'm just glad you're home. It feels like we barely see you these days."

"I know," Palmer said softly, facing his wife. "But I promise, I'm working hard for all of us."

Sophie looked at him with a mixture of admiration and longing. "Are you ever going to take a break?"

Palmer chuckled. "Maybe one day, sweetheart."

The three turned their attention to the food, a warm tranquility falling over the family. But this tranquility wasn't to last.

As they neared the end of their meal, the sound of the front door opening resonated through the house, followed by the heavy thud of footsteps making their way across the hallway toward the dining room. The family exchanged puzzled glances, the warm atmosphere disrupted by a sudden wave of unease.

The dining room door creaked open, and the silhouette of a figure appeared in the doorway. A veil was thrown over the family's cozy little meal, the sound of eating replaced by a tense silence. The figure stepped into the light, and Palmer's eyes widened as he recognized the man standing before them.

All eyes at the table turned toward the seven-and-a-half-foot giant as he ducked under the doorway, stepping into the dining room, followed by two other men of normal size but just as menacing.

They took positions around the table, their presence

casting a shadow over the warm dinner scene. Palmer, Emily, and Sophie exchanged confused and fearful glances.

The huge man was Brennon Krol. He was the result of the Council's genetics program—a program Palmer had helped develop.

"What is this about?" Palmer demanded, trying to keep his voice steady.

"I think you know, Doctor," Krol replied with a cold smile. He turned to one of the operatives. "Check the basement."

The operative headed off, and Palmer's heart dropped. He now knew exactly what this was about.

"Wait," Palmer said urgently.

Krol's smile vanished. "No. You wait, Doctor."

Emily, her face pale with fear, clutched Palmer's hand. "Tony, who are these men?"

"They're from work," Palmer replied, squeezing her hand reassuringly.

Emily's voice trembled. "Why have they just barged into our house?"

"Emily, just hold tight for a moment," Palmer said, his voice strained.

His daughter Sophie's eyes were wide with fear. "Daddy, I'm scared."

Palmer forced a reassuring smile. "It's going to be OK, honey."

But it wasn't. Just as he said this, the operative returned, holding the glass container with Atlas inside.

"The intel was correct," the operative said. "The lab was right where he said it would be, and I found this in it."

Krol took the container, holding it up to his eyes and

peering inside at the halved cow's brain and the writhing organism within.

"This is it," Krol said, his voice filled with satisfaction.

"Look, I can explain," Palmer started, his tone desperate.

Krol held up a hand, silencing him. "No need, Doctor. I take it this is a working prototype?"

Palmer nodded, his voice barely a whisper. "Yes."

Krol's smile returned, cold and predatory. "Then we have everything we need. Your colleagues back at the lab will be able to find out how to duplicate your findings."

Krol nodded at the operatives, who moved around the table toward Emily and Sophie.

"Wait. Wait!" Palmer shouted, panic rising in his chest.

Emily and Sophie cringed as the men came behind each, then stopped. Krol took his phone from his pocket, made a call, then held it out to Palmer. The call was answered, and a face appeared on the screen. Emily and Sophie had no idea who the man was, but Palmer did. It was Number Seven of the Council.

"You've been deceiving us, Dr. Palmer," Number Seven said, his voice cold and emotionless.

"You have it all wrong, sir," Palmer pleaded. "I needed to take the research out of the lab to finally get the breakthrough I've achieved here. I was days away from revealing my findings. I just needed a few more tests."

Seven's reply to this was jarring. "Then why have you been sabotaging the equipment in the main lab? Our investigation has been very thorough. We have evidence of at least six experiments failing due to your subversion."

A cold shock washed down Palmer's spine. "Please, I was trying..."

"To do what? To undermine us? To take the research for your own? Remember, without our backing, you would still be peddling your ideas around college campuses. We made you, Dr. Palmer. It is, therefore, *our* research."

"Then let me work it... Let me show you what I have achieved here, at home."

"We are well aware of what you have achieved at your home. No. We no longer need your assistance, Dr. Palmer. You and your family are condemned to death."

The screen went blank, the call ending.

The next seconds were the worst of Dr. Anthony Palmer's life. He pleaded for the lives of his wife and daughter as the men rounded on them. In the commotion, Sophie got free and made a run for it, heading upstairs, the two operatives going after her as Krol pulled Emily from her chair while she screamed.

"Please!" Palmer begged, tears streaming down his face, his useless legs pinning him to the wheelchair. "Tell them I'll give them everything! All of it! Just, please, stop!"

Krol held Emily by the neck, her feet dangling somewhere around his knees. His head swiveled on his gigantically wide neck, his poison eyes pointed at Palmer. He opened his mouth.

"Orders are orders," Krol said coldly.

With a jerk and a sickening crack, he broke Emily's neck, dropping her limp body to the floor.

Palmer's head exploded with grief and horror, his ears ringing, his heart pounding in his skull. In the background, he could hear the faraway sounds of his daughter upstairs slamming the bathroom door and the two operatives banging on it, her screams echoing with each pound as they charged the door to get at her.

Everything came snapping back to Palmer—all the sounds, all the emotions, all the horror, all of it. Krol stood over him, a menacing shadow blocking out the light.

"Time to die, Doc," Krol growled.

With terrifying strength, he lifted Palmer out of his wheelchair by the neck and slammed him down on the table —right next to the glass container with Atlas. The impact sent the container into the air, then crashing down. Atlas began emerging from the piece of cow's brain.

Krol used one hand to press Palmer to the table by the chest, the other hand cuffing his throat. The huge hand closed easily around Palmer's slender neck, like a farmer strangling a goose. He held it for now, not squeezing, just letting Palmer know it was right there and there was nothing he could do about it.

Palmer lay there powerless, holding on to Krol's huge arm, neither of his hands able to get around the giant appendage. It was like holding on to solid stone.

"Please... no..." Palmer gasped for air.

Krol smiled wickedly and began squeezing harder, hoping to slowly crush Palmer's neck to jam. He was enjoying this.

But Palmer wasn't done. Not yet. His hand reached for the container, his fingers snatching at the clasp and finally opening the lid. Reaching into it, he allowed the worm to loop around his fingers, then brought it out.

As Krol throttled him, he raised his hand toward the giant's head.

"It is useless to struggle," Krol said.

Palmer's hand reached the ear, and Atlas came alive, finding its way into Krol's ear canal, quickly slipping out of Palmer's hand and into the head.

Krol instantly felt it as Atlas began burrowing, working its way into the subarachnoid space between the skull and brain. He let go of the neck, leaving Palmer gasping for air. Krol then began wheeling around the room, knocking into things as he grasped at his ear, a small thread of blood pouring down his neck from it. He fought a little longer, crashing about as he grabbed at his head, and then—he was still.

Just like that, Brennan Krol stood there, completely frozen, staring blankly into space.

Upstairs, the door finally gave way. Sophie let out a bloodcurdling scream, followed by two suppressed gunshots, then nothing. A silenced Beretta had silenced his daughter forever.

"No... Sophie..." Palmer gasped, tears streaming down his face.

Anger twisted his face, but he knew he had to act quickly. He crawled to his wheelchair, pulling himself into it. His mind raced. He couldn't let his family's death be in vain. He had to survive. He had to finish his work.

He wheeled himself to the basement stairs, his hands shaking as he lifted himself into the chairlift. Soon, he was at the lab. Inside, he activated the emergency protocols, setting the lab to self-destruct in ten minutes. He began gathering the most important data files and samples, packing them into a secure case—including the eight incubation subjects.

The Council would pay for this. They would all pay.

Palmer took a deep breath, wiping away his tears. "I'll make sure of it," he whispered to himself.

RIGHT AT THAT MOMENT, the operatives joined Krol in the dining room above.

"Where's the doctor?" one of the men demanded.

There was a moment of silence.

"Hey! You hear me, big guy?"

The second operative then spoke. "What's the matter with him?"

"I don't know," the first operative replied.

"He ever do this before?"

"No, never," the first operative answered, worry creeping into his tone.

Meanwhile, downstairs, Palmer pulled himself up onto a chair before taking a microphone headset that sat next to a laptop and placing it over his head. His hands trembled as he typed a few commands into the laptop, then pressed an icon labeled: *Run Program*.

"Hey, Krol? You in there?" one of the operatives called out.

"And where's the doc?" the other added.

"He can't be far. The guy's a cripple. Go find him," the first operative instructed.

Downstairs, the program initiated. Shaking all over, uncertain if this would work, Palmer spoke into the microphone. "I'm in the basement. Come down to me."

Upstairs, Krol suddenly moved.

"Oh, you are alive. OK, buddy," the first operative said, relieved.

The sound of Krol's heavy footsteps reverberated across the ceiling of the basement. He passed the other operative at the top of the basement steps.

"OK, so you're good now. Krol?" the second operative called after him, confused.

Krol reached the lab, stopping in front of Palmer. The two operatives followed closely behind.

The second operative was the first to arrive. Seeing Palmer, he said, "Ah, so this is where he is."

The other operative then arrived, and all four men stood inside the room. Palmer looked coldly at Krol and commanded, "I want you to kill them in the most terrible way you can imagine."

Krol turned on the operatives with terrifying speed. He grabbed the first operative by the chin and mouth, ripping out his lower jaw and then grabbing his head in both hands, crushing his skull within them.

The pop of the bone giving way made the second operative shudder as he watched in horror. As Krol dropped what was left of the other man onto the floor, the second operative was reaching for his pistol, but it was too late. Krol grabbed his head in one hand and drove it into the wall, crushing it like a ripe melon as the guy screamed out.

In the aftermath, Palmer gazed at the dead men, malicious satisfaction burning in his eyes. "Now take me to my wife."

Krol gently carried Palmer to the dining room, laying him next to Emily's body. Palmer cradled her face, sobbing uncontrollably. Krol then brought Sophie's body to him from upstairs, laying her beside her mother.

Palmer whispered through his tears, "I promise you both, those who harmed you will pay."

Krol then gathered the eight specimens from the lab along with other essential equipment, loading them into two holdalls. He carried everything to a car, carefully placing Palmer in the passenger seat before climbing into the driver's seat himself.

Palmer looked at Brennan Krol, his eyes burning with resolve. "Are you ready, Mr. Krol?" he said as the giant started the car. "Ready to get busy. We have so much work to do."

ONE

SIX MONTHS LATER...

THE EVENTS IN CUBA HAD EXPOSED THE COUNCIL
to the world in a way E & E couldn't cover up entirely. The
widespread coverage of the Cuban base unleashing
microwave radiation across a fifty-mile radius and the subse-
quent death toll reaching into the hundreds created global
shock and outrage.

News outlets and social media continuously broadcasted
stories about the Council, some of it true, most of not, thus
creating urgency and paranoia among the public. US President Jackson T. Whitmore and other world leaders assured
their nations that they were leading the charge against this
global threat, promising increased security measures,
international cooperation, and investigations to root out
Council influence in their own governments.

US intelligence and law enforcement agencies worked
around the clock, uncovering and dismantling Council cells.

High-profile arrests and exposés dominated the news. Governments worldwide launched their own investigations, leading to purges, arrests, and resignations of high-ranking officials found complicit. Paranoia was rife amongst the world's political apparatus.

On the ground, Noah Wolf and the rest of teams Camelot and Cinderella did the grunt work, fishing out the Council's operations piece by piece. Through intelligence and investigative work, they uncovered a series of bases, all buried deep beneath the earth, all in various countries across the globe—and all showcasing the ominous reality of just how far-reaching, entrenched, and organized the Council's operations were.

The silence in the underground base was shattered by the high-pitched whine of a cutting torch as it carved its way through the sealed vent. Sparks flew down from the ceiling, illuminating the darkened corridor. The vent finally gave way with a kick, landing with a loud clang that spread in an echo throughout the network of tunnels that made up the base.

Ropes fell from the hole into the corridor, followed by black-clad operatives lowering themselves down into the freezing depths below. As they descended, their breath formed icy clouds in the cold air, a sign that the climate control had been off for a while. It must only be a few degrees centigrade above freezing.

As the boots of the first two operatives touched the ground, they spread out, their red laser sights cutting through the darkness.

"Clear left," Marco whispered into his comms, acting as point man of Team Camelot, his laser sweeping the corridor.

"Clear right," responded Jenny, point man of Team Cinderella, her eyes scanning the tunnel's recesses through the green tint of her NVGs.

As the last man touched down on the metal walkway, the soft clink of his boots echoed faintly through the cavernous space. The two teams of six then split up, fanning out as they moved.

At junctions, they snapped red chemlights, dropping them there to mark their way before splitting up, the operatives spreading out within the sprawling labyrinth. The silence of the corridors was as thick as the darkness itself, the base devoid of any signs of life.

Two operatives arrived at a set of windows overlooking a vast and very empty room. Looking out the window, both men knew for a fact that it wasn't always so empty.

One of the men brought his hand to his earpiece. "This is Noah," he said, his voice steady and low. "Jenny, you at the operations room yet?"

"Affirmative, Team Leader," came the reply. "We are in. But it appears that Grandma isn't home."

"We've got nothing on our end either," Noah said, staring at the empty chamber. "Looks like they stripped this place clean. No sign of the microwave machine or the EMP equipment."

"Copy that, Team Leader. Looks like they've stripped everything here, too."

The operative next to Noah lifted his goggles. It was Marco.

"Feels like a ghost town, boss," he muttered, his Louisiana drawl barely above a whisper. "Ain't no sign of life."

"They're always one step ahead," Noah said, his jaw clenched.

The massive installation the two teams had just infiltrated was buried six miles beneath the Chihuahuan Desert. It was a Council base, the third they'd uncovered since Cuba.

Noah and Marco moved on, as did the others. The corridors twisted and turned, the temperature dropping the deeper they went, until they eventually converged on the operations room. Frost rimed the edges of control panels and doors.

Noah and Marco found Jenny and Neil at the back of the room, standing by a large blast door, its control panel gutted and lifeless. Neil was already at work, tools in hand, bypassing the dead circuits.

"Whoever was in charge of the base had their quarters through there," Jenny said, her breath puffing in the cold air.

With a final click, the door groaned open, revealing a large set of living quarters, one that had been stripped bare, just like everywhere else.

"They cleared everything out," Neil noted, stepping into the room. "Knew we were coming."

Noah nodded, his eyes scanning the bare walls for any clues. "We need to find out where they went and fast. Let's gather what intel we can and get out."

———

THREE HOURS LATER, the teams emerged from the underground base into the blistering heat and blinding sun of the Chihuahuan Desert. The harsh light assaulted their eyes, especially after the darkness below, and the dry, sandy air blew relentlessly around them, scratching their skin and stinging their eyes.

They made their way to the field tent, ignoring the throng of people waiting nearby. Military personnel, CIA agents, Mexican government officials, and members of the press all jostled for position. In the background, news reporters with cameras prepared to broadcast the latest developments to the world.

Noah strode past them, his face set in a grim expression, his mind focused purely on the mission. Within the shade of their field tent, Renée sat by the comms equipment.

"Patch me through to Allison," Noah instructed as he and the others arrived.

Renée nodded, quickly establishing the connection. The screen flickered to life, showing the face of Allison Peterson, Dragon Lady, framed by what Noah took for a government office.

"Noah," she said. "What's the situation?"

"It's the same as Honduras and Mongolia," Noah replied. "They knew we were coming and have moved out."

Allison frowned. "That's not good. I'm just about to see the president. I was hoping I'd have some good news for him."

As she spoke, Neil approached Noah, a tablet in hand. "Noah, you need to see this," he said. "I just got these images from a video captured by one of the local goat herders here. He handed it over to some CNN reporter earlier on."

Noah took the tablet and watched the footage. The video, taken at night from the nearby foothills, showed a massive convoy of vehicles moving out, carrying large loads of equipment. The time stamp indicated it was four days ago.

Allison's voice came through the video call. "Look, Molly and I are about to step inside the Oval Office. It looks like you've got your hands full out there. We'll speak later. Allison out."

Noah's grip on the tablet tightened, his lip curling as he watched the footage of the convoy disappearing into the night.

Marco came beside him, placing a hand on his shoulder. "Don't worry, bossman," he said, "we'll get them. They can't keep running forever."

TWO

THE SUN STREAMED THROUGH THE TALL WINDOWS of the Oval Office, casting a warm glow on the Resolute desk, as well as the many documents and reports that cluttered its surface.

Molly Hanson and Allison Peterson were ushered into the room by a White House aide. As they entered, Vice President Gina Brown was leaving, exchanging a brief nod with Allison as they passed one another. Unseen by anyone else.

President Jackson T. Whitmore rose from behind his desk, his demeanor both welcoming and serious. "Molly, Allison, thank you for coming," he greeted, extending his hand to each of them.

"Mr. President," Molly replied, shaking his hand firmly. Allison followed suit, her face as composed and professional as always.

Whitmore gestured for them to sit. "We have a lot to discuss," he began, settling back into his chair. "The international disputes over the Council bases found in

Cuba, Honduras, Mongolia, and now Mexico are escalating. However, we have a plan to address this."

Allison and Molly exchanged a glance.

"Tomorrow, I'll be meeting with the head of the United Nations to flesh out a unification between NATO and the UN," Whitmore continued. "The goal is to bring all 193 member states under NATO jurisdiction, thereby making the bases found on those territories NATO-controlled. This new global alliance will leave the Council nowhere to go."

Allison's eyes narrowed. "And you've managed to get Iran, China, and Russia to agree?"

"Not yet. But they will."

"How?"

"I'm going to buy Russian oil and gas at five times its price, create zero interest export costs for Chinese manufacturing, and send American scientists in to help Iran build its first nuclear reactor. We'll iron out any other concessions they want when the meetings begin. But I need their compliance in this if we're gonna win. It has to be a global effort."

While Allison thought about the implications of such concessions, Molly nodded. "It's an ambitious step, Mr. President," she said. "It could change the dynamics of our fight."

"Indeed," Whitmore agreed. "I see it as a necessary step. The world is at a critical juncture, and it's imperative that we stand united against the Council."

Allison leaned forward. "With you at the helm, sir, the world is safe."

Whitmore gave a brief, appreciative smile. "Thank you, Allison. I also wanted to showcase our new department of the FBI, tasked with rooting out Council stooges from all parts of American life."

He handed them a dossier, the cover emblazoned with the FBI emblem. "We're due to sign over the budget for this department in the next few days. This will provide the resources needed to conduct thorough investigations and bring these operatives to justice."

Allison felt a chill but didn't let it show. Molly flipped through the dossier, her eyes scanning the detailed plans.

Whitmore went on, "We have to be meticulous. The Council's influence runs deep, and we need to root it out at every level. This is not just about immediate security; it's about safeguarding our nation's future. You saw with your own eyes what those bastards did in Cuba. Saw the way they deal with ordinary people. They're monsters."

"The Council won't see this coming," Allison said confidently. "They've underestimated our ability to unite and act decisively."

"Exactly," Whitmore said, leaning back. "That's why we need everyone on board. Your roles, both of you, are critical in this fight."

Molly closed the dossier. "We're ready to do whatever it takes, Mr. President."

Whitmore stood, signaling the end of their meeting. "I have no doubt. Together, we will dismantle the Council's network and restore stability to our world."

———

As THEY LEFT the meeting with President Whitmore,

Allison turned to Molly. "Go on without me. I need to speak with someone."

Molly nodded, a hint of curiosity in her eyes. "All right. I'll see you in the car."

As Molly walked away, Allison made her way to the vice president's office. She moved with purpose, her mind focused on the task ahead. She knocked on the door and was promptly invited in by Gina Brown.

"Have a seat," the vice president said.

Allison took her seat, her eyes scanning the room out of habit. Gina Brown reached into her desk, retrieving a small device. She switched it on and placed it on top of the desk. "We're safe now," she said.

"I have mine on, just in case," Allison replied, pulling a similar device from her handbag. The jammer pulsed with a faint blue light, ensuring that their conversation would remain private.

Vice President Brown leaned back, her eyes narrowing. "What's the update?"

"There's been a change of plan," Allison said, her voice low. "The Council has decided to eliminate him. Everything is in place for you to take over in time for the summit."

The vice president's expression tightened, but she nodded. "I thought they were developing something to control Whitmore. I heard it was going to involve some type of mind manipulation."

Allison shook her head slightly. "I'm afraid the research for that has gone south for the time being. That means Plan B will have to suffice."

"Assassination," Gina Brown stated, her tone flat but resolute.

"Yes," Allison confirmed. "Everything is in place. You must be ready to step in immediately."

"So assassination it is," Gina Brown repeated. "It has to look natural, of course. He's been eating a lot of junk food lately. The White House physician has been on to him to diet and take up running."

"I'm aware of his health issues. I'll handle it," Allison said firmly.

Gina Brown nodded. "Whitmore's unification plan will hurt the Council and ultimately the world. And not just that. His concessions to our enemies will cause global instability that will take decades to correct. We can't afford any mistakes."

"There won't be any," Allison assured her. "Once Whitmore is out of the way, you'll have the authority needed to steer the summit in our favor."

Vice President Brown leaned forward, her eyes locking on to Allison's. "I've waited a long time for this. The Council's vision is within reach, but we're treading on thin ice. Your execution needs to be flawless."

"It will be," Allison promised. "Just be ready. As soon as Whitmore is eliminated, you'll need to act fast. The Council's plans depend on it."

As their conversation concluded, a heavy silence filled the room. The enormity of their plan and the stakes involved cast a shadow over them. Leaving the office, the weight of their conversation settled on Allison's shoulders, knowing that the fate of nations hinged on the success of their plan.

THREE

When Dr. Anthony Palmer had told Brennan Krol about how busy they would be, he hadn't been lying. Over the past six months, the two of them had worked nonstop, and what started one terrible evening over dinner had now become something else entirely.

The dense canopy of the Sumbanese jungle filtered the midday sun into a mosaic of shadows and light. Hidden deep within this verdant expanse was a compound, heavily guarded and shrouded in secrecy. Hidden deep within that was Dr. Palmer's new laboratory.

Inside its bare walls, Anthony Palmer sat at the center of this technological haven, his intense blue eyes focused on the screen of data in front of him. Around him, assistants and lab technicians moved efficiently. Not far from where he sat, two technicians were busy wheeling a shelved cart of equipment into a walk-in dry heat sterilization oven.

The sounds of the metal lab tools rattling as the cart passed over the threshold was jarring to Palmer, and he was about to say something when one of the assistants, a young woman with a tablet in hand, approached cautiously. "My Lord, we have a visitor."

Outside, at the edge of the sprawling compound, Dr. Jonathan Taylor stumbled through the undergrowth. His clothes were torn and dirty, his face streaked with sweat and grime. Each step was a struggle. The terrain had been unforgiving and treacherous. He could feel the weight of his backpack digging into his shoulders, the thick, humid air adding an extra weight to it all.

As he reached the first of the newly built buildings, his heart pounded in his chest, not just from the physical exertion but from the gnawing anxiety that had been his constant companion since he had set out on this journey four days ago. The farther he had gone, the more he had questioned his decision. But he had to see Palmer. He had to try and reason with him.

The village was a maze of narrow, winding streets lined with small, wooden houses. As he walked through, the locals emerged from their homes, their eyes fixed on outsider. They didn't speak; they merely stared, their silence more unnerving than any hostile words could have been. Walking past, their heads turned in unison on their necks as those vacant looks followed him.

Jonathan pushed forward, the villagers' scrutiny adding to his growing sense of unease. He could feel their eyes on him, following his every move, more and more of them emerging from the houses. They began following him, a large crowd forming in his wake as he made his way to the heart of the village. There, the temple Pura Luhur rose atop a hill, its ancient stones covered in moss and vines.

When he was halfway up the weathered temple steps, the doors of Pura Luhur creaked open, and out emerged Dr. Anthony Palmer, carried by the towering figure of Brennan Krol.

"Jonathan," Palmer said, his voice carrying a note of cold curiosity. "So they've sent *you* this time."

"I'm here as a friend, Tony," Jonathan replied, his voice trembling. "As a friend."

Palmer's lips curled into a faint, humorless smile. "I'm afraid there are no friends anymore."

As if commanded by his words, the villagers began closing in around Jonathan, their presence menacing and overwhelming, their hands reaching out, taking hold of him.

"Please, Tony," Jonathan pleaded. "Let me talk with you. Please. This has gone too far. Please! I was the godfather to your daughter, for Christ's sake!"

At this, Palmer raised a hand, and the crowd halted instantly. His command over them was absolute, their obedience unquestioning. "Fall back," he ordered.

The villagers stepped back, their eyes still locked on Dr. Jonathan Taylor, who was on his knees, panting and shaking. A shadow loomed over him, and he looked up to find Krol and Palmer standing above him, their expressions cold and impassive.

"Say what you've come to say," Palmer instructed, his voice devoid of any warmth.

Pura Luhur's grand chamber was vast and imposing with high, arched ceilings adorned with intricate carvings that told stories of gods and warriors from a forgotten time. Dim lighting from torches and small oil lamps cast eerie shadows on the walls, adding to the mystical atmosphere of the place.

Dr. Jonathan Taylor was guided by the silent locals through the massive stone doors and into the heart of the temple. The weight of their eyes upon him never lifted, their gaze unyielding and intense. They moved with an eerie synchrony, their steps almost mechanical.

Jonathan's backpack was taken from him without a word, and he was led to a long, ornately carved wooden table that stretched across the chamber. The surface of it was polished to a sheen, reflecting the flickering light from the torches. Krol, ever imposing, carried Dr. Palmer to his place opposite Jonathan, setting him down with a gentle but firm touch.

Palmer's eyes met Jonathan's. "You must be tired and hungry," Palmer mentioned, gesturing to the table before them.

Jonathan nodded slowly, taking a seat, his movements cautious.

The locals began to serve them with a reverence that was unsettling. They brought platters of food, laying them gently on the table. Fruits, meats, and delicacies were presented before him.

"Eat," Palmer encouraged, picking up a piece of mango. "You need your strength."

Jonathan hesitated but then took a piece of bread, his mind racing. The silence of the locals, their unwavering attention on Palmer, and the grandeur of the chamber all contributed to a growing sense of unreality. He felt as though he had stepped into another world, one ruled by the iron will of his former friend.

As they ate, the silence between the two men grew heavier, punctuated only by the soft sounds of their meal and the quiet rustle of the locals moving around. Jonathan's mind flashed back to their days at MIT, to the camaraderie they had shared and the ambitious dreams they had pursued together. How far they had come since those halcyon days and how drastically things had changed.

Palmer broke the silence. "You know, John, I've missed our conversations. It's been too long since we last spoke as friends."

Jonathan swallowed hard. "This isn't what I wanted, Tony. This isn't how it was supposed to be."

Palmer's gaze hardened. "And yet here we are. The Council's betrayal, their attempt to control me—this is the only path left."

Jonathan shook his head, his eyes pleading. "There has to be another way. This... this isn't you."

Palmer leaned back, his expression unreadable. "You don't understand. The Council's reach is vast, their power insidious. My work—our work—was supposed to protect humanity, to bring order. But they will twist it for their own ends. Use it to destroy humanity, not save it. I had to break free."

Around them, the locals continued their silent service, bringing more food and refilling their bowls with the mechanical precision of robots.

"Tony, you talk about saving humanity," Jonathan said. "But what about these people? They're not your tools. They're human beings."

Palmer's eyes flickered with a hint of regret but then

steeled over. "They are necessary. Mindweaver is the key, Jonathan. It is the only thing that can defeat the Council."

Jonathan felt a surge of anger and desperation. "Defeat them? This is ridiculous. This has to stop, Tony. You have to stop this madness before it consumes everything you ever stood for."

Palmer's expression softened momentarily. "Jonathan, I respect your passion. But you're too late. The wheels are already in motion. You can either stand with me or be swept away."

The words hung in the air, a chilling ultimatum.

Jonathon Taylor took a deep breath, trying to steady his nerves. "Tony, I've come with a message from the Council."

At the mention of the Council, Palmer's eyes narrowed.

"They want you back," Jonathan continued, his voice trembling slightly. "Orders from Number One themself. They apologize for their mistakes, but they need you—"

"They need my research!" Palmer snapped.

"All will be forgiven if you return now," Jonathan pressed.

Palmer's eyes narrowed further. "They say mistakes. Like when you accidentally set the thermal cycler at half a centigrade too low and lose your specimens. Mistakes are why we have erasers. But their mistakes cost me everything, John. You know that. And now they think they can just apologize? There is no eraser for what they did to me—and what they continue to do to me."

Jonathan swallowed hard, his hands shaking slightly. "They acknowledge it was wrong to kill your family and that it was also wrong to send an extraction squad to—"

"A kill squad," Palmer corrected sharply. "They sent a kill squad to the island."

"They were sent to come get you. To bring you safely home, Tony. Not to kill you."

"Then why were they so heavily armed?" Palmer's eyes bore into Jonathan's.

"Because you're all the way out here in the middle of the jungle surrounded by your... cult."

"They are my children," Palmer said softly, almost tenderly. "Even those who attempt to wrong me."

As he said this, four men emerged through the crowd of people surrounding them. These weren't local like everyone else. They were foreigners dressed in Special Forces garb—body armor, fatigues, pistols on their belts, rifles strapped to their shoulders. They moved with the same blank, mechanical precision as the villagers. They came to a stop beside Krol, their expressions devoid of emotion, their eyes vacant.

Jonathan's heart sank as he recognized one of the men. "Corporal Hendricks?" he called out.

The man didn't react in the slightest, his eyes empty, his stance rigid.

Palmer's voice cut through the silence. "These men no longer serve the Council. They serve me now. They are part of the future, John. A future where loyalty is absolute and dissent is eliminated."

Jonathan felt a wave of despair wash over him. "Tony, please. I know you feel betrayed by the Council. But this—this isn't the answer. One man can't have this much power. To control and guide all these people."

"And so what? I hand it over to your Council? Let them guide it?" Palmer's voice dripped with sarcasm.

"Yes, Tony. That's exactly what you do. They are exactly the right people for this."

"With President Whitmore declaring war on them?"

"The Council has faced tougher tests than Whitmore."

"I'm sure it has," Palmer said, a sinister edge to his voice. "And I'm sure it'll beat this one. But—" Looking Taylor right in the eyes, he added, "Will it beat the next big test?"

"And that'll be what, Tony? You?"

"Yes, John. Me. Me and my army."

Right at that moment, everyone else in the room stopped moving. The waiter pouring Jonathan's glass of water had frozen, the liquid overflowing from the cup. Another thing: every one of them was staring right at him, even harder than before, their empty, unblinking eyes homed on him.

Jonathan did his best to ignore them. "But it's not a real army, though, is it?" he put to his oldest friend, trying to keep his voice steady.

"Not yet," Palmer replied, a chilling calm in his voice. "But people can be trained. Especially people as attentive as these. And with more experts turning up to train them each day, it won't be long." He gestured with a wave of his hand at the four Special Forces men standing just behind him.

Jonathan felt a shiver run down his spine. The sheer control Palmer exerted over these people was terrifying. It was a glimpse into the future they had both envisioned—a future where the individual was completely stripped of free will, and all were subject to the whims of a single, controlling mind. A human hive, they had called it.

"You see, John," Palmer said, his voice soft but menacing, "this is just the beginning. The Council's time is over.

It's time for a new order, one where true scientific enlightenment and clarity reign supreme."

Jonathan took a deep breath. "Tony, there's still time to stop this. We can find another way."

Palmer's eyes flashed with anger. "There is no other way. You're either with me, or you're against me."

Jonathan's desperation grew. "Come back to life, Tony. Don't stay out here rotting in this temple. Would Emily have wanted this for you?"

"Don't mention her name."

"But she was my friend as well," Jonathan said softly.

Palmer's fist slammed onto the table. "No! You don't get to mention her name."

"But I loved Emily as well. What happened to her—"

"Shut up!" Palmer shouted, and everyone in the room echoed, "SHUT UP!"

Taylor was shocked into silence, his face paling.

Seething, Palmer struggled to get his words out. "You loved her, did you, John? Loved her?" He leaned forward, his voice a menacing undertone. "If you loved my Emily, my love, then why did you turn on me, on her?"

Jonathan's face lost all remaining color. "Tony, I... I didn't..."

"Yes, you did. I've seen the transcripts. I know it was you who was liaising with them the whole time, wiring them reports on me, showing them evidence that I was stalling research. That I'd taken it out of the lab and was doing experiments at home. That I had my own thing going. I know it was you."

Jonathan began shaking all over. He knew now that it

was a terrible mistake to have come out here. "But I didn't know they would…"

"But they did, John. Didn't they? They did."

The locals began crowding around Jonathan Taylor, their presence menacing. "Please, Tony. I did what I thought was right. I never knew what they'd do. They said you'd just get a warning. All I wanted was the research back on track, for you to stop stalling, stop hiding stuff from us all."

Palmer's voice was eerily calm. "That's OK, John. You're forgiven. All you have to do is go fetch something for me."

Jonathan screamed as the locals grabbed him, their hands rough and unyielding. Soon, they were carrying him out of the temple, his cries echoing off the ancient walls, a haunting sound of desperation and fear.

FOUR

ON THE OTHER SIDE OF THE WORLD, SPIRIT'S BAR
and Grill in Kirtland was a haven of warmth and familiarity,
a place where the scent of grilled meat mingled with the hum
of friendly conversations. The wooden beams of the ceiling,
strung with fairy lights, cast a soft glow over the room.
Patrons filled the tables, laughter and chatter creating a lively
atmosphere.

Yet despite the inviting setting, Noah and his team sat
around their table, their mood flat in comparison to the bar's
vibrant energy. Plates of ribs, brisket, and cornbread lay
untouched, and their drinks sat mostly full. Their usual
camaraderie was replaced by a heavy silence, each member
lost in their thoughts.

Sarah, Noah's wife and the only one not involved in the
day-to-day operations of E & E, looked around at the down-
cast faces. Determined to lift their spirits, she leaned
forward, her voice bright and hopeful. "Come on, guys. This
is our night out. We should be celebrating. Having fun."

Marco sighed, running a hand through his long black hair. "It's hard to celebrate when we're always one step behind."

Jenny nodded, her fingers tracing the rim of her glass. "Feels like all we do is chase our tails out there. Every base we find is empty. It's like they know our every move."

Renée poked at her food, her expression frustrated. "Yeah, it's like we're playing their game and losing every round."

Sarah, refusing to give up, smiled encouragingly. "But you're still out there fighting, making a difference. That has to count for something, right?"

Noah, who had been staring at his drink, finally looked up. His eyes were distant, filled with the weight of their recent failures. "We're trying, Sarah. But it feels like a losing battle."

The table fell silent again. The sounds of the bar seemed distant, almost surreal against the backdrop of their collective disappointment.

Neil reached out and placed an arm around Jenny's shoulders. "We'll figure it out. We always do."

Jenny managed a small smile, though it didn't quite reach her eyes. "I hope you're right, baby."

Marco leaned back in his chair, his gaze drifting around the room. "Remember the first time we came here? We were celebrating our first big win—Nicolaich Andropov. Feels like a lifetime ago."

Renée nodded, a faint smile playing on her lips. "Yeah, we were so optimistic back then. Felt like we could take on the world."

Sarah seized on the moment of nostalgia. "And you still

can. You've faced so much and come out stronger each time. This is just another challenge."

Noah's shoulders slumped slightly, his fingers drumming absently on the table. "It's more than that, Sarah. It's not just about us anymore. The stakes are higher, and the enemy is smarter."

Sarah looked at her husband, her heart aching at the sight of his burdened expression. She reached out and took his hand, squeezing it gently. "Noah, you're doing everything you can. We all believe in you."

Noah looked at her, the corners of his mouth lifting in a small, grateful smile. "Thanks, Sarah."

Marco raised his glass, attempting to break the tension. "To better days ahead?"

The others lifted their glasses, though the gesture was half-hearted. "To better days ahead," they echoed, their voices subdued.

———

THE DRIVE HOME WAS SILENT, the evening hanging heavily over Noah and Sarah. Parking outside the farmhouse, Noah sighed heavily, breaking the stillness. He turned to Sarah, his expression weary.

"I feel overwhelmed, Sarah," he admitted, his voice low. "The Council... it's like a shadow that we can't shake."

"Come on, Noah. You can..."

Her voice died as he held a hand up.

"I have to tell you something," he said.

"What?"

"I didn't tell you this before because I've been trying to process it."

"Process what?"

He took a deep breath before admitting, "Back in Cuba, I almost cracked. I almost took their offer. I almost joined the Council."

Sarah's concern deepened. "What do you mean, Noah?"

Noah rubbed his face with his hands, trying to find the right words. "It started to make logical sense what he was telling me. Look at the world, Sarah. The way it just seems set on tearing itself apart."

Sarah reached out, placing a hand on his arm. "It's because of things like the Council that it is. It's because of people who have given up on humanity and only want to speed up its demise that the world is falling apart. It's because of people who profit from doom. That's what the Council is, Noah. You know that."

Noah leaned back against the seat. "But it's so hard to see the light when all we keep getting is darkness."

Sarah's voice softened, but her conviction was clear. "Noah, I didn't just join E & E because I had no other choice. I joined because I wanted to see justice prevail. I wanted to see people like the Council punished. You can't lose hope. You *are* hope. You and your team, you're fighting for something bigger than all of us. And it's worth it. Every step you take, every move you make, it's a blow against the darkness."

Noah nodded slowly, a glimmer of determination returning to his eyes. "You're right. We can't give up. We won't give up."

Sarah smiled. "That's the Noah I know."

They embraced over the center console of the Durango, holding on to each other for a moment, drawing strength from their connection. As they pulled back, they looked toward the farmhouse. The lights were on, and they could see the silhouettes of their daughter and the babysitter through the curtains.

"She should be in bed," Noah said with a small, affectionate smile.

Sarah chuckled softly. "Looks like someone wanted to wait up for us."

They got out of the car, the cool night air wrapping around them. Hand in hand, they walked toward the farmhouse. Inside, they were immediately set upon. Their six-year-old daughter, Norah, full of excitement, came running at them from across the hallway.

"Mommy! Daddy! You're home!" Norah's voice was bright and cheerful as she threw herself into her parents' arms.

Sarah smiled, kneeling to hug her daughter. "*You* should be in bed."

Norah's eyes sparkled with a mischievous glint. "I know, but I missed you. And Carol said I could stay up a little longer."

Carol was the babysitter.

Noah was next to scoop his daughter up, lifting her high with a playful grin. "Did she now? Well, I guess we're lucky to have such a good babysitter."

Carol, standing nearby with a slightly sheepish look, chimed in. "She was very convincing."

Sarah let out a chuckle. "That's our girl."

The atmosphere in the house was filled with warmth and love, a welcome reprieve from the heaviness of their earlier conversation. The coziness of their home, with its well-worn furniture and family photos lining the walls, was a reminder of what they were fighting to protect.

FIVE

Meanwhile, in DC, the Jefferson Memorial was standing stark and silent against the moonlit sky, the columns casting long, eerie shadows on the marble steps. At this late hour, the usually bustling site was deserted. The only sounds were the faint rustling of leaves and the distant hum of the city.

Allison Peterson waited on the steps, her eyes scanning the darkness for any sign of movement. She pulled her coat tighter around herself, the chill in the air doing little to ease the tension in her shoulders.

Out of the darkness, a shadow emerged, a figure, moving with careful, deliberate steps. The man's face was obscured by the brim of his Yankees cap, his dark clothing blending seamlessly with the night.

He stopped a few feet from Allison and reached into his coat, pulling out a small vial.

"This is it," he said, holding it out to her.

Allison took the vial, holding it up to the moonlight to

examine its contents. The liquid inside was clear, almost innocuous in appearance. "What exactly is it?" she asked.

"One of our specialties," the man replied. "A genetically mutated poison that induces heart attacks. Completely undetectable to normal science. Only our own scientists will be capable of spotting it."

Allison nodded. "Understood."

The man glanced around, ensuring they were still alone. The stillness of the Memorial seemed to swallow their conversation, the shadows deepening as the moonlight shifted. "Make sure it's administered soon. Timing is crucial."

"I know," Allison replied, slipping the vial into her coat pocket. "It will be done."

———

DANE CHAVERS EXITED the White House, the cold night air hitting him as he made his way to the street. Pulling out his phone, he called the president, going over the last details of tomorrow's trip to the UN Council.

"Yes, Mr. President, everything is set," Dane said, his voice steady but his eyes scanning the street nervously. "Yes, sir. I'm just getting a ride home now. My Uber's here."

"All right, Dane. Safe travels," the president replied over the phone.

"Thank you, sir," Dane said, spotting the approaching car. He hung up and entered the Uber, giving his address to the driver. "134 Maple Street, please."

As the ride began, Dane settled back into his seat, his mind racing through the preparations for tomorrow.

However, it wasn't long before the silence was interrupted. As the city lights blurred past the window, the driver spoke, cutting through Dane's thoughts with an ominous question.

"Do you recall the promise you made to the Council, Dane?"

Dane's eyes snapped to the driver, his heart skipping a beat. It was Allison Peterson. Swallowing hard, he replied, "Yes."

"Plan B," Allison said, her voice calm and firm, her eyes never leaving the road.

Dane nodded. "Yes, ma'am."

"Slip your hand into the pocket at the back of the passenger seat," she instructed next.

With trembling hands, Dane reached forward, feeling around until his fingers closed on a small container. He pulled it out and opened it to reveal the vial of poison, its contents shimmering faintly in the dim light of the car.

"Tomorrow morning, you are to get that inside the president's food or drink," Allison said. Her tone left no room for hesitation.

Dane's throat tightened, and he could barely manage to speak. "Yes, ma'am." He closed the container, slipping it into his work satchel.

The rest of the ride was silent, for obvious reasons. Dane stared out the window, the familiar streets of DC now feeling alien and foreboding. The car's interior felt like a prison, the vial a deadly reminder of the choice he had made a long time ago.

As they approached his address, Allison slowed the car and pulled over. "We'll be watching, Dane. Don't disappoint us."

Dane Chavers nodded, feeling the cold sweat on his brow. "I won't," he promised.

He stepped out of the car, his legs feeling unsteady. Allison drove off into the night, leaving him standing alone on the quiet street, the vial of poison making the satchel feel twice as heavy as it had before.

Once she was a couple of blocks away, Allison dialed a number, the encrypted line ensuring that their conversation would remain private.

When the call was answered, she spoke in a low voice, her words precise and measured. "It's done. He has the vial."

The voice on the other end was equally calm. "Good. Make sure everything goes according to plan."

"I will," Allison replied, her eyes scanning the empty road ahead. "I'm flying back to Kirtland in the morning. Do you have the next location for us?"

There was a brief pause before her handler responded. "No. We're going to shelve the wild goose chase for now."

Allison raised an eyebrow, surprised. "Oh?"

"Yes. Instead, we have something else to keep Mr. Wolf and his team busy, while also helping us directly, of course."

"And what is that?" Allison asked, curiosity piqued.

"What do you know about Dr. Anthony Palmer?" the handler inquired.

"Genius is the best word. Why?" Allison replied.

"Have you heard about him going rogue?"

"Only whispers," Allison said. "But you know me, I prefer to concentrate on my own."

"Yes. Well, six months ago, we discovered that our esteemed doctor was not only delaying his own research but had also taken the project further on his own at his private home laboratory."

"He was developing the program for himself?" Allison asked, her interest growing.

"Yes. And now he's run off and started his own project in the jungles of Sumba, Indonesia. He's enlisted the local population and is running around like some deity—or a modern-day Kurtz. The Council needs him back, and we need that research. I want you to send Noah Wolf and his team into the area to extract the scientist and take his research. You can tell him that the doctor is working for the Council, tell him that the whole thing is a Council project. Make him think he's breaking apart our plans. Do whatever it takes to get Palmer and his research out of there, OK?"

"Understood. I'll handle it," Allison affirmed.

"But be careful, Number Eleven. Palmer is very dangerous. I've already lost a team of elite operatives on this, as well as a scientist who thought he could persuade Palmer. Tell Wolf and his people to tread carefully. They will be stepping into the lion's den on this one."

SIX

The early morning air was crisp, carrying a faint chill that cut through the orderly chaos of the preparations for takeoff. The hum of Air Force One's engines provided a steady backdrop to the buzz of activity surrounding the plane. Staff and security personnel moved with determined efficiency, their movements a well-choreographed dance.

Dane Chavers arrived early, his every sense sharpened to the mission in hand and what he must do. As he passed through the security checks, his mind raced with the details of the plan ahead. Each step felt heavy as he tried to maintain his composure, his usual excitement of boarding Air Force One overshadowed by a deep sense of dread.

The press was gathered at one end of the plane, every one of them animated by the rumors surrounding the potentially historical nature of the day. Cameras clicked, reporters murmured to one another, and the energy was electric with the anticipation of the president's upcoming UN Council trip.

"Can't wait to see what the president's speech is," one reporter said to another, a smile on his face.

"Absolutely. Let's hope he delivers a strong message," the second reporter replied.

"You think the rumors about him making concessions to the Russians and Chinese to get them into NATO are true?"

"I don't know. But whatever he's going to say, this is going to be a historic trip."

It would be historic all right. Just not in the way they were expecting.

Dane, standing off to the side, watched as President Jackson T. Whitmore approached the press. The president's charisma and composure were evident in the way he carried himself, his smile genuine and his eyes bright with confidence.

"Good morning, everyone," President Whitmore addressed the press. "I just wanted to say a few words before we head out. This is a crucial trip, and I'm confident that together, we can make a significant impact. Thank you all for being here."

The press responded with various acknowledgments and questions, their excitement and respect clear. Whitmore's presence was commanding, his optimism infectious. That was why he was so dangerous to the Council.

Dane's heart pounded in his chest as he watched the president interact with the press. The contrast between Whitmore's calm demeanor and his own nervousness was huge. He took a deep breath, trying to steady himself. "Stay focused, Dane. Just stay focused," he muttered under his breath.

The president finished his impromptu interview and made his way to his seat. The voices of the press quieted down as the seatbelt sign came on, and inside the president's cabin, he and his advisors huddled together, making last-minute adjustments to his speech.

Dane made his way to his own seat. Sitting down, he carefully went over his surreptitious preparations, ensuring that everything was in place. The vial of poison felt like a leaden weight in his pocket, a constant reminder of what was about to transpire.

As the plane cruised at altitude, President Whitmore turned from his advisors, fixing his eyes on his personal assistant. "Hey, Dane?" the president called out.

Dane swallowed hard, his heart pounding in his chest. "Yes, Mr. President?"

"Dane, could you get me a Diet Coke, please?"

"Of course, Mr. President. Would anyone else like one?"

His advisors all shook their heads. Good. It would make it easier.

Dane moved to the galley, his movements precise and controlled. He retrieved a can of Diet Coke, ensuring no one was watching. His hands shook slightly as he discreetly poured the can over a glass of ice, then poured the vial over that. Allison had said it was tasteless. He hoped to God she hadn't been lying.

Taking a deep breath, he steadied himself and took the drink to the president. "Here you go, sir. Your Diet Coke," he said, his voice steady despite the turmoil inside.

President Whitmore smiled warmly, his demeanor relaxed. "Thanks, Dane. You always know what I need."

He took the glass and raised it to his lips. Dane watched, his heart in his throat, as the president took a sip. Time seemed to slow, the world narrowing to the single moment of that sip.

The president set the can down, none the wiser. "Perfect, as always," he said, his attention already turning to the documents in front of him.

Dane felt a cold sweat break out on his brow as he retreated to his seat. The droning hum of Air Force One's engines seemed to echo with the weight of his actions, marking the beginning of a day that would change the course of history forever.

SEVEN

ALLISON AND MOLLY HAD RETURNED TO KIRTLAND from DC only an hour before and were visibly tired. But despite their exhaustion, they were present and ready for the morning's briefing. With the imperturbable Dragon Lady seated behind her desk and Molly standing next to her, occasionally stifling a yawn with the back of her hand, they were set to begin.

Noah, Neil, Jenny, Marco, and Renée stood on the other side of the desk.

"I hope this isn't another chasing our tails mission," Noah commented in a tone edged with frustration.

"No," Allison assured him. "This one may have some teeth in it."

"OK," Noah said. "I'm all ears."

"Has anyone here ever heard of Dr. Anthony Palmer?"

The five of them exchanged glances, all shrugging and shaking their heads.

"That's because before he could make a name for

himself publicly, he was recruited by the Council, straight out of MIT, where he was running their PhD program at twenty-five. The guy's a genius by all accounts. But his work has been kept underground for the past twenty years."

Neil raised an eyebrow. "And he's the target?"

"Yes," Allison confirmed.

Noah's eyes narrowed. "Extraction or elimination?"

"Extraction," Allison replied firmly. "We want him alive."

Noah nodded. "So who is he and where is he?"

"First who," Allison said, turning to Molly. "Ms. Hanson."

Molly stepped forward, tapping on a tablet that brought up a picture on a telescreen behind her. She stifled yet another yawn before speaking. "Dr. Palmer was born in Ohio in 1971. He got a scholarship to MIT at sixteen and had his PhD in neuroscience and molecular biology by twenty. Not long after that, the Council stepped in. They recruited Dr. Palmer in 1997, and after that, the doctor was kept hidden away from the public, his work completely secret."

The image on the screen showed Dr. Anthony Palmer sitting in a wheelchair. He was tall and gaunt, with sharp features, graying hair, and intense blue eyes that seemed to reflect both brilliance and madness. As well as being a paraplegic, there was a scar that ran from his left temple to his jaw.

"Our intelligence tells us that by thirty, Palmer was the lead scientist at the Council's largest lab," Molly continued, fighting off another yawn. "The scar you see running down his face and the paralysis of his legs is from a gas explosion in one of the labs ten years ago. But he is not to be underestimated. Anthony Palmer is highly intelligent, obsessive, driven, morally ambiguous, manipulative, and charismatic. He is highly regarded by the Council and vital to our fight against them."

Molly tapped the tablet again, and another image appeared on the screen. This one was of a hulking figure, standing at seven and a half feet tall, a mountain of muscle.

"What is *that*?" Neil exclaimed, eyes widening.

"This is Dr. Palmer's bodyguard, Brennan Krol," Allison explained.

"Another experiment, like Gruber?" Noah asked, his expression hardening.

"Yes, but a little different," Allison replied. "Whereas Gruber was instilled with exceptional intelligence, Krol is merely a physical form. His IQ is around average, but his strength outweighs even Gruber's."

"Great," Noah grunted. "Because it only nearly killed me fighting Gruber."

"Twice," Jenny added. "You fought him twice—and it nearly killed you twice."

"Yeah," Marco added with a smirk. "And it took a car crash to kill him."

"Actually," Neil chimed in, "if you recall, Marco, the car crash only incapacitated him—having broken every bone in his body. It was Noah shooting him in the—"

"OK," Allison interrupted, holding up a hand. "We get the picture."

"Anyway," Molly continued, "our intelligence states that Krol is extremely loyal to Palmer and will likely have to be taken out if you are to extract the doctor."

"Which begs the question: where?" Renée asked.

Molly brought up another image on the screen, displaying a map of the Indonesian archipelago, zooming in on a medium-sized island south of the larger Nusa Tenggara Islands.

"Dr. Palmer is currently running one of the Council's biggest projects on Sumba, Indonesia. Sumba is a remote island with low tourism, part of the Lesser Sunda islands. Unlike Bali and Java, it doesn't attract many visitors, so it maintains a low population and a quiet atmosphere. It has a total population of around 800,000 and an area of a little over 11,000 square kilometers—mostly jungle, some low mountains. Where exactly Palmer's lab is among those 11,000 kilometers is going to take some detective work from yourselves. Your mission is to investigate the island, find Palmer, and extract him and his research."

Noah's eyes narrowed as he studied the map. "What about resistance?"

"Allison and I will provide more details, but expect significant resistance," Molly replied, yawning. "Wherever Palmer's lab is, you can guarantee he doesn't just have Krol. He'll have armed guards, as well as most of the local population under his and Council control. This will not be an easy mission."

"Understood," Noah said.

Allison leaned forward, her eyes meeting each team member's. "This mission is critical. Palmer's research could be the key to turning the tide against the Council. I trust you all to handle this with the utmost precision." Having said this, she turned to Molly, adding, "Ms. Hanson, you can continue."

Molly cleared her throat. "We suspect Dr. Palmer and his lab are in the southeast of Sumba but can't be sure. You'll need to be separated into groups and approach the island from three different locations."

"Once you've located Palmer," Allison added, "extract him alive, along with all his data and any test subjects."

Neil's frown deepened. "Test subjects? What does that mean?"

Allison's expression was somber. "I guess you'll have to decide what that means when you find out what they're up to in Sumba. Whatever it is, it looks very big. The intelligence we're getting from Council sources is that they've put a lot of eggs in Dr. Palmer's basket. Get him—and we get them."

Marco crossed his arms. "Wait. I have a question."

Allison looked his way. "I'm all ears, Mr. Turin."

"So correct me if I'm wrong," Marco put to the Dragon Lady, "but not only are we going in blind, but we've also got to start asking people questions? We'll be exposed the second we start sniffing around."

"Marco's right," Noah said. "The Council will have eyes and ears everywhere. They'll see us coming from a mile away."

"No they won't," Allison said resolutely.

"And why not?" Noah retorted.

"Because Wally has something special for you down at R&D."

Noah raised an eyebrow. "What kind of special?"

EIGHT

THE LABS OF RESEARCH AND DEVELOPMENT (R&D) were a hive of cutting-edge technology, filled with sleek machines, advanced robotics, and interactive displays. The air buzzed with the faint hum of churning machinery, and the walls were lined with monitors displaying streams of data and holographic interfaces. Noah, Jenny, Neil, Marco, and Renée stood around Wally Lawson.

"In this mission, communication will be vital," Wally began. "In order to be able to interact with the locals during your investigations, you'll need to understand their language as well as speak it. Does anyone here know Kambera or East Sumbanese?"

The team exchanged glances, rolling their eyes and shaking their heads.

Wally chuckled. "So that's a no, then. Well, that'll be where our little friend here comes in." He held up a small earpiece and a mouthpiece contraption, displaying them in the palm of his hand. The earpiece was sleek and wireless, equipped with tiny advanced microphones and speakers, while the mouthpiece was a lightweight device designed to fit snugly over the user's mouth, similarly equipped with a microphone and speakers.

"This," Wally announced proudly, "is the world's most advanced NLP: natural language processor."

Noah raised an eyebrow. "How does it work, Wally?"

Wally smiled and began explaining. "The earpiece is small, wireless, and equipped with advanced microphones and speakers. It fits comfortably in your ear." He demonstrated.

"The mouthpiece," he continued, "is lightweight and covers your mouth. It's equipped with a microphone and speakers for speech translation." He held the mouthpiece up for them to see before placing it over his mouth.

Neil looked skeptical. "So this thing is supposed to translate languages in real-time?"

"Exactly," Wally confirmed. "The earpiece and mouthpiece use advanced speech recognition algorithms to capture spoken language. The captured speech is transmitted wirelessly to a central processing unit, a cloud-based server, where it's processed by sophisticated translation algorithms."

Jenny leaned in, intrigued. "Can you break that down for us, Wally?"

"Sure," Wally replied. "It involves several key steps: First, natural language processing (NLP) breaks down the speech into understandable components. Then contextual understanding uses context and local dialect nuances to accurately translate phrases and sentences. Finally, machine learning leverages vast databases of linguistic patterns and continuously learns from interactions to improve accuracy."

Renée frowned, still not entirely convinced. "And the translation happens in real-time?"

"Yes," Wally assured her. "The translated speech is sent back to the earpiece, providing real-time audio output in your preferred language. The mouthpiece uses text-to-speech technology to convert your translated text into spoken words, adjusting tone and accent to sound natural."

Marco nodded slowly. "So if someone speaks in East Sumbanese, the earpiece's microphone captures the audio and transmits it wirelessly to the central processing unit."

Wally nodded. "Correct. The CPU, equipped with powerful processors and access to cloud-based translation databases, quickly processes the speech using NLP algorithms. The speech is translated from East Sumbanese to English in real-time. The translated English speech is transmitted back to the earpiece, which plays it back to the user."

Noah looked thoughtful. "And when we respond in English?"

"The mouthpiece captures your speech," Wally explained, "transmits it for translation, and then uses text-to-speech synthesis to play the translated speech in East Sumbanese through the mouthpiece's speakers."

Jenny looked impressed. "That's pretty advanced."

Wally grinned. "It is. This technology should give you a significant edge in communicating with the locals and gathering the information you need without drawing unnecessary attention."

"What about communication between us?" Noah asked. "Can we use it to talk to each other?"

"I'm glad you asked," Wally said, patting Noah on the shoulder. He held up the mouthpiece of the NLP, his enthusiasm undiminished. "The NLP is also capable of being used for encrypted communication between team members while on the island. But not just that. There's another feature of the NLP that I haven't mentioned yet. This device doesn't just translate languages; it also has a voice concealment feature."

Noah was interested. "Voice concealment? How does that work?"

"Great question, Noah," Wally replied. "The mouthpiece can project ambient sounds that mask your voice, making it seem like you're not speaking at all. This means you can communicate with each other without anyone around you hearing a thing."

Renée raised an eyebrow. "So we can call in to the other team members without those nearby noticing?"

Wally nodded. "Exactly. It's perfect for maintaining covert communication in sensitive situations. Let me show you."

Wally put on the mouthpiece and activated the ambient sound projection. "Esmeralda, activate voice concealment mode."

"Voice concealment mode activated," the AI responded.

Wally spoke normally. "Can you hear me?"

The team saw Wally's lips moving behind the mouthpiece, but all they heard was the sound of the lab's machinery humming in the background, the buzz of the overhead lights—perfectly masking his voice.

Jenny's eyes widened in amazement. "That's incredible. We can actually talk without worrying about being overheard."

"Exactly," Wally confirmed, switching it off. "The device

uses a combination of white noise and ambient sound recordings tailored to your environment to mask your voice. It's highly effective in noisy areas, like markets or busy streets."

Marco looked impressed. "And this won't interfere with the NLP's translation capabilities?"

"Not at all," Wally assured him. "The translation and voice concealment features work seamlessly together. You'll be able to communicate and translate while staying completely discreet."

Neil nodded. "That's going to be a game-changer for us."

"That's the idea, Mr. Blessing," Wally said with a grin. He then gestured to his right, where an elderly man of Sumbanese ethnicity had quietly entered the lab and now stood behind them. "But it isn't the only invention that will help you out there. This here"—he indicated the man—"is Jane."

The team frowned and mumbled, "Jane?" looking at one another. The Sumbanese man, appearing to be in his late 60s, certainly didn't look like any 'Jane.'

"Jane," Wally said, "show them."

The man pressed his palm with a thumb and suddenly flickered like a television before transforming into a woman standing in what looked like a wetsuit with a full mask, only her mouth, nostrils, and eyes showing. The suit was covered entirely in tiny dots that caught the light in the room.

As Jane removed the mask to reveal herself, the team muttered, "What the...?"

Wally explained, "Jane is wearing an advanced holographic disguise system. The suit she's wearing can project holographic images the size of a pinhead. Combined all together, it projects an image straight over a person. One that the naked eye cannot differentiate."

He nodded at Jane, who pressed the function pad on her palm once more. The suit flickered, and before their eyes, the woman transformed back into the elderly Indonesian man.

Wally continued, "The Hologram Suit is designed to project a completely realistic holographic image over the wearer, allowing you to blend in perfectly with the locals. Added to the NLP, you may as well have been born on Sumba."

Neil stepped forward, intrigued. "What about battery life and durability? We'll be out in the field, so it needs to last and withstand some wear and tear."

Wally nodded. "The suit is designed with efficient power management for long-lasting performance, and it's built to be durable yet comfortable. It can also handle various lighting conditions and environments, adjusting its images, ensuring it performs well in the field."

Noah smiled, clearly impressed. "That's impressive, Wally."

"And that's not all," Wally continued. "The Hologram Suit has an additional feature that could prove indispensable for your mission: camouflage."

He nodded to Jane, who gave a small, knowing smile. "Jane, could you demonstrate the camouflage mode for us?"

Jane pressed her palm again, and before their eyes, she began to disappear. The suit melded seamlessly with the environment of the lab, mimicking the colors and textures of the walls, machinery, and even the floor. The team watched in awe as she vanished completely, only a faint shimmer giving any indication of her presence. Suddenly, Jane waved, and for a brief moment, the suit struggled to keep up with the rapid movement, revealing her outline before blending in perfectly once more.

Wally stepped forward to explain the science behind the suit. "The Hologram Suit employs nano cameras embedded throughout its surface. These cameras capture the surrounding environment in real-time and relay the data to a central processor in the suit. The processor then generates a live feed that is projected over the surface of the suit using the micro-scale projectors."

Neil, clearly fascinated, asked, "So it's like the suit is wearing a live video feed of its surroundings?"

"Precisely," Wally confirmed. "The nano cameras continuously scan the environment, and the projectors display the captured images, effectively rendering the wearer invisible by blending them into their surroundings. This process happens almost instantaneously, ensuring that the camouflage adapts dynamically to changes in the environment."

Noah nodded, clearly impressed. "This technology is incredible. Between the NLP and the Hologram Suit, we'll have significant advantages in the field."

Wally smiled, pleased with their reactions. "That's the goal. With these tools, you'll be able to sink right in and operate without drawing any unwanted attention. But just in case blending in isn't enough, I have something else for you."

Taking a pen-sized device from his pocket, Wally held it up for everyone to see. "You may or may not recognize this from Cuba," he told the team. "Neil certainly does."

Neil's eyes lit up with recognition as he spotted the device. "Oh, yes," he said, a hint of suffering in his voice.

Wally continued, "This here is a cognitive harmonizer. You place it directly to the skull and press the button. It then temporarily disrupts neural pathways, making the subject highly suggestible for up to an hour. He or she is essentially your slave. You can reverse the effects by placing it back to the skull and pressing the button twice. It's perfect for quick intel extraction, as well as making potential prisoners more cooperative. It could come in handy with those unwilling to share vital information with you."

Noah examined the device with a mixture of curiosity and caution. "So it basically turns someone into a puppet for an hour?"

Wally nodded. "That's right. The cognitive harmonizer disrupts the brain's normal functioning, making the subject highly suggestible and open to commands. It's a powerful tool, but it must be used with care."

Noah was nodding. "It will be very useful for when we come into contact with Council agents."

The team nodded with him, each member absorbing the importance of the new technology. Nevertheless, the positive mood was short-lived.

As Wally finished up the presentations, a lab technician burst into the room, his face pale with urgency. The team turned to look at him, a sense of foreboding entering the room with him.

"Have you heard yet?" the technician asked breathlessly.

"Heard what?" Neil responded, the unease spreading through the team.

"It's all over the news, the Internet, everything. Turn it on," the technician urged.

Wally, sensing the gravity of the situation, quickly directed Esmeralda. "Esmeralda, put the news on."

"Yes, Wally," the AI responded, and the large screen on the wall flickered to life.

The images showed chaotic footage taken by a camera-phone aboard Air Force One. People were rushing toward the president's cabin, led by the president's personal physician. Over the top, the newscaster's voice relayed the shocking events.

"What the images you're watching show are the moments directly after the president went into cardiac arrest aboard his plane, Air Force One," the newscaster narrated.

The team stood frozen, the color draining from their faces as they watched the footage. The gravity of the situation hit them like a punch to the gut.

News anchor: "President Jackson T. Whitmore was pronounced dead before the flight touched down in New York. He joins the list of presidents who died in office, including William Henry Harrison, Zachary Taylor, Warren G. Harding, and Franklin D. Roosevelt. President Whitmore was about to address the UN Council in New York. The honor will now be taken by Vice President Gina Brown."

The screen cut to live footage outside the United Nations building, where Vice President Gina Brown was addressing the nation.

"Today, we mourn the loss of a great leader and a dear friend. President Jackson T. Whitmore was not just a president; he was a visionary who dedicated his life to serving our nation. It was my honor and privilege that he chose me as his running mate, and it has been my honor to serve alongside him ever since.

"President Whitmore and I have worked closely for many years, and I am committed to continuing his legacy. However, in light of this tragedy, we must take a moment to reconvene and carefully consider our next steps. The signing of the UN-NATO alliance pact will be stalled as we navigate this period of mourning and transition.

"Our nation is without a leader at this critical moment, and we must step carefully to ensure stability and security. I ask for your patience and understanding as we move forward together. Thank you."

Inside the lab, the news was greeted with a stunned silence. The abrupt shift in mood almost took their breaths away.

Jenny was the first to speak. "Does that mean they're pulling the plug?"

Noah said nothing, his jaw clenched in fury, his eyes fixed on the screen. The news of Whitmore's death and the implications for E & E filled him with a boiling rage.

Renée shook her head. "It really does sound like Whitmore dying is the end of the alliance."

The weight of the situation bore down on Noah. Inside, he was seething. The loss of President Whitmore and the potential collapse of the alliance felt like a personal blow. Without a word, he turned on his heel and stormed out of the lab.

NINE

THE KIRTLAND GRAVEYARD LAY IN THE SHADOW OF the majestic Rockies, the mountains towering in the background, their snow-capped peaks glistening in the morning light. The air was crisp and clear, a gentle breeze rustling the leaves of the ancient trees that dotted the gravestones.

Noah stood alone over a grave marked with Allison Peterson's name. The gravestone was simple and unadorned, yet it held a profound significance for him. Like he had done during the three months they thought she was dead, Noah stood there before that empty grave, contemplating their situation and the seemingly unbeatable Council.

As he stared at the inscription written on the headstone, the silence was broken only by the distant call of a bird—and something else.

Noah sighed, his breath visible in the chilly air. "Are you going to speak?" he said aloud. "Or are you just going to stand there watching me?"

Behind him, Allison Peterson stepped forward, her presence almost ghostly in the quiet of the graveyard. "Can't sneak up on the great Noah Wolf, I guess," she said with a wry smile, coming to stand beside him.

Gesturing to the gravestone with her own name on it, Allison shook her head slightly. "A little weird this thing still being here."

Noah shrugged, his eyes never leaving the gravestone. "I guess no one knows what to do with it. After all, we've all got our own plots up here. This is yours." Pointing off to the west, he added, "Mine, Sarah's, and Norah's are over there."

"A nice thought," Allison quipped dryly.

"Practical," Noah replied, his tone matter-of-fact.

"Yeah. But that still doesn't explain why you're standing next to my empty grave," Allison said.

Noah sighed again. "I used to come up here to think, back when we all thought you were gone. I guess I haven't lost the habit yet."

The peaceful yet eerie atmosphere of the graveyard enveloped them, watched only by the birds and the mountains.

"It's a big shame the president dying like that," Allison said.

"With Whitmore gone, things are looking even more uncertain," Noah said. "Bleak would be my word for it."

"It's a huge loss," Allison agreed. "He was a strong leader, but we can't let his death derail everything we've been fighting for."

Noah sighed, his gaze fixed on the gravestone. "Where do we go from here? The Council seems more unstoppable than ever."

"We keep fighting. We adapt. We find their weaknesses

and exploit them. Whitmore's death is a setback, but it's not the end," Allison replied firmly.

Noah shook his head slightly. "It feels like we're always one step behind."

"That's because we are," Allison acknowledged. "But that doesn't mean we stop. It means we push harder, smarter. This thing with Palmer in Sumba. Get him. Get his research. Get a win."

A moment of silence fell between them, both lost in their thoughts. Allison had to admit to herself that even she never knew she was capable of this level of manipulation. Sending him to Sumba, thinking he was getting a win against the Council when all he was doing was acting as their errand boy was despicable. But it had to be done. Her work had to be done.

Noah turned to Allison, meeting her gaze. "You've never spoken of what happened between you and the Council during those three months they had you as their captive."

He let the statement hang between them, the unspoken question thickening the air.

"Why not?" Noah asked quietly.

Allison looked right back at him, her eyes unwavering. "What do *you* think happened?"

"They tried to turn you," Noah said instantly, his voice steady. "Just like they tried with me."

Allison nodded. "Yes, they did. For three whole months. You only had it for three days. Can you imagine what..."

"Yes, I can," Noah interrupted, his voice barely above a whisper. "I can imagine giving in after all that time."

They held each other's stare, the weight of shared experiences and unspoken fears passing between them.

"But you didn't," Noah continued. "You stayed strong. That's why they decided to kill you on that platform."

"That's right. Three months of torture and then death," Allison confirmed.

"Lucky Marco and I turned up when we did," Noah said, a faint smile touching his lips.

Again, they held each other's stare.

"The Lord works in mysterious ways, Noah Wolf," Allison said, her tone softening.

"He certainly does," Noah agreed, a hint of a smile playing on his lips.

Allison's tone lightened further, bringing a touch of normalcy back to the moment. "Now come on, you can't stay up here all day moping. You need to go down there and say goodbye to your family because after that, you've got a scientist to catch. Let's get a win for E & E for once. OK?"

Noah nodded, the determination returning to his eyes. "OK."

TEN

Dr. Jonathan Taylor arrived at the entrance to the highly secured Council lab H9-3, located deep beneath the vast expanse of the Sahara Desert. The facility was a fortress hidden far below the desert sands.

There were five entrances to H9-3. The main one, designed to look like a medium-sized warehouse, was linked by road and accepted deliveries of equipment. Another entrance opened into a vast chamber in the desert, allowing helicopters to lower even larger equipment down. Then there were three staff entrances for the daily access of personnel. These small entrances were disguised as simple pump stations for wells, surrounded by fences and monitored by CCTV but appearing as nothing more than harmless buildings. Hidden inside, however, were elevators that transported staff miles underground.

The entrance Jonathan Taylor was arriving at was one of these. Unlike most pump stations, this one was guarded by a state-of-the-art biometric scanner and a heavily armored door that only allowed access to those with the highest clearance.

Jonathan approached the scanner, his demeanor calm and confident. The device scanned his retina, fingerprint, and voice pattern before the massive door slid open with a soft hiss. He stepped through, entering a platform that began descending into the earth. Almost half a mile down, he exited the elevator into a sleek, high-tech world far removed from the harsh desert environment above.

The underground lab was a maze of sterile white corridors illuminated by soft, ambient lighting. The walls were lined with advanced security cameras, and every few feet, there were security checkpoints manned by vigilant guards. Jonathan moved through the facility with purpose.

A security officer nodded to him as he passed. "Afternoon, Dr. Taylor. We weren't expecting you. Is everything in order?"

Jonathan responded with a professional smile. "Yes. Just some routine checks. Everything is as it should be."

The officer nodded, and Jonathan continued on his way. The air was cool and sterile, filled with the hum of advanced machinery and the occasional beep of electronics.

As he walked nonchalantly down a corridor, he caught the eye of a passing scientist who did a double-take. "Hey John," the man called out.

Jonathan stopped and turned to him, his expression blank. "Hello, Barry."

"You're back then?" Barry asked, curiosity evident in his tone.

"Yes," Jonathan replied curtly.

They stared at one another for a moment. "So how did it go?" Barry asked. "Did you find him?"

"Unfortunately not," Jonathan said.

"So he wasn't out at your old research grounds like you thought."

"No. He wasn't."

Barry looked puzzled. "What did management say?"

"They've left agents in the area," Jonathan responded flatly.

"You still think he's on Sumba?"

"No." With that, Jonathan turned and walked away, his steps echoing in the silent corridor.

"OK, John. Bye then," Barry called after him, adding under his breath, "Dick."

Dr. Jonathan Taylor continued through the lab. Several levels down, he reached the entrance to the power room. The door was reinforced with layers of steel and advanced biometric locks. Jonathan quickly accessed the control panel, his fingers moving with precision as he entered his high-level security clearance. Then the door slid open, revealing the heart of the facility.

Jonathan's eyes scanned the power room until he found the main control panel. He approached it, his focus intense. Pulling a small device from his pocket, he plugged it into the system's interface. The device immediately began to work, uploading a sophisticated virus designed to wreak havoc on the lab's security systems.

Jonathan stood staring as the progress bar on the screen slowly filled until finally, the upload was complete. The virus took hold, the room's lights flickering before plunging into darkness. A moment later, emergency lighting activated, bathing the room in an eerie red glow.

Throughout the facility, alarms blared as the security system spiraled into disarray. The blast doors separating each section of the lab slammed shut with a resounding thud, trapping everyone in whatever area they happened to be. Jonathan could hear the people crying out, their voices muffled by the thick steel doors. Frantic banging echoed through the corridors, a cacophony of fear and confusion.

Jonathan moved swiftly toward the fusion reactor at the back of the room, his path illuminated by the red emergency lights. Reaching it, he paused for a moment, taking in the sight before him. The cold fusion core, a compact cylindrical device about the size of a coffee can, was housed within a reinforced containment unit bristling with cooling fins and data cables. This containment unit was securely plugged into the reactor with a faint blue glow emanating from the core. It was limitless energy. Enough to run this lab forever.

With a final, determined breath, Dr. Jonathan Taylor stepped forward and with steady hands began the extraction process. The core was nestled deep within the reactor, held in place by a series of intricate locking mechanisms. He methodically disengaged each lock, the hum of the reactor growing louder as he worked.

Beads of sweat formed on his forehead as he carefully lifted the fusion core from its housing. The core pulsed with a faint blue glow, a concentrated source of immense energy. Taylor held it steady, knowing that even the slightest mistake could result in catastrophic consequences.

"Got you," he muttered to himself as he gently placed the core into a specially designed container he had brought with him. As the core settled into place, the container emitted a soft hiss, sealing it inside.

With the container secure, he turned his attention to the large ventilation shaft nearby. Removing the grill, he hoisted himself into the narrow, dark passageway, the sounds of distant alarms and voices echoing around him. Taking one last look at the power room, he turned and began crawling toward the service ladder that would take him back to the surface—after, of course, climbing the half mile up.

ELEVEN

INSIDE THE TIGHT CONFINES OF A SUBMARINE, Noah, Jenny, Neil, Marco, and Renée were packed and ready for deployment, their gear meticulously arranged.

The alarm blared suddenly, its sharp tone reverberating through the metal corridors. "Surface! Prepare for deployment."

The team members looked at each other, a mix of determination and camaraderie in their eyes. Noah stood at the center. "All right, everyone. This is it. See you on the other side."

Jenny and Neil exchanged a nod. Marco and Renée did the same, a silent understanding passing between them. They were all ready.

Noah moved to the hatch, the cramped space of the submarine feeling even tighter as the mission loomed. The hatch opened with a hiss, and Noah climbed through, emerging into the night air. He climbed into a small motorized dinghy, the cold sea spray hitting his face as he started the engine and headed toward the island of Sumba.

The submarine began to submerge once more, its sleek silhouette disappearing beneath the waves as it prepared to circle the island and drop the other teams off. Inside, the others steeled themselves for their own deployments.

Jenny and Neil would land on the northwestern edge of the island closest to Waitabula. Marco and Renée were set to hit the southern coast near Lalindi, prepared to move inland. As for Noah, he and his dinghy were approaching the northeastern shore, near the large town of Waingapu.

Glancing back at the dark sea where the submarine had vanished, Noah felt the gravity of the mission settle over him. He was all alone now. The night was quiet except for the gentle lapping of waves against the dinghy. The dense jungle loomed ahead, a dark and unknown expanse waiting for him.

He reached a lonely stretch of shore, the sand glistening under the moonlit sky. Quickly, he deflated the dinghy and dragged it into a small cove of shallow caves. He stashed the deflated dinghy and its motor inside one of them, hoping no one would bother to investigate. If they did, he reasoned, they'd likely take the motor and leave the rest, reporting nothing—that was unless the Council had a significant presence here.

Changing out of his wetsuit, Noah swiftly donned the hologram suit, including the mask. It clung to him as he dressed in a pair of shorts, a T-shirt, and flip-flops, mimicking the typical clothing of the locals. He was almost finished when he spotted flashlight beams piercing the darkness at the edge of the beach. Two local fishermen were making their way toward him.

Noah hurried, activating the suit and the NLP just in time. As the fishermen approached, the suit's micro-LEDs projected the image of a local man beneath the casual attire. By the time the fishermen got a good look, he appeared just like them.

"Hello there," Noah said to both men.

The fishermen, both weathered by years of salt and surf, regarded Noah curiously. Their flashlights flickered across his figure, casting long shadows on the sand. One of them, a tall man with a wiry frame, spoke first in the local dialect, his voice rough like the sea.

"Out late, aren't you?" he asked, his tone more curious than suspicious.

Noah nodded, maintaining the calm demeanor of a local. "Just finished a night dive," he replied in the same dialect, the suit's NLP translating his English seamlessly into the local tongue. "Needed to check the nets before dawn. Caught a few good ones, but it's quiet tonight."

The shorter fisherman, with a bushy mustache and a slightly wary expression, glanced at Noah's feet, noting the flip-flops. "You're not from Waingapu, are you?"

Noah smiled, a small, disarming gesture. "No, I'm from further inland, near Lewa. Just visiting some family here and thought I'd help out. The sea's always been a part of me, you know."

The fishermen exchanged a glance, then relaxed. The tall one chuckled. "Ah, Lewa. A beautiful place. You must know the old man Arman there. He has the best betel nuts."

Noah nodded again. "Old Arman's a friend of my

father. His betel nuts are the only reason I visit him!" he joked, eliciting a laugh from the men.

"Well, safe travels, brother," the tall fisherman said, adjusting the strap of the net slung over his shoulder. "The night's calm, but the tides are unpredictable this time of year. Don't get caught out there."

"Thanks, I'll keep that in mind," Noah replied, stepping aside to let them pass.

As the fishermen continued down the beach, their flashlights bobbing in the darkness, Noah watched them go, his muscles gradually unclenching.

Walking away in the opposite direction toward the road, he reflected on the encounter. He noted how easily people were put at ease when they saw a familiar face and heard a familiar accent. It struck him how different the interaction would have been if they had seen him in his true state.

TWELVE

Jenny and Neil left their dinghy at a small harbor where it would be inconspicuous among the other dinghies, their hologram suits already activated. The night air was warm, filled with the hum of nocturnal insects and the subtle scents of cooking wafting from the small wooden houses dotting this part of the coastline. They soon moved off the beach, with the denser part of Waitabula township looming ahead.

They entered narrow streets lined by closely packed buildings, each one a patchwork of vibrant colors and makeshift materials. The suits worked flawlessly. As they walked, they appeared as locals, dressed in the common garb of the area. Neil's face was that of an older Sumbanese, his skin weathered and his eyes sharp with years of experience. Jenny's guise was that of an old woman, his wife. Their cover was that they were an old retired couple from Bali looking for their son.

The deeper they got into Waitabula, the more streets

became alive with activity. Even at this late hour, people moved about their business, some carrying baskets of goods, others engaged in animated conversations. The soft glow of streetlights cast long shadows, adding to the sense of bustling intimacy.

As they moved through the throng of a night market, they were met with nods and smiles, receiving the respect due to their supposed seniority. No one looked twice at them. They were just another part of the tapestry of night life in Waitabula.

In a hushed tone, Neil said, "The suits are working perfectly. No one's giving us a second glance."

Jenny nodded. "It's amazing how different it feels to blend in like this. But even still"—her tone darkened—"we need to stay sharp. The Council's agents could be anywhere."

"Agreed. We'll gather intel here, then move on to the next location if and when needed."

"Right," Jenny replied. "We should stick around this market. See if we can pick up any local chatter about unusual activities or newcomers."

"And keep an eye out for any signs of the Council."

They continued walking, their senses heightened, taking in every detail of their surroundings.

THIRTEEN

Marco and Renée walked down the bustling streets of Lalindi. Nighttime in Sumba meant night markets, and Lalindi was no different. The market stretched out before them, a lively tapestry of stalls, colorful lights, and a mix of people from all walks of life.

The market was a sensory overload, the air filled with the tantalizing aromas of street food, the sizzle of meat grilling, and the sweet scent of tropical fruits. Stalls overflowed with a kaleidoscope of goods—handmade crafts, vibrant textiles, and an array of spices that added a rich scent to the air. Strings of lights crisscrossed overhead, casting a warm, festive glow over the scene. The chatter of the crowd created a constant hum, punctuated by the occasional shout of a vendor hawking their wares.

Marco and Renée moved through the thronging alleyways, their hologram suits ensuring that they went unnoticed. The few tourists that were there were being set upon by the locals, eager to sell their goods or offer guided tours, but Marco and Renée moved freely, protected by the suits' deceptive appearances.

"I wish we could've used these during our honeymoon to Cairo," Marco remarked, a smile playing on his lips. "The way those locals set on us at the bazaar."

Renée chuckled as her eyes scanned the crowd. "They sure were, hon. These suits would've made things a lot easier."

They stood among the people at the night stalls, blending in perfectly with the ebb and flow of locals. They listened to the chatter around them, picking up snippets of conversation and noting the interactions between locals and tourists. Like Jenny and Neil, their plan was to hit the local spots, use the NLPs to listen in to any conversations, work from there. They knew that in the midst of this colorful chaos, vital information awaited, and they were determined to find it.

As they stood, listening to the myriad of conversations around them, a local trader leaned over his stall and fixed them with a curious gaze. "You're not from around here," he stated matter-of-factly.

Caught off guard, Marco and Renée exchanged quick glances, momentarily lost for words. For a brief, tense moment, they feared their cover had been blown. But then the trader added, "You're either from another island or from the north."

Renée, recovering quickly, asked, "How do you know we're not local?"

The trader raised an eyebrow and smiled knowingly. "There are just over a thousand of us here in Lalindi. Generations of the same families, including my own. So trust me, I know my own people."

Marco seized the opportunity to probe further. "Are there many other outsiders who come by here? Foreigners, maybe?"

The trader nodded, his expression growing serious. "There are now. Foreigners have taken over the jungles. Some say they're building a city out there. Employing the locals to build it."

Renée leaned in. "Are any of those foreigners here?"

"Maybe you mean the priest," the trader suggested.

Renée's brow furrowed. "The priest?"

"Yes," the trader confirmed. "He came here years ago, but lately, he has been recruiting people for work in the jungle."

Marco pressed on. "Whereabouts in the jungle?"

The trader shrugged. "I don't know. People come from all around for the work. They go off with the priest, and that's it."

Renée's mind raced as she asked, "Where is this priest?"

The trader pointed in the direction of the jungle. "He lives at the old mission house at the edge of the valley. It's about an hour's drive from here. I can take you when I finish here if you like. There are some others I'm already taking up there for work. Maybe you could join them."

Marco and Renée exchanged a glance, silently agreeing on their next move. "We'd appreciate that," Marco said, nodding. "Thank you."

The trader smiled. "No problem. I'll finish up here in about an hour. Meet me back here then."

As the trader returned to his stall, Marco and Renée

blended back into the crowd, their minds now focused on the lead they had just uncovered.

FOURTEEN

Jenny and Neil navigated through the dimly lit streets of Waitabula, their senses heightened as they approached the source of a large commotion. The sound of anxious voices had drawn them closer to the town's police station, where a crowd of locals had gathered, their expressions fraught with worry and frustration.

The scene was chaotic. Under the flickering streetlights, families stood huddled together, their voices loud and angry. The police station, a modest building with peeling paint and a few barred windows, seemed almost overwhelmed by the number of people pressing against its entrance.

Jenny and Neil joined the crowd. They listened intently, picking up fragments of conversation as the villagers pleaded with the police.

"Please, you have to find my son!" a woman cried, clutching a worn photograph.

"My brother's been missing for three weeks now," another man added. "You have to do something!"

A weary-looking police officer stood at the entrance, hands raised in a gesture meant to calm the crowd. "We understand your concerns," he said. "Investigations are ongoing. We're doing everything we can."

Jenny exchanged a look with Neil. They moved closer, straining to hear more.

"They were recruited for work in Lalindi," a man shouted, his voice cutting through the din. "Some priest, they said. None of them have been heard from since!"

The crowd murmured in agreement, voices rising again in a chorus of pleas and demands.

Neil leaned in toward Jenny, his voice low. "Did you hear that? Lalindi. That's where Marco and Renée are."

Jenny nodded, her eyes scanning the faces of the distressed islanders. "We need to let them know."

The police officer continued to placate the crowd with empty reassurances. "We're following every lead. I promise you, we will find them."

As the scene unfolded, Jenny spotted two men—foreigners—standing across the street. Just like Jenny and Neil, they too appeared interested in what was happening outside the police station.

Jenny whispered to Neil, "You see the two goons on the other side of the street? They're at nine o'clock—Easy!" she snapped under her breath as Neil went to turn their way. "Don't let them see you looking."

Neil glanced over without turning his head, just with his eyes. The two men looked exactly like you'd expect Council agents to look; dressed in khaki fatigues and black T-shirts.

Jenny added in an undertone, "We should get out of here before we draw too much attention."

Neil nodded in agreement. "Let's go."

They slipped away from the crowd, moving through the shadows to avoid drawing notice. The dimly lit streets of Waitabula seemed even more foreboding now, the sight of their enemy sharpening their focus. They needed to regroup and share their findings with the others, especially Marco and Renée.

However, just as they were looking for a quiet street to use the radio, Jenny and Neil rounded a corner and observed a group of locals hurriedly getting into a series of cars.

"The police will do nothing but sit on their backsides," one man was complaining loudly to those who urged him to let the authorities handle the situation. "We're going ourselves to find them. It is all we have left."

Neil, sensing an opportunity, stepped forward. "We'll come with you," he offered.

A local man looked Neil up and down, skepticism written across his face. "Eh, that's OK. I don't need passengers."

"But you might need help in a fight."

The man frowned. "From you? I appreciate the offer, but you're a little too old for fighting," he said dismissively.

Neil's jaw tightened as he stepped forward, ready to argue. "I'm not—"

But before he could continue, Jenny placed a firm hand on his arm, shaking her head when he turned. "Yes, you are old," she whispered, her tone brooking no argument. "We'll make our own way there."

Neil reluctantly nodded, stepping back as the locals piled into their vehicles. The cars roared to life, headlights cutting through the night as they sped off, determined to find their missing loved ones.

FIFTEEN

Waingapu's bustling streets were alive with activity. Vendors lined the sidewalks, their stalls overflowing with goods. The hum of conversation, the clinking of cookware, and the occasional honk of a motorbike created a lively backdrop as Noah made his way through the town.

He kept to the edges, his keen eyes taking in every detail, hunting for evidence of Palmer and the Council. At a busy street corner, he found something.

A local man stood, surrounded by a large, curious crowd. The man appeared to be recruiting people for work. His voice carried over the din, drawing in more passersby as he enthusiastically described job opportunities.

Noah watched from the periphery, observing the recruiter. The man was adept at engaging the people, his tone inviting and confident.

"What type of work?" one man asked, stepping closer to the recruiter.

"Labor," the recruiter replied with a broad smile. "But well-paid labor. They have hospitals up there, too, so there's complete medical care for all employees. There's accommodation for your family, too. Everything you could need."

A local woman, her face etched with worry, voiced her concern. "I heard from a cousin in Madala that people are going out there and never being heard of again."

The recruiter's smile didn't falter. "Absolute garbage. There'll always be husbands who don't report back to their wives right away, but anything else is just speculation and mischief."

Noah's eyes narrowed as he continued to listen. The situation confirmed his suspicions about the Council's influence in the area. These jobs in the jungle were likely tied to Palmer's operations, and the recruiter was a key player in funneling labor to the secret project.

The bustling energy of Waingapu's streets seemed to pulse around him, but Noah remained focused. He needed to find a way to get closer to the operation without drawing attention to himself. It was then, as he discreetly glanced around, that Noah noticed two foreigners watching the scene from the front of a nearby café. The men were dressed casually, but their alert eyes and poised demeanor betrayed their true purpose. One was tall and muscular with a shaved head, while the other was shorter and wiry, with a perpetual smirk. Both had the cold, calculating look of Council agents.

Recognizing the threat, Noah decided to communicate with his team using the NLP's voice concealment feature. He moved discreetly to the side and activated the setting, masking his voice with ambient sounds to ensure privacy.

"Team, this is Team Leader. I've found more evidence of

the work they're offering. Looks like they're heading your way, Marco."

Marco's voice crackled softly in his ear. "Copy that, Team Leader. Renée and I are heading inland right now. On our way to meet this priest guy out in the jungle."

Jenny joined the conversation, her tone laced with urgency. "Us, too. We're about to board a bus that is part of a convoy heading southeast. Do you know exactly where this work is taking place?"

Renée answered, "No. The guy who's driving us to the priest doesn't know. Just says it's the jungle. Which could be anywhere because most of the island is jungle and mountains."

Noah glanced at the two Council agents, maintaining his calm exterior. "Well, the Council are certainly here. I'm right this moment looking straight at two of their goons. They're watching their friend recruit people."

Neil's voice came through. "Just like the guys we saw in Waitabula. What do you think they do with the locals?"

Noah's answer was cold. "Experiment on them, probably."

Renée's response was determined. "Well, Marco and I will find out soon enough. We're almost there."

Just then, the recruiter pointed directly at Noah, his voice carrying over the noise of the crowd. "You there, sir! Do you need work that pays five times the average salary?"

Noah quickly deactivated the voice concealment feature. He stepped forward, adopting the demeanor of a curious local. "Yes, actually," he said, keeping his tone neutral. "What kind of work are we talking about?"

The recruiter's eyes lit up with enthusiasm, sensing a

potential recruit. "Labor in the jungle, but it's well-paid and includes full medical care, accommodation, everything you could need."

As the recruiter detailed the job, Noah kept a close eye on the two Council agents, who were now watching him intently. He knew he had to tread carefully.

"A wise person once told me," Noah said, keeping his tone skeptical, "that if something sounds too good to be true, then it isn't true."

The recruiter's eyes widened slightly, his voice taking on a slightly mechanical tone. "I assure you, sir, this opportunity is very real. You won't find a better offer anywhere else. We provide medical care, accommodation, and a stable income."

Noah feigned curiosity, leaning in slightly. "What kind of work is it exactly? And why so far into the jungle?"

"It's labor work, but well-compensated," the recruiter replied smoothly. "Our project requires a lot of manpower, and we have everything set up to take care of our workers. The jungle location is strategic for the resources we need."

"Resources, huh?" Noah probed. "What kind of resources are you extracting from the jungle?"

The recruiter hesitated slightly but quickly regained his composure. "That's confidential information, but rest assured, it's perfectly legal and safe. Our workers' safety is our top priority."

Noah glanced at the Council agents, who were still watching him intently, then back at the recruiter. "I've heard rumors that people go out there and aren't heard from again. Can you guarantee that won't happen to me?"

A flicker of discomfort crossed the recruiter's face. "Those are just rumors. We have strict protocols to ensure everyone's safety and well-being. If you join us, you'll see for yourself."

"I'm still not convinced," Noah said. "Can I speak to someone who's been there and come back?"

The recruiter's nervousness increased. "I'm afraid that's not possible right now. Our current workers are in the middle of a critical phase, and communication is limited. But trust me, you'll be well taken care of."

"Limited communication, huh?" Noah said, raising an eyebrow. "Sounds a bit too secretive for my taste. Who's running this operation anyway?"

The recruiter glanced around, clearly nervous. "Our management prefers to stay anonymous for security reasons. But I can assure you, they are highly reputable."

"Anonymous management and jungle labor... sounds like a recipe for disaster. I think I'll pass," Noah said firmly.

Desperation crept into the recruiter's voice. "Please reconsider. This is a once-in-a-lifetime opportunity. You won't regret it."

Noah shook his head. "I appreciate the offer, but I need more transparency before I commit."

The recruiter, sensing he was losing Noah, handed him a flyer. "At least take one of these."

As Noah took the flyer, he did something sneaky. In a flash of movement, he deftly slipped a miniscule tracking device on to the recruiter's clothing, the action taking less than a second, the recruiter feeling nothing.

Then Noah walked away, the streets of Waingapu

buzzing around him, but his focus was on the task ahead. As he moved deeper into the market, Noah glanced back, catching a final glimpse of the recruiter, who was now busy with another group of locals. The two Council agents were still there, eyes scanning the crowd. He'd avoided their scrutiny for now, but he knew it wouldn't last.

SIXTEEN

THE TRADER'S PICKUP TRUCK RUMBLED ALONG THE winding road, its headlights cutting through the thick darkness of the night. The road twisted and turned, climbing steadily uphill into the heart of the jungle. Marco and Renée sat in the front seat beside the trader. Huddled in the back, lining the bed, were six other people, their expressions a mix of apprehension and fatigue. All of them had come for the work.

The houses they passed were eerie silhouettes against the night sky, their yards overgrown with weeds, the uncut foliage reclaiming the land. The once-inhabited homes stood abandoned, their doors locked, their windows shuttered— evidence of an exodus.

Renée glanced out of the window, her eyes tracing the outlines of the deserted buildings. "Looks like people have abandoned their homes," she remarked.

The trader, a middle-aged man with a weathered face,

nodded casually. "They're all out in the jungle, earning money," he explained.

Marco asked, "And you have no idea who they're working for?"

The trader shrugged, his tone nonchalant. "Some foreign corporation. Big corporation. Just like my uncle back in the '80s when big tobacco started planting all over Indonesia. He left to work away. Never bothered to come back. Last I heard, he had a family in Jakarta. I guess that's life."

The eerie quiet of the road was punctuated only by the steady hum of the truck's engine. The darkness seemed to press in around them, the jungle alive with unseen activity. The trader's words hung in the air.

Renée turned to him. "You mentioned earlier a priest."

"Father Sanchez."

"Yes. Do you think he knows who the company is?"

The trader's eyes flicked to her briefly before returning to the road. "Oh yes. Father Sanchez knows everything about these parts."

The pickup truck continued its journey, the headlights casting long, flickering shadows on the abandoned houses as it wound its way up the hills.

As they got deeper into the jungle, there were no more houses, and the road grew narrower and more rugged. The thick canopy of trees overhead blocked out most of the moonlight, but soon, Marco and Renée began to notice a faint glow in the distance. They hit a flat area of ground, and for the first time since they'd left Lalindi, they saw electric lights piercing through the darkness.

It wasn't long before they arrived at a large compound, the source of the light. The centerpiece was a wooden Jesuit church with a pointed steeple, its stained glass windows glowing warmly from within. Around the church, rows of tents and a giant dormitory spread out, creating a small, bustling community.

The grounds were covered in people wearing overalls, methodically working away, cutting back at the jungle, which grew in at the edges. It appeared that their community was growing and needed more space. Renée and Marco felt strange watching them work at such a late hour. After all, it was almost ten. But not just that. It was the way they moved. Their movements were almost robotic, each task performed with precise, mechanical efficiency. As the truck pulled to a stop, all the workers paused in unison, turning to stare at the newcomers with blank expressions.

Marco and Renée, along with the six other passengers, stepped out of the pickup. The silent, staring crowd created an unsettling atmosphere, their eyes fixed on the new arrivals.

Suddenly, the church doors swung open, and a man in a dog collar emerged. His presence seemed to break the spell, and the workers immediately returned to their tasks, their eyes no longer on the newcomers.

Father Sanchez had a big, wide smile on his face as he approached. He was in his mid-50s, short, with a friendly face and a confident gait. His demeanor was charming, and he spoke Sumbanese with a distinct accent.

"Welcome," he greeted them warmly. "I am Father Sanchez. It is a pleasure to meet you."

Stepping forward, the trader exchanged a few hushed words with Father Sanchez, who then handed him a small bundle of money. The trader pocketed it and turned to Marco and Renée. "Good luck," he said, nodding at the others. "You too."

With that, the trader climbed back into his truck and drove away, leaving Marco and Renée in the care of Father Sanchez.

"So you've all come for work," the priest said, his smile broadening.

"And good pay," one of the men added, making the others chuckle. The priest's smile widened to breaking point in response.

"Good pay. Exactly," he said, pointing at the man. "And that is what I am offering you, friends."

One of the others who had come for work stepped forward, his expression inquisitive. "You don't sound like you're from around here. Where're you from?"

Father Sanchez's smile never wavered. "I'm originally from the Philippines, but I've been out here now for over thirty years, so I consider myself somewhat of an islander. And where are yourselves from?" He pointed at Marco.

Marco recalled his cover story. "Kodi."

Father Sanchez nodded appreciatively. "Kodi, ah. We have several people already from Kodi. You make good farmers."

"Cattle," Marco added.

"Yes. Well, we have cattle up on the sites. Meat for the workers. We process it up there too. Can you butcher cattle?"

"Absolutely. I'll butcher an alligator if I have to."

The odd comment made everyone frown, but Father Sanchez continued smoothly. "Well, we don't get alligators around here—saltwater crocodiles occasionally, but they usually stick to the coastline. It is good to hear we have a rancher and a butcher, though. What do the rest of you do?"

The others listed their professions: two rice farmers, a laborer, a fisherman, a carpenter, and an electrician.

"Excellent. The company needs more electricians. The way the site is expanding, the need for power maintenance has increased tenfold," Father Sanchez said.

One of the men, a carpenter by trade, stepped forward. "And who exactly is the company? It doesn't say on the posters."

Father Sanchez's eyes narrowed slightly. "Palmer-Tech," he answered. "They deal primarily in pharmaceuticals but are currently branching out into other areas."

The carpenter frowned. "And what does a pharmaceutical company want out here in the jungle?"

Father Sanchez gave him a pointed look. "You do ask a lot of questions."

"I'm curious. So?" the carpenter pressed.

"There is a rare life form that is specific to this part of the world," Father Sanchez replied.

"What type of life form?" the carpenter asked.

Father Sanchez's smile turned thin. "One which grows in the forest. Now do you want the work or not?"

The carpenter fell silent, sensing the priest's impatience.

"So without further ado," Sanchez went on, the smile returning, "you all look hungry. I'll show you to the bathrooms where you can clean up, and then you'll join the rest of us in the dining hall where we'll all eat together. How does that sound?"

"Sounds good," the workers chorused, the tension easing.

SEVENTEEN

As the coach moved southward, the landscape began to change, the urban environment giving way to jungle. The journey was grueling. Without air conditioning, the oppressive heat inside the vehicle made it difficult for passengers to find any semblance of comfort. Beads of sweat trickled down foreheads, and the air felt thick and heavy. Young children cried and fidgeted restlessly, their parents doing their best to soothe them despite their own exhaustion.

Jenny glanced out the window, her eyes scanning the passing landscape. The coach rolled by dark, quiet houses with overgrown yards and neglected porches.

"Look at all these empty houses. It's like entire villages have been cleared out," Jenny remarked.

Neil nodded. "They've taken so many people. This operation must be huge."

A local woman seated nearby overheard their conversation and leaned in. "My village used to be full of life," she said. "Now it's just a handful of us left behind. No one to even tend to the rice paddies."

Jenny and Neil turned their attention to the woman. "What happened to everyone?" Jenny asked gently.

"They said they were taking my brother to work on a big project deep in the jungle, near Mount Wanggameti," the woman explained.

Neil leaned closer. "Did they say who they were working for?"

A gray-haired elderly man seated across the aisle chimed in. "They told my son that it was a foreign corporation."

"They said the same to my brother," the woman added.

As they continued to gather testimonies, another local man unfurled a tattered poster and showed it to Jenny and Neil. "This is what recruited my father," he said, his voice tinged with bitterness.

The poster read, *Join us for lucrative opportunities in the heart of Sumba! Contact Father Sanchez at the mission.*

Jenny exchanged a meaningful glance with Neil. "Father Sanchez... that's who Marco and Renée talked about."

Neil nodded thoughtfully. "Looks like we're heading in the right direction."

The coach continued its journey through the night, the oppressive heat and cries of children adding to the sense of urgency and despair. As the hours passed, the passengers grew quieter, each lost in their thoughts. The coach rumbled along the dark, winding roads, taking them deeper into the heart of Sumba. Jenny and Neil knew they were on the verge of uncovering something significant, and their resolve to find answers for these families only strengthened with each passing mile.

EIGHTEEN

THE DINING HALL STOOD AT THE EDGE OF THE mission compound, an impressive structure built from bamboo and dried, woven banana leaves. The warm glow of candlelight flickered from within, casting dancing shadows on the intricately constructed walls. Marco and Renée, having freshened up, were ushered into the hall by the workers of the mission.

As they entered, they marveled at the scene before them. The hall was filled with the soft, glimmering light of countless candles, creating a serene and almost ethereal atmosphere. In the center, a long dining table was set, laden with a sumptuous feast. Platters of steaming rice, grilled fish, fresh fruits, and aromatic vegetables were arranged artfully, the scents mingling in the air. At the head of the table sat Father Sanchez, his presence commanding yet welcoming.

He rose from his seat, his smile broad and inviting. "Come, newcomers. Come eat. You must be starving."

Everyone took their seats, the workers lining the benches

with an eerie synchrony. The newcomers, including Marco and Renée, stood in awe of their precision before taking seats themselves. A few of them went to begin eating, but upon observing that the workers sat perfectly still before the food, they held back.

"Before eating," Father Sanchez intoned, "let us bow our heads and give thanks."

In perfect unison, the locals dipped their heads and laced their hands together. Marco and Renée exchanged uneasy glances. The six newcomers, including the carpenter, also looked bewildered by the display.

Father Sanchez's voice echoed through the grand hall. "Heavenly Father, we thank you for the food before us, for the hands that prepared it, and for the fellowship we share. As it is written in John 10:14-16, 'I am the good shepherd; I know my sheep and my sheep know me—just as the Father knows me and I know the Father—and I lay down my life for the sheep. I have other sheep that are not of this sheep pen. I must bring them also. They too will listen to my voice, and there shall be one flock and one shepherd.'"

Father Sanchez paused, glancing at Marco and Renée with a hint of something deeper in his eyes, something that sent a shiver down their spines.

"May we all listen to the shepherd's voice, come together as one flock, and work for the greater good, united in purpose and spirit. Amen."

As if on cue, the locals raised their heads and let out an almighty "AMEN!" that shook the bamboo structure of the hall. Then, they took up their spoons with a rapidity and exactness that made Marco and Renée shudder. The unsettling synchrony continued as everyone served themselves from the trays in the center of the table, their movements smooth and coordinated.

Marco leaned slightly towards Renée, whispering, "This is getting weirder by the minute."

Renée nodded, her eyes scanning the room. "Something's not right here. We need to be careful."

The carpenter, seated a few places away, looked equally unnerved. He caught Marco's eye and gave a slight nod, indicating that he too was aware of the oddity around them.

Father Sanchez noticed that Marco, Renée, and the carpenter were hesitant to eat. He smiled broadly at them. "Eat. It's good food. My cooks are the best. You like fried chicken?"

Marco and Renée nodded and began to load their plates from dishes of crispy fried chicken, the golden-brown crust glistening in the candlelight.

Renée glanced at Father Sanchez, her voice casual yet inquisitive. "When do we go to work?"

Father Sanchez finished chewing a mouthful of grilled fish before replying. "We move out tomorrow."

Renée frowned slightly. "It's not here?"

Father Sanchez shook his head. "No. It's up in the hills. About a half day's drive from here and then a short trek."

"A trek?" Renée echoed, trying to mask her concern.

"Yes," Father Sanchez confirmed. "We haven't quite connected the site to the road yet. We're still delivering supplies by helicopter. But don't worry. Once you're there, it is quite decent living. Fresh water, air-conditioned buildings."

Marco and Renée exchanged a quick glance, silently processing this new information. The carpenter, seated nearby, seemed equally intrigued, his eyes flicking between Father Sanchez and the others.

Father Sanchez continued. "Now come. Eat. Get your strength for tomorrow. It's going to be a long—"

The priest's words were cut off when the woman seated next to Renée began choking, her face contorting with signs of distress. The jovial atmosphere of the grand hall shifted abruptly as all eyes turned to the woman, who appeared to be in severe pain. A rivulet of blood began trickling from her ear, quickly followed by another from her nose. She covered her face with a hand as she rose shakily from the bench.

Renée immediately got up, placing a steadying arm around the woman. "She's having a seizure," she said urgently, her voice rising above the sudden silence. "I have medical training."

The woman let out a groan. Her face twisted in agony as more blood flowed from her ear. Her eyes rolled back in their sockets, and she screamed, a sound that pierced the quiet and sent a shiver through everyone present.

Renée quickly laid her down on the ground. "She needs space," she commanded. "Someone—"

A sputter of blood burst from the woman's ear. As Renée recoiled, one of the mission workers stepped forward, his face calm but his actions swift. "She is sick. She needs medicine," he said. The next thing, he began forcibly pushing Renée away.

Before she could do anything, more of them moved in, lifting the woman and carrying her off as she continued to writhe in pain, taking her out of the hall.

Renée stood there, watching them, her heart racing. The atmosphere in the hall had changed dramatically. The swift, almost mechanical response of the locals to the woman's distress was unsettling. It was as if they were following a script or some type of programming, their actions devoid of genuine concern or empathy. They had simply wanted to get her out of the way.

As the meal recommenced, the tension in the hall was obvious. Resuming their places at the table, Marco and Renée realized that they'd need to stay alert, to watch every move and listen to every word.

NINETEEN

Noah had tracked the recruiter to a modest house on the outskirts of Waingapu. He was now hidden in the scrub of the man's backyard, his hologram suit set to camouflage mode, its images blending seamlessly with the surrounding vegetation. He lay perfectly still, his eyes fixed on the back window, the parabolic microphone in his hand aimed precisely to capture every sound.

Inside, the recruiter was making himself something to eat, his actions methodical, almost mechanical. The scene was mundane, yet the recruiter's movements felt oddly robotic.

Noah adjusted the parabolic microphone. It began picking up the faint sounds of the recruiter's actions: the clink of cutlery against a plate, the scrape of a chair, the dull thud of footsteps on the wooden floor. The recruiter sat at a table, staring into space, his fork moving to his mouth with the regularity of a machine.

What are you up to? Noah thought, his eyes narrowing as he focused on the recruiter's expressionless face.

It was as his mind mulled over exactly what was wrong with the guy that Noah's eyes narrowed. A set of headlights had just shone down the street, followed by a car pulling up a few houses down. Through the gaps between the buildings, Noah saw the two Council agents from before get out. He expected them to casually stroll up to the house, let themselves in, and join the recruiter, assuming they were all part of the same team. But they didn't.

Instead, they separated. One agent circled around to the back of the house, while the other approached the front. They didn't knock. Noah watched as they expertly picked the locks and slipped into the house from opposite ends.

Noah adjusted the parabolic microphone as the agents crept stealthily through the house, their movements almost silent. As they converged in the kitchen, the recruiter noticed them. He stood up abruptly, stepping back in alarm. Noah turned the volume up on the microphone.

The recruiter spoke in Sumbanese. "Who are you?"

The larger of the agents replied in English. "We don't speak the local dialect, but we know you can speak English."

"Yes, I speak English," the recruiter confirmed. "What do you want?"

"Your boss. Where is he?" the shorter, smirking agent demanded.

The recruiter's eyes widened. "My boss? He is not my boss. He is my Lord."

The first agent scoffed. "He's not your Lord. You're merely—"

CRRRRKKKK!!!

Noah ripped the headphones off, startled by the huge bug that had just landed on the end of the parabolic microphone. He quickly shooed it away and placed the headphones back on.

"Where is he?" the agent's voice demanded again.

"I would rather die than tell you," the recruiter responded.

"That's exactly what will happen if you don't," the second agent threatened, smirking.

In a flash, the recruiter lunged at the shorter agent, lashing out with unexpected strength, attacking him. The sudden transformation was brutal. The recruiter's strength was unnatural, and both agents struggled desperately to subdue him. The kitchen erupted into madness as the recruiter fought the two men with a ferocity that belied his squat appearance.

"Shoot him! Shoot him now!" the larger agent yelled as he grabbed ahold of the recruiter, desperately trying to control him, his voice filled with panic.

The other agent drew his gun and fired six shots into the recruiter. Each bullet tore through him, but it wasn't until the sixth that the recruiter finally collapsed lifeless on the floor.

The larger agent stood back, panting. "Jeez, Tom, did you see that? He took six hollow-tips. Not even an elephant can take that amount of lead."

Tom nodded, still shaken. "Yeah, I saw it."

Noah remained perfectly still as he observed the agents begin to search the house. Once they had, finding what appeared to be nothing, the two men returned to the body. The smaller agent, Tom, glanced at his partner, his expression grim, devoid of its usual smirk. "Come on, help me remove the head. We'll ship it back to base for analysis."

The agents left the house and retrieved a large container from their vehicle. Bringing it back to the house, they placed it on the kitchen floor next to the recruiter's lifeless body. They then crouched over him. While the larger man held the body steady, Tom used a surgical saw to decapitate the recruiter. The process was gruesome, the wet sounds of flesh and bone being severed resonating through the headphones of the parabolic. The agents did the job with a clinical detachment, placing the head into the container and sealing it tightly once it had been released from the body.

Noah then watched them leave the house, Tom carrying the container to the car. He waited until they were a safe distance away before bursting from his cover. His eyes darted to the side of the house where the recruiter kept a scooter. Moving quickly and efficiently, Noah used a skeleton key to start the vehicle.

The engine grumbled to life, and Noah set off in pursuit of the agents as they drove away, keeping a careful distance to avoid detection. A determined urgency fueled him. He had to know where the agents were going and what they planned to do with the recruiter's head.

TWENTY

Following the meal, Marco and Renée were led into a large dormitory, its sparse furnishings illuminated by dim overhead lights. The room was filled with rows of simple beds, each one occupied by new recruits ready to be taken out into the jungle.

There were more than the six who had traveled with Marco and Renée. At least fifty others occupied the large dorm, none of them wearing the overalls of the mission workers, and each recruited from Lalindi or the surrounding villages, some by the same trader that had brought Marco and Renée up here.

The quiet, almost eerie atmosphere was punctuated by the occasional cough or murmur. As they settled into their assigned beds, they began to interact with the others who had been gathered over the past week.

A young man with wide eyes and a nervous demeanor leaned over to Marco and Renée. "It's weird," he whispered. "The people who work here hardly speak. No chit-chat.

Nothing. Just work and duty. The priest says they are building a new world out there."

"Building a new world?" Renée replied. "That sounds pretty ambitious."

A woman with short-cropped hair and a determined look nodded. "I heard we're heading to the east side of Mount Wanggameti. They've set up a massive camp there. Thousands, I hear."

Marco asked, "Does anyone know exactly who is behind this or what we'll be doing up there?"

An older man with a scraggly beard shook his head. "You get no real answers from the priest or the others. Just speculation. Some say it's a foreign corporation, others think it's some kind of religious movement."

Three hours later, almost everyone was asleep. The dormitory was bathed in the soft chorus of cicadas, their rhythmic chittering blending with the faint snores of the sleepers. Marco and Renée weren't asleep, though. They were wide awake, moving like shadows through the dark, slipping soundlessly from their bunkbeds.

Outside, the night air was thick and warm, the sounds of the jungle a constant backdrop as they navigated the quiet compound. Marco and Renée moved with practiced stealth, their footfalls silent on the dirt path leading to the mission house.

The doors were unlocked, so they slipped in easily. Inside, they ducked past the mechanical mission workers, who moved with an unsettling precision as they swept the floors or performed other duties, their eyes vacant.

Marco and Renée reached a door with the words *Father Sanchez's Office* written in Bahasa.

This door was also unlocked.

Inside, the room was dimly lit by the faint glow of an oil lamp. The office was cluttered with papers and documents. Marco and Renée moved quickly, their eyes scanning the shelves and desk for anything useful. The faint light illuminated their path as they searched through the documents, their fingers flipping through pages and files.

Renée's eyes widened as she pulled a file folder marked *Project Site* from a drawer. "Marco, look at this," she whispered, opening the folder to reveal maps and schedules.

Marco leaned in, his eyes narrowing as he examined the documents. "There's plans for a hospital, schools, a large church up there. Roads," he murmured, tracing a finger along the detailed maps.

Renée's brow furrowed. "There are plans for another eight sites. It looks like they're building a bunch of towns out there."

Marco shook his head. "Why does the Council need that many people?"

Before they could ponder this further, the sound of approaching footsteps reached their ears. They exchanged a quick glance, their eyes widening in alarm. Silently, they closed the folder and moved toward the window. Marco carefully lifted the latch, and they slipped out just as the door to the office creaked open.

Outside, they stayed low, pressing themselves against the side of the building. A set of footsteps stopped inside the office. They could hear the rattling of keys, followed by the sound of a video call being connected, then the low murmur of voices.

"My Lord, everything is going to plan at our end,"

Father Sanchez began, his voice low and deferential. "Tomorrow morning I will set out with fifty new recruits ready for Communion."

Renée, crouching beside Marco, whispered using the voice concealment setting on the NLP, "It sounds like he's talking to Palmer."

The voice from the computer, cold and authoritative, confirmed her suspicion. "Good," Palmer responded. "Soon, we will have enough for the first phase."

Father Sanchez hesitated for a moment before continuing, "There was another issue with one of the members' Communion tonight. It appears that the binding process with our Lord has caused an embolism to form. Too much grace, I suppose."

"Not everyone is suitable. I shall improve testing," Palmer replied.

"Your benevolence is commendable, Lord."

Palmer's voice took on a sharper edge. "Another thing. Our takeover of the area's police force and judiciary hasn't stopped some in the western part of the island from forming a militia. They're coming down to find out what is happening."

"A militia? Here?" Father Sanchez's voice wavered slightly, the first hint of unease breaking through his calm façade.

"Yes. But do not worry. I will deal with it," Palmer assured him.

"Thank you, my Lord. Your power and wisdom will surely see us through," Father Sanchez said, his voice returning to its reverent tone.

"Ensure that everything proceeds smoothly. We cannot afford any more mistakes," Palmer commanded.

"Of course, my Lord. All will be ready for Communion," Father Sanchez promised.

"Good. Keep me informed. Palmer out."

The call ended.

Outside, Marco and Renée gazed at each other, the gravity of what they had overheard settling heavily between them. They needed to report back to Noah and the others immediately.

As they silently retreated, they retraced their path back to the dormitory. However, they were in for a surprise.

Upon reaching the dormitory door, they collided with a solid form in the dark. The sudden impact sent a jolt of adrenaline through them, and they instinctively tensed, ready for a confrontation. But instead of an alarm being raised, a startled, yet familiar voice whispered urgently, "Who's there?"

Marco exhaled sharply, recognizing the voice. "Shh! It's us. What are you doing sneaking around?"

The carpenter, his face barely visible in the dim light, looked equally relieved and surprised. "I could ask you the same thing. I couldn't sleep and wanted to look around."

Renée leaned closer. "Us too."

The carpenter's eyes widened. "And what did you see on your walkabout?"

Marco glanced around, ensuring no one else was within earshot. "Not here," he said in a low murmur. "Let's get inside first."

TWENTY-ONE

NOAH FOLLOWED THE AGENTS ALL THE WAY TO THE coast. The dark, quiet coastal area was eerily serene, the only sounds being the faint lapping of waves against the shore and the occasional distant call of a seabird.

Having dumped the scooter, he reached a hidden vantage point among an outcrop of rocks. Pressed low to the rough ground, Noah pulled out a pair of field glasses and focused on the agents. They approached a motorized dinghy, which was tethered to a small, weathered dock. Beyond the dock, a large boat bobbed gently in the water, anchored off the coast. The boat's silhouette was dark against the night sky, but the faint glow of lights from it hinted at activity within.

Adjusting the field glasses, he saw that the vessel's sleek, white hull was dotted with an array of high-tech sensors and instruments, including massive radar dishes and towering communication masts.

That's a science vessel. So what kind of experiments are they running out there?

Noah watched the agents climb into the dinghy. They then started it, the motor humming softly as the small boat cut through the water, heading straight for the larger vessel. Noah immediately began readying himself for the water, his thoughts reeling.

Where are you taking that head? And what are you hiding out there?

TWENTY-TWO

IN THE DIMLY LIT DORMITORY, MARCO, RENÉE, and the carpenter huddled together at their bunkbed, their heads nearly touching as they whispered urgently.

"My name is Garin Antara," the carpenter began, his eyes scanning the room for any sign of eavesdroppers. "I'm a detective with the Indonesian police force. I'm stationed in Jakarta but have been sent here undercover by my superiors to find out what is going on in Sumba."

Marco's eyes widened. "A detective?"

"Yes," Garin Antara confirmed. "We've had numerous reports of people being recruited for work and then never being heard from again. A colleague of mine, Detective Bintang, was sent out here but went missing. Recently, he got back in contact."

Renée leaned in. "What did he say?"

"On the eve of me coming out here, Detective Bintang told us not to come looking for him. He said he was emigrating to Sumba and had told his wife and two sons to join him. It was crazy," Antara explained.

"So you came out anyway?" Marco asked.

"Yes. I arrived in Lalindi on Wednesday. I intend on finding out what has been going on. Local law enforcement in the area insists that nothing is the matter. So whatever is happening here, it's happening with the knowledge of the local PD."

Renée's eyes narrowed. "You think they've been taken over?"

"I do," Antara replied. "But by who or what? Whoever is behind this, they're controlling the police and even some military units. It's why I had to come disguised and in secret. The usual channels can't be trusted."

Renée nodded. "We're here for the same reason. To find out what's going on."

Antara's eyes narrowed further. "Which makes me ask the question: who are you?"

Marco exchanged a quick glance with Renée before answering, sticking to their cover story. "Our son came out here looking for work three months ago. We haven't heard from him since."

Antara's expression softened slightly. "So many have lost people out here. I am sorry for your loss. But if it's any consolation, he is most likely still out there, alive. People don't go entirely missing. They just don't come back. It's like there's some cult out there."

"A cult?" Renée echoed.

"Yes. That's what it seems like. They recruit people, and those people vanish into the jungle, never to be heard from again. But the local authorities keep insisting everything is normal. That's why I'm here."

"Whatever it is, it's big," Marco said. "We found maps and plans in Father Sanchez's office. They're building a city out there."

Antara nodded, his expression grim. "We need to find out what they're doing and who is behind it. We need to get proof and bring it back to the authorities in Jakarta."

"Agreed. We can work together," Renée said.

"Yes, together. We'll stand a better chance. But we need to be careful. They're watching everything," Antara cautioned.

"We'll be careful," Marco said. "Let's start by sticking to our cover stories and gathering as much information as we can."

"And if we find out anything significant, we share it immediately," Renée added.

"Agreed. We'll work together. Stay safe and keep your eyes open," Antara said.

The three of them nodded in agreement, their partnership solidified as they prepared for the challenges ahead.

TWENTY-THREE

Noah swam silently through the dark, cool water, the large research vessel looming ahead of him like a shadowy fortress. Armed men patrolled the deck, their figures silhouetted against the dim glow of the spotlights at the bow and stern. The spotlights cut through the darkness, scanning the water with a relentless, searching beam.

Each time he surfaced, Noah scanned the deck, noting the positions of the patrolling guards and the soldiers manning the spotlights. He paused behind a large buoy, catching his breath and planning his next move. The spotlights swung past, leaving a brief window of opportunity. Noah took it, gliding silently through the water, his strokes smooth and powerful. He reached the ship's hull, pressing himself against the cold metal surface and listening for any sounds from above.

Once he felt safe to do so, Noah swam along the side of the vessel, looking for a way to climb aboard without being seen. A rope ladder hung from the stern, swaying gently with the movement of the ship. Gripping the rungs tightly, Noah hauled himself up.

The sound of footsteps made him pause, clinging to the ladder and watching the deck above. But the armed men continued past, unaware of his presence.

Sure that they were gone, he climbed the last few rungs and slipped onto the deck, crouching low behind a stack of crates. It wasn't long before another patrol passed by, their footsteps soon receding into the distance.

Noah took a deep breath and moved swiftly and silently, blending into the shadows as he navigated the deck. *Stay low, stay quiet. Don't get caught*, he reminded himself, his mind laser-focused on the task at hand.

Entering the inner part of the boat, he quickly ducked into an alcove as the two agents from before suddenly emerged from a door farther along the corridor, their voices low but urgent as they spoke into a radio. Noah held his breath, his body pressed against the cool metal of the ship, listening intently.

"What do you mean all hell's about to break loose?" the shorter agent said into the radio.

The radio crackled, and the voice of the operator came through. "Like I said. There's a convoy on its way, and from what I can see, Palmer's people have formed a blockade just outside Kataka. It won't be long before the convoy reaches it."

The taller agent shook his head, glancing at his companion. "OK, OK. We'll head out to the location. Maybe Palmer will make an appearance or at least someone who can lead us to him."

"You do that, Harry," the operator replied. "Keep me informed."

The two agents marched off in the opposite direction to where Noah hid, their footsteps echoing down the narrow, dimly lit corridor.

Why would they need to be led to Palmer? Noah couldn't help thinking. *Aren't they all part of the same team?*

Coupled with the murder of the recruiter, things were beginning to make less sense to Noah by the second. Was Dr. Anthony Palmer working for the Council, like their intelligence insisted, or had he gone rogue?

With the agents gone, Noah left his hiding spot and slipped into the room the two men had just vacated. Inside, he found himself in an empty observation room. A large glass screen separated it from a laboratory on the other side.

Noah crouched low, moving silently to the glass screen. The laboratory beyond was brightly lit, providing the only illumination inside the observation room. Two scientists in biosafety suits entered, their white suits and face shields giving them an almost otherworldly appearance.

They were carrying the container with the head. Noah watched as they placed it on top of a gurney. The voice of one of the scientists voice broke the silence, emerging through a speaker in the observation room. "OK," he said. "Let's take a look."

The man then opened it, revealing the severed head of the recruiter, while the other prepared a series of instruments on a nearby tray.

Noah's eyes narrowed as the first man lifted the head out carefully, placing it on a metal dish. The eyes were still open, the wet black hair plastered to the forehead.

"Place it in the vise," the second scientist instructed.

They positioned the head in a vise, securing it firmly. Then the first scientist, his gloved hands steady, retrieved a scalpel from the tray and made a precise incision along the top of the skull. With a practiced hand, he carefully peeled back the skin and underlying tissue, exposing the bone beneath.

The second scientist handed over a bone saw. The sharp whirring sound of the electronic saw filled the observation room as it began cutting through the skull. Once the top was detached at the crown, they gently lifted the section of bone away, revealing the brain within.

"Look at that," the first scientist murmured, his voice barely audible through the speaker. "It's still perfectly latched on to the cerebral cortex and the oblongata."

The other scientist handed him a pair of bent-tip tweezers. He held down the brain with the fingers of one hand while trying to pull something from it.

"Don't struggle. Easy does it," he murmured.

"Try not to break it," the other man cautioned.

"I know. I know," the first replied.

Noah's eyes widened as the scientist eased something from the brain, finally lifting out a long, thin, writhing, wormlike creature. The first man held it away from himself, even through his suit, as the other brought an open glass box underneath it. With the worm inside, the lid was quickly slammed down, sealing it in.

"Let's hope this one survives long enough to get it to the lab," he said.

What the hell are they doing? What is that thing? Noah's mind spun from what he'd just seen. Maybe that was why he failed to notice someone approaching the door to the observation room.

As Noah continued to watch the scientists, the door creaked open. He barely had time to react before someone stepped inside and saw him in his wetsuit. The man's eyes widened in shock, and without hesitation, he lunged for the alarm on the wall.

The alarm blared instantly, a deafening siren filling the air. The vessel was instantly plunged into chaos.

Time to move.

Noah sprang into action, tackling the guard. They grappled briefly, but Noah's skill was of a much higher level. Avoiding the guard's clumsy attempts, he landed a swift punch to the man's jaw, knocking him off his feet before hitting him with a knee to the face as he was halfway down.

With the guard sprawled out on the floor, Noah bolted out of the observation room. The sound of footsteps and shouts echoed throughout the tight spaces as armed men came looking for him.

Spotting the feet of two men descending the stairs at the end of the corridor, Noah ducked into an alcove, his breath steady and controlled as he waited until the guards passed before slipping back into the corridor, his movements fluid and silent.

Noah reached the main deck, where more guards were stationed. The second they spotted him, he launched himself over the edge, plunging into the water below.

"He's in the water! Light him up!" a guard yelled.

Spotlights swept the water, their beams cutting through the night in a frantic search. But Noah was already swimming deep, his powerful strokes carrying him away from the boat and into the safety of the dark. He stayed low, using the cover of the water to evade further pursuit.

Moving fluidly through the water, he pushed forward, determined to put as much distance as possible between himself and the science vessel.

As his lungs began to burn, Noah surfaced briefly, taking a deep breath and orienting himself. The boat was a distant silhouette against the horizon, the frantic activity on deck barely visible. He dove again, swimming with strong, steady strokes toward the shore.

It wasn't long before he reached the shallows, his feet finding purchase on the sandy bottom. He emerged from the water, dripping and cold but alive and resolute. The jungle loomed ahead, offering a temporary refuge.

Noah took a moment to catch his breath, his eyes scanning the darkness for any sign of movement. Satisfied that he was alone, he began to make his way into the jungle, his mind already planning his next steps.

After a few minutes, Noah found the hidden spot where he had earlier stashed his things. He checked his surroundings, ensuring that he was still safe, then knelt down and brushed away the loose foliage to reveal his rucksack.

Noah removed the hologram suit, swapping it for his wetsuit. The suit felt like a second skin as he switched it on, transforming once again into a local Sumbanese man— though a little tall, it had to be said. He carefully stowed the wetsuit and secured his belongings. Then he initiated a covert radio call to the others through the NLP.

However, only static filled the air in response. Frustration gnawed at him as he adjusted the radio, trying different frequencies, hoping to reach someone.

Come on, someone pick up. But the static continued to crackle, an oppressive white noise that grated on his nerves.

Despite the radio silence, Noah pressed the transmit button and began speaking into the coms. "If any of you can hear me," he said, "they're infected with some type of parasite. It's serious. Be careful."

TWENTY-FOUR

Jenny slept peacefully in Neil's arms as the convoy rumbled onward into the jungle. The rhythmic motion of the vehicle and the steady hum of the engine provided a semblance of comfort in the otherwise tense journey.

But all was not well.

As the coach climbed the winding, hilly roads of Kataka, the convoy began to slow, the rumbling of the vehicles gradually diminishing as they came to a halt.

Passengers slowly awakened, the whole bus beginning to stir, their sleepy gazes turning to the front of the bus. The murmurs of confusion and curiosity grew as the driver announced the situation.

"The road is blocked ahead," he said, his voice barely masking his own unease.

Neil and Jenny left their seats and moved to the front of the bus. Through the windshield, they could see a mass of flaming torches and the flashing lights of police vehicles up ahead. The coach was several vehicles back from the front of the convoy, but the flickering lights illuminated the scene enough for them to discern the uniforms of police officers and army soldiers blocking the road.

The driver opened the door of the coach, allowing the humid night air to flood in. Neil and Jenny stepped out, feeling the oppressive warmth immediately. The flickering torchlight cast dancing shadows on the road, mingling with the harsh, intermittent flashes of blue and red from the police lights. The uneasy murmurs among the convoy passengers grew louder, a mix of confusion and fear spreading through the crowd.

A woman from one of the vehicles at the front of the convoy stepped forward, her eyes wide with recognition as she spotted someone among the crowd blocking the road. Her voice trembled with emotion as she called out, "Ramlan? Ramlan, is that you?"

The woman moved closer to the line of police and soldiers, her hands outstretched, pleading for one of the soldiers to respond. "Ramlan, it's me, Nadya! Where have you been? Why haven't you called?"

Ramlan stood rigidly among the army members, his expression blank and unresponsive. Nadya's desperation grew as she continued to call out to him. "Ramlan, please! What happened to you? Why haven't you come back?"

Neil leaned into Jenny. "They're not going to let us pass," he whispered. "We need to be ready."

Jenny nodded, her eyes fixed on the unfolding scene. "This is bad. Really bad."

Nadya's pleas became more frantic. "Ramlan, don't you recognize me? It's Nadya! Please, say something!"

Ramlan remained unmoved, his eyes staring straight ahead. The convoy passengers watched anxiously, some starting to panic, as Nadya continued to plead with her husband. "Ramlan, please! Come home with me. We can figure this out together. Just come back to me."

A police officer next to Ramlan stepped forward, his face stern. Ignoring Nadya, he addressed the crowd through a bullhorn. "All of you are to surrender to us now. This is your only warning."

Suddenly, several police officers forcefully grabbed Nadya's arms, pulling her away from the line. She struggled, crying out for her husband as the convoy passengers gasped in fear.

"No! I need to talk to him! Ramlan, please!" Nadya screamed. "Ramlan! Don't let them take me! Please!"

Many of the people from the convoy surged forward to help Nadya, a scuffle breaking loose. That was when more torches appeared along the edges of the road, surrounding the convoy as people emerged from the jungle, as though they'd been there the whole time lying in wait. The flickering torchlight illuminated the road, casting eerie shadows that jittered menacingly like dancing devils. The increasing number of torches and the people emerging from the jungle was very intimidating.

The police officer's voice boomed through the bullhorn again, commanding, "Everyone, step out of the vehicles and surrender to us."

"We need to get out of here. Now," Neil said urgently to Jenny.

"Agreed. This is about to get a lot worse," Jenny replied.

The tension escalated as police officers approached the

vehicles. A driver, his face etched with confusion, leaned out of his window.

"What's happening? Why are we being stopped?" he asked.

"Everyone, step out of the vehicles," the police officer commanded, his tone leaving no room for argument.

Some people in the convoy, angered and fearful, began to put up fights. But their resistance was short-lived as police officers quickly subdued them, using force when necessary. One man, his voice filled with defiance, cried out, "We have a right to travel!" before being struck in the back of the head by the butt of a rifle, collapsing to the ground.

All of a sudden, the people blocking and surrounding the road began moving toward them, grabbing ahold of those from the convoy. "Hey! Hey! What are you doing? Let him go!" voices shouted in panic and anger.

As if on cue, the police, army, and local villagers began grabbing and subduing the passengers. Men and women, their expressions blank and mechanical, forced people to the ground and tied their hands and feet with rope. The road became a scene of chaos and confusion as more people emerged from the jungle, adding to the overwhelming force restraining the convoy passengers.

Neil and Jenny watched the chaos unfold, their minds racing.

"We need to go. Now!" Neil urged.

Jenny nodded.

They began to edge away from the bus, trying to avoid drawing attention. The scene was bedlam, with people being forced to the ground everywhere they looked.

Making a run for it, they fought their way through the

chaos, their skills in hand-to-hand combat being tested by the sheer number and determination of their opponents. As one man attempted to grab him, Neil landed a swift punch to the assailant's jaw, sending him reeling, while Jenny used a well-placed kick to disarm another as he came at her with the butt of his assault rifle. They moved with well-trained precision, but the swarm of people was relentless. They were almost being overwhelmed. Neil elbowed another attacker in the ribs and grabbed Jenny's hand, pulling her through the throng as a multitude of hands grabbed at them. "This way!" he shouted, their path to the jungle opening momentarily before another wave closed in.

They managed to break free, sprinting toward the closely packed vegetation at the edge of the road. The foliage then swallowed them up as they headed downhill. The sounds of pursuit followed close behind, shouts and heavy footsteps echoing through the trees.

The jungle was dense and dark, the thick canopy blocking out most of the moonlight. Neil and Jenny ran, branches whipping at their faces and undergrowth snagging at their clothing. Their breath came in ragged gasps as they pushed themselves to keep moving.

"Where do we go?" Jenny panted.

"Just keep running. We need to get as far away as possible," Neil replied.

The physical effort was immense, every step a battle against the terrain. They stumbled over roots and branches, the fear of capture spurring them on, adrenaline pumping through their veins.

They emerged from the jungle into the alleyways of small rural properties that sat along the banks of a river. The water glimmered in the moonlight. The houses were modest with flickering lights in some windows suggesting the presence of families within. As they navigated the narrow passages that led between the houses, they almost ran into a patrol of police officers.

Neil quickly pulled Jenny down behind the tangled roots of a large mangrove, the two of them holding their breath as the patrol passed just inches away.

"They can't have gone far," muttered one of the officers. "Spread out and search the area. No one escapes."

Once they passed, Neil and Jenny continued to weave through the alleys, their movements silent and cautious. As they reached a bridge, the searchlight from a police vehicle parked on top swept the area, illuminating the houses and the river below. Neil and Jenny ducked behind the corner of a nearby property just in time, the beam passing them.

"That was too close," Jenny whispered.

"We need to find somewhere to hide," Neil replied.

"Over there!" came the urgent calls of their pursuers.

The sound was emanating from the way they had come. Panic surged through them as they realized the search was closing in. They were trapped, the people on the bridge watching the river, the others closing in from the jungle.

They were about to bolt from the house when a cellar door close to their feet creaked open slightly, revealing the face of a small girl peeking out. Her eyes were wide with curiosity and a hint of fear.

"Come quickly!" she whispered, opening the door wider.

Neil and Jenny hurriedly slipped into the cellar, the girl closing the door quietly behind them. Inside, the dim light revealed a modest space filled with jars of preserved food and basic supplies. The girl led them farther in, where a man she said was her father stood.

"You look exhausted," the father said, his voice low and kind. "You can rest here. I have food and water."

Neil and Jenny sank onto a bench, their bodies trembling with exhaustion. The father handed them blankets and a jug of water, which they gratefully accepted.

"Thank you," Neil said, his voice hoarse. "We're very grateful."

"You're safe here. No one will find you," the father assured them.

Their relief, however, was abruptly shattered by a scream. Neil and Jenny's heads snapped toward the door of the cellar. Lifting it slightly and peering out, they saw the locals dragging a woman away by her feet as she clawed at the ground, her cries piercing the night.

The father quickly pulled them away, his expression urgent and fearful. "You mustn't let them see you," he whispered, his voice trembling. "If one sees you, they all do."

TWENTY-FIVE

INSIDE PALMER'S LAB, STAINLESS STEEL SURFACES gleamed under the bright, clinical lights. The lab was meticulously organized, every instrument and tool precisely placed, reflecting the clinical detachment of its overseer, Dr. Anthony Palmer.

The doctor sat beside Brennan Krol, who was strapped to a medical chair in the center of the room. Palmer held an injection gun in his hand, filled with a serum of a strange, iridescent color. He pressed the gun against Krol's wide neck and pulled the trigger, pumping the serum into his bloodstream with a quick hiss.

Krol's muscles began to writhe under his skin almost immediately, twitching and bulging in unnatural ways. His face contorted in a mix of pain and confusion, but he remained silent, enduring the procedure with grim determination. Palmer watched intently, his eyes cold and analytical, observing every reaction with a clinical detachment that bordered on the inhuman.

The lab's equipment beeped and whirred, capturing data and displaying it on a series of monitors. Palmer glanced at the readouts, satisfied with the results. The serum was working as intended, triggering the desired physiological responses in Krol.

Just then, a lab assistant entered the room, breaking the silence. "My Lord, Brother Taylor has arrived," the assistant announced.

A smile spread across Palmer's face, a rare expression that carried a hint of anticipation. "I'll be right up," he replied.

He set the injection gun down on a nearby tray and released the restraints holding Krol to the chair. The giant man, his muscles still twitching from the serum, groaned as he flexed his arms and legs.

Palmer looked up at him. "Krol," he said firmly, "carry me outside. We mustn't keep John waiting."

With surprising gentleness, given his enormous size and the violent reactions his body had just endured, Krol bent down and lifted the paraplegic Palmer from his chair. He cradled him as if he were a fragile piece of equipment or a newborn, careful not to jostle him too much.

He carried Palmer to the elevator, and the assistant quickly pressed the button, causing the doors to slide open with a quiet hiss. Krol stepped inside, carefully adjusting his hold on Palmer. As the elevator began its ascent, Palmer's gaze remained fixed, his thoughts occupied with the machinations and plots that lay ahead.

The moment they emerged from the grand temple of Pura Luhur, Dr. Jonathan Taylor dropped to his knees, presenting the fusion core to Palmer with a deep, respectful bow. The device gleamed under the flickering light of the flaming torches that lined the temple entrance.

"Lord, I have it for you," Jonathan said, his voice filled with reverence.

Krol gently lowered Palmer so he could take the fusion core. He examined it with a mixture of scientific curiosity and satisfaction, his fingers playing over its smooth, polished surface.

Krol then lifted Palmer again, the fusion core now securely in his hands. His followers watched in silent awe, their obedience and dedication evident in their eyes.

Holding the core aloft, Palmer announced, "Now our new civilization has power! Unlimited power!"

The crowd let out a roar that traveled all around the jungle, every man, woman, and child in a ten-mile radius shouting in triumph.

Johnathon Taylor remained bowed, his posture one of complete submission. Palmer shifted his gaze from the fusion core to the man kneeling before him, his expression unreadable.

"Now I have one last job for you, John," Dr. Palmer said, his voice calm and authoritative.

"Anything, my Lord," Johnathon Taylor replied.

"Now I wish for you to commit suicide," Palmer commanded, his tone chillingly casual despite the subject of his words.

Without a moment's hesitation, Jonathan drew his pistol and placed it to his temple, ready to obey. But Palmer quickly stopped him, a hand raised in a gesture of control.

"Not that way. That way would spoil things. No, we must preserve what is inside your head. So it must be done another way," Palmer explained in a voice devoid of emotion.

He nodded at one of the followers, who approached carrying a seppuku knife. The handle of the knife was intricately designed with two snakes twisted together, their scales meticulously detailed. The follower handed the knife to Palmer, who held it out for Jonathan to see.

"Do you recall our college years watching samurai films?" Palmer asked, a hint of nostalgia in his voice.

"Yes, Lord," Jonathan replied, his eyes fixed on the knife.

"Do you remember how the samurai committed seppuku?" Palmer continued, his gaze piercing.

"Yes," Jonathan answered.

"That is how you shall do it," Palmer decreed, his words hanging in the air—a literal death sentence.

Jonathan immediately ripped his shirt open, exposing his bare chest. Without a moment's hesitation, he took the seppuku knife from Palmer's hand. His movements were deliberate and calm, a testament to his unwavering obedience and the chilling control Palmer held over him.

The tension in the air was palpable as Jonathan positioned the knife. The followers watched in silence, their faces blank. The flaming torches cast long shadows that seemed to dance in anticipation.

With a steady hand, Jonathan plunged the knife into his stomach, committing seppuku with a brutal efficiency. His face contorted in pain, but he made no sound, his resolve unbroken. Blood spilled from the wound, staining the stone steps beneath him.

Palmer watched with a cold, detached interest, his eyes never leaving Jonathan as he performed the act. The control

Palmer wielded was absolute, his power over his followers unquestionable. Jonathan's body wavered but remained upright, his strength and determination holding him steady as he completed the ritual of disembowelment.

Dr. Palmer's expression remained unchanged as Jonathan took his final breaths, the life draining from his eyes. The stone steps were slick with blood, the crimson liquid running down the ancient stone, reflecting the flickering torchlight. *This is for Sophie and Emily*, Palmer thought, and, just as he did, as though this thought had commanded it, Jonathan Taylor took one last breath, then fell sideways onto the steps, dead.

"Place me next to the body," Palmer commanded.

Krol obeyed without hesitation, placing Palmer beside Jonathan's head. The scene was a chilling tableau of life and death, power and submission. Palmer's presence exuded control, his eyes focused on the task at hand.

Holding a small device, the rogue scientist leaned over Jonathan's ear. The device emitted a soft hum as he carefully positioned it. The followers watched in silent awe, their eyes fixed on Palmer's every move. The device pulsed, and a thin, worm-like parasite began to emerge from Jonathan's ear, writhing as it was drawn out.

Palmer cooed softly to the parasite, his voice almost tender. "That's right. Come to your master."

The worm responded, wrapping itself around Palmer's fingers with an unsettling familiarity. The scene was both grotesque and mesmerizing.

One of the followers stepped forward, a containment box in hand. Palmer transferred the parasite carefully, the nematode curling and writhing as it was placed inside the box. The follower sealed the container, handling it with the same reverence and care that marked all their actions.

Palmer's expression remained detached, his focus solely on the parasite now contained within the box. The blood-soaked steps and the lifeless body of Jonathan were mere backdrops. The jungle around them seemed to hold its breath, the sounds of nature muted in the presence of such a chilling display of power and obedience.

With the parasite and fusion core secured, Krol picked up Palmer once more and carried him back into the temple, the followers trailing behind them like some solemn procession.

Palmer directed Krol to a massive machine at the center of the main chamber, a complex structure of metal and circuitry designed to house the fusion core. The followers gathered around as they watched their 'Lord' prepare for the next phase.

With precise movements, Palmer placed the fusion core inside the machine. The machinery whirred to life, lights flickering and indicators flashing as the system powered up. The low hum grew into a powerful, steady vibration, filling the chamber with a sense of imminent transformation.

"For decades, the Council has used cold fusion for their own, while peddling expensive, inefficient, environmentally disastrous energy to the masses," Palmer announced. "Now we, my brethren, have that power."

Outside, the newly built jungle village that surrounded the temple began to glow with electric light. Streetlights flickered on, illuminating the paths that wound through the dense foliage. Floodlights bathed the construction sites in bright, harsh light, revealing the skeletal frameworks of new buildings rising from the earth. Houses glowed warmly as electric lights blinked to life within, casting a comforting radiance through the windows. Water pumps roared to life, sending fresh water coursing through newly laid pipes. Communication towers sprang to life, their lights blinking rhythmically as they connected to the wider network, bringing the village online with the rest of the world.

Palmer watched from an archway of the temple as the transformation unfolded. The once primitive jungle settlement was evolving into a modern city, powered by the very technology he had harnessed. His eyes gleamed with the possibilities that lay ahead. "This is our destiny," he murmured, more to himself than to anyone else. "And nothing will stand in our way."

TWENTY-SIX

ALLISON SAT IN THE BACK OF A LIMOUSINE, THE cityscape of New York flashing past the tinted windows, when the phone rang. The screen lit up with Molly Hanson's name, and she accepted the call.

"Molly, what's up?"

"I've got Noah on the line with urgent news about the mission." Molly's voice crackled over the speaker. "You want me to patch him through?"

"Yes," Allison replied, her tone steady.

Noah's voice came through a moment later, filled with concern. "Allison, do you read me?"

Adjusting her position in the limo, Allison responded, "Loud and clear, Noah. What's the situation?"

"I've lost contact with the other teams."

"That's troubling," Allison said, a slight frown creasing her forehead. "Do you have any idea where they might be now?"

Noah's voice lowered, becoming almost conspiratorial.

"Last I knew, Marco and Renée were heading to a mission house an hour north of Lalindi, where some priest was offering work. Neil and Jenny had joined a convoy of people from the northwest who are looking for missing relatives, but I overheard two Council agents discussing how Palmer's people were going to intercept it at Kataka. That was last night. I don't know what the situation is there now. Everything is pointing to the southeast of the island. I'm about to buy some transport here in Waingapu and head there myself."

Allison nodded slowly. "Good. You need to keep moving forward. What else have you discovered?"

"Last night, I witnessed something disturbing. Two scientists were pulling some kind of parasite from a man's head. It's got to be what Palmer is working on."

Feigning surprise, Allison replied, "A parasite? Are you sure?"

"Positive. And it gets worse. I think Palmer has gone rogue. It seems like the Council and Palmer are at odds. These Council agents aren't working with him; they're after him. They executed the guy who the head belonged to. He was recruiting for the same priest Marco and Renée were heading to see. I get a feeling the Council are here trying to clean up a mess."

Allison pretended to consider this, her expression thoughtful. "Palmer going rogue? That sounds odd, Noah. Are you sure you're not over-interpreting the situation?"

Noah's voice was firm. "No. I'm not. The way these agents are behaving—it all points to him working against the Council. He's not just a rogue scientist; he's a threat to both us and them."

Keeping her voice calm, Allison said, "Keep digging, Noah. If Palmer is truly rogue, we need to bring him in and get to the bottom of this even more than we did before. If he's gone against the Council, he may be more willing to come to us. But remember, he's incredibly dangerous. Proceed with caution."

"I will. I'm heading southeast to Kataka the second I can. I'll report back as soon as I find anything," Noah said. "But I might get hit by whatever is blocking the others' signals. So I might be radio silent for the foreseeable future."

"Be careful, Noah. We're counting on you."

"Understood. Noah out."

Allison disconnected the call, leaning back in her seat, a small, satisfied smile playing on her lips.

The driver glanced back at her through the rearview mirror. "Everything all right, ma'am?"

Allison smiled, her eyes cold and calculating. "Just fine. How long until we're there?"

"No more than a few minutes, ma'am," the driver replied.

He wasn't lying. A few minutes later, the sleek, black limousine was gliding to a stop outside the United Nations building, its polished exterior reflecting the 39 national flags lining the plaza of the iconic structure. Allison Peterson stepped out, her tailored suit impeccable, her demeanor calm and collected. She adjusted her sunglasses, scanning the crowd of diplomats and dignitaries bustling toward the entrance.

Inside, the hall was abuzz with anticipation. Delegates from every corner of the globe filled the seats, their chatter a cacophony of languages and dialects. Allison moved through the crowd with purpose. She found her assigned seat, settling in with a composed smile as she watched the proceedings.

The podium stood at the center, illuminated by spotlights. Vice President Gina Brown, now the acting president, approached it with a steady gait. The room fell silent, a hush of expectation enveloping the delegates. Allison's eyes fixed on Brown, already knowing every word she was about to speak. After all, it was Allison who had meticulously crafted the speech on behalf of the Council.

Brown's voice echoed through the hall, firm yet measured. "Today, we stand at a crossroads. In the wake of President Whitmore's tragic passing, we must reconsider our path forward. While he advocated for a merger between the United Nations and NATO, we must ask ourselves if we are ready to take such a monumental step."

A murmur rippled through the room. Delegates exchanged puzzled glances, whispering among themselves.

Brown continued, "Perhaps it is not wise to spiral the world into conflict, not until we know for sure who our true enemy is. The Council remains an elusive and powerful force, but we are yet to truly understand it. We must move forward with caution, ensuring that our actions are guided by clarity and certainty, not by fear or haste."

Allison's face remained impassive as she observed the reactions. Confusion and disappointment filled many of the faces. The anticipated new era of international military cooperation was slipping away, replaced by the uncertainty of former times.

Brown concluded, "Let us take this moment to reflect and reassess. We owe it to our nations and our people to proceed with prudence. Thank you."

A smattering of applause broke the silence, hesitant and scattered. The delegates were unsure how to respond. The initial promise of unity and strength was now overshadowed by caution and hesitation.

Allison rose from her seat, weaving through the throng of delegates toward the podium. As she left the stage, Brown was surrounded by advisors and diplomats, their faces a mix of concern and curiosity. Allison waited for a moment before cutting in, her smile calculated and warm.

"Madam President," Allison said, extending her hand. "Congratulations on a well-delivered speech. It was exactly what was needed in these uncertain times."

Brown nodded, a hint of relief in her eyes. "Thank you, Ms. Peterson."

Allison gave a slight nod, her eyes meeting Brown's with a knowing glint. "You're welcome. You may have just saved the world from war."

With a final nod, Allison turned and made her way out of the building. The limousine awaited, its door held open by the driver. She slipped inside, the soft leather seats embracing her as she removed her sunglasses.

The driver looked at her through the rearview mirror. "Where to, ma'am?"

Allison replied, "I fancy eating lunch in the park. Drive me to Central Park."

"Yes, ma'am," the driver responded, and the limousine pulled smoothly away from the curb, merging into the flow of city traffic.

———

Twenty minutes later, the limousine glided to a stop at the edge of Central Park. Her driver stepped out and opened the door for Allison. She exited gracefully, holding a brown paper bag filled with pastrami on rye from a nearby deli. The driver leaned in and said, "I'll swing around in an hour to pick you up."

"Thank you," Allison replied. She turned and walked into the park, her heels clicking softly on the pavement.

Passing a trash bin, she casually dropped the lunch bag inside without breaking stride. Her path led her not to a lonely park bench for lunch but to the Inscope Arch. Pausing in the middle of the underpass, she glanced around to ensure that no one was nearby. The park was thankfully quiet on this chilly morning.

Satisfied she was alone, Allison pulled out a keycard and swiped it against a nearly reader embedded in the southern wall of the underpass. A metal door clicked open, revealing a dark walkway. She slipped inside, letting the door close silently behind her.

The passageway was pitch black, but Allison navigated it with practiced ease, moving beneath East Drive toward the zoo. Halfway through, she encountered another thick metal door. This time, she leaned in, and a scanner read her eyes. The door unlocked, and she stepped into a small, window-less room, no larger than a closet.

As soon as the door sealed shut behind her, the floor began to descend. As she dropped slowly through a ceiling, lights flickered on, revealing a vast chamber as the elevator lowered her deep beneath New York City. The illumination spread across a massive space, revealing industrial scaffolding and high-tech equipment lining the walls.

As the elevator touched down, a walkway lit up, connecting it to a door on the far side. A man emerged from this door, his footsteps echoing as he approached her.

"Number Eleven," he greeted her, reaching her just as the elevator came to a halt.

"Seven," Allison responded in an even tone.

"Come," he instructed, turning and leading her across the walkway.

They moved into the heart of the underground base. The walls were lined with screens displaying streams of data and surveillance feeds from around the world. Uniformed personnel moved briskly through the corridors.

Seven led her to a secure briefing room, gesturing for her to take a seat at a large conference table.

"How close are your people to Palmer?" Seven asked, taking a seat and then leaning back in his chair.

Allison steeled herself, maintaining her composure. "They're getting closer. Everything points to the southeast of the island. That's where his lab must be."

Seven nodded thoughtfully. "My people are getting the same vibe."

Allison leaned forward slightly. "That brings me to something. You should keep Council agents out of the area. They're getting in the way of my teams, and they're making Noah suspicious. He's already figured out that Palmer has gone rogue."

"Does it matter?" Seven said. "You said yourself you can spin anything to him."

"Yes, but what if he figures out that he's playing errand boy?"

"OK. I'll pull my people out. Nevertheless," Seven said,

his voice going cold, "your man doesn't have forever to get the scientist."

Allison's eyes narrowed. "What is that supposed to mean?"

"It means that we have a contingency plan in place."

Allison's gaze sharpened. "What type of contingency plan?"

Seven's expression remained impassive. "What Palmer is doing out there is genius, yes. But if we can't get the doctor and his research under our control, then we must stop it from leaving the island entirely."

A chill ran through Allison. "You're going to nuke them."

"Good guess," Seven confirmed. "Palmer has recently gained control of a cold fusion drive. He now has limitless power. It is only a matter of time before he has farmed and incubated millions of those parasites. Then he will have amassed the ability to take over the world. That cannot be allowed to happen. Mindweaver must not leave that island in the hands of Palmer. Your people have three days to get him."

Allison's resolve hardened. "Then I'll pull them," she said firmly.

Seven shook his head. "Oh no, you won't. You work for us, not E & E, and certainly not the United States of America. We still want Palmer and that project in our hands. Your man Wolf is to stay in Sumba until the bitter end."

Allison opened her mouth to protest, but Seven held up a hand to silence her.

Leaning forward, his tone turned icy. "And this isn't like Cuba. I don't want you showing up with a rescue party."

Allison's blood ran cold, the color draining from her face. She glanced around the room, suddenly aware that several armed guards were watching her through the windows of the conference room.

"Oh, yes," Seven continued, a hint of menace in his voice. "We know it was you who led them to Cuba. You who killed Four."

Allison's eyes widened in shock.

"You didn't think we would find out?" Seven's voice was scornful. "You're lucky we find you so important. Four was an idiot for capturing Wolf in the first place. Not when we already had you. He lost the base through his myopia."

"You're not going to..." Allison began, her voice trembling.

"Kill you, no," Seven interrupted. "Count it as a strike. But not one of three. One of two. The next one burns you. Now we have a lot of work to do here, so you can see yourself out."

With that, he stood and left the room, joining the others, leaving Allison to exit sheepishly.

By the time she reached the surface and was getting back into the limousine, she was shaking all over.

"How was your lunch, ma'am?" the driver asked.

"Oh, it was OK," she mumbled, her mind a million miles away from sandwiches and delis.

TWENTY-SEVEN

IN THE CELLAR, THE ATMOSPHERE WAS TENSE AS Jenny whispered into her radio, "Noah, Marco, Renée, can anyone hear me? We're safe for now, but we need help. Please respond." Her frustration mounted as she received only static in return.

Shortly after the woman's screams had died down last night, the four of them had partaken in a whispered introduction. The father's name was Damu, and the daughter was Kiya.

The eerie silence of the village outside was unsettling. Damu peered through the gap in the cellar door, his eyes scanning the empty passageways for any sign of movement. The searchers had been thorough, working all night, all the way through dawn and into the morning. Every so often, they'd hear a scream break out from somewhere in the distance as another person was found.

It had been at least two hours since the last cry of horror.

"Do you see anyone?" Neil asked quietly, his eyes locked on Damu.

Damu shook his head, his voice a low whisper. "Doesn't mean they're not still out there, though."

Kiya clung to her father's side, her wide eyes reflecting the fear that gripped them all. The static that filled the earpieces of their NLPs only added to the oppressive silence, each crackle and hiss a reminder of their precarious situation.

Jenny tried again, her voice a mix of desperation and determination. "Noah, Marco, Renée, please respond. We need help."

Damu stepped away from the door with cautious movements. "We have to stay hidden until we're sure it's safe," he whispered.

Neil nodded, his expression grim. "I agree."

Kiya, clutching her father's hand, whispered, "Daddy, are they going to find us?"

Damu knelt down beside her, his face softening as he looked into her eyes. "No, sweetheart. We're safe here. We just need to be very quiet."

The reassurance did little to ease the tension, but it was enough to keep Kiya calm for the moment. They huddled together in the darkness, Jenny continuing to try the radio as Damu and Kiya began to recount their experiences to Neil, their voices filled with fear and sorrow.

"My wife went away to work in the kitchens of the place they're building out there," he said. "When she came back, she wasn't the same."

Neil leaned in closer. "What do you mean?"

"She acted strangely, like she was possessed. She tried to

convince us to come back into the jungle with her, and when that didn't work, she tried to force us, wouldn't take no for an answer. Others came, those who had also taken jobs in the jungle. They tried to take us away, but we escaped."

Neil asked, "Where is she now? Your wife."

Damu shook his head, the pain evident in his eyes. "I don't know. Ever since, we've been living hidden from the others. Everyone in our village and all the surrounding villages is now infected with the same sickness."

"Sickness?" Jenny echoed.

"Yes," Damu replied. "Whatever it is, it changes them. Makes them different."

Kiya, her small frame huddled against her father's side, spoke quietly. "We're safe here, but we always have to be careful."

Damu's eyes were filled with caution as he looked at Neil. "They're everywhere. And they're always—"

Before he could finish, the cellar doors burst open, sunlight flooding the tight space. A wild-eyed attacker charged into the light, his gaze fixed on them with murderous intent.

Jenny was first into action. She positioned herself between the attacker and the father and daughter, her curved karambit knife flashing in the light as she braced for the onslaught.

The struggle was immediate and intense, the attacker's ferocity almost overwhelming, his strength driven by an unnatural rage. But he was unskilled. He left himself open, Jenny's knife plunging into him repeatedly. With a final, powerful thrust straight into the man's heart, the attacker fell to the ground, his body twitching before finally going still.

They stood over the body, Jenny's chest heaving from the exertion and adrenaline. Blood smeared her hands and clothes, and the room filled with the metallic scent of it.

"He took seven blows," she said. "Each one of them should have killed him."

Damu kneeled beside his daughter, clutching Kiya tightly to him, her eyes buried in chest, his hands covering her ears. His own eyes were wide with fear and horror. "We need to move," he said. "They'll all know we're here now."

TWENTY-EIGHT

THE MORNING LIGHT BATHED THE DORMITORY IN A warm, golden hue as Marco and Renée prepared to leave for the jungle. The quiet rustling of clothes and the soft thud of items being placed in bags mingled with the low murmurs of conversation. The atmosphere was a little on edge as everyone prepared to leave for the hike into the hills.

Renée tried once more to reach the others through the NLP, but it was no good. "Still nothing but static," she said afterwards, her voice edged with worry.

Marco frowned. "I don't like it."

"Me neither. The signal must be jammed," Renée replied.

Marco sighed thoughtfully. "Then it must be the Council."

Detective Antara approached them, a rucksack slung over one shoulder. His expression serious, his eyes scanned the room. "You two ready for what comes next?" he asked, keeping his voice low.

Marco nodded. "Ready as we'll ever be."

"Let's get this over with," Renée added.

They nodded in unison, joining all the others leaving the dormitory. The golden glow of the morning sun created a solemn ambiance that matched the mood of the fifty or so people ready to depart. Around twenty followers stood with Father Sanchez, their expressions reverent and serious. A convoy of trucks waited nearby, their engines idling softly, ready to transport the group on their journey.

Father Sanchez stood at the center, preparing to lead a prayer and bless the group. Once everyone was present, he raised his hands, his voice resonant and steady. "Good morning, everyone. Before we embark on our journey, let us bow our heads in prayer and seek the Lord's blessing."

The followers bowed their heads as one, the quiet rustle of movement the only sound as they prepared for the prayer. As for the recruits, they all looked at one another before sheepishly joining in, bowing their heads.

"Heavenly Father," Sanchez began, "we gather here today to embark on a journey of purpose and unity. We ask for Your divine guidance and protection as we venture into the unknown. Grant us strength and courage to face any challenges that may come our way. Just as You led Your people through the wilderness, lead us now to fulfill the mission set before us.

"Bless our hands to be steady and our hearts to be pure so that we may carry out our tasks with dedication and faith. May we remain united as one flock under Your watchful eye, ever faithful to Your will. Let Your light shine upon us, illuminating our path and dispelling any darkness that seeks to hinder our progress.

"We place our trust in You, O Lord, knowing that with Your blessing, we can achieve greatness in Your name. Guide us, protect us, and keep us steadfast in our purpose. Amen."

The followers echoed a quiet "Amen," their voices united in solemn reverence.

After the blessing, the group began boarding the backs of military trucks, the fifty recruits distributing themselves among the vehicles. Additional equipment trucks, six in total, joined the back of the convoy. These were loaded with machine parts, medical supplies, and other equipment.

Marco leaned into his wife and Antara, keeping his voice low. "You seeing this?"

"Oh yes," Antara replied, his eyes scanning the convoy.

Renée nodded at one of the trucks. "Looks like parts for some kind of electric generator."

"Look at that one at the back," Marco said, gesturing subtly. "It's loaded with sewage pipes, the type you lay under towns."

Father Sanchez, standing nearby, raised his voice to address the group. "We'll be driving the first fifty miles, but after that, it'll be on foot. The hike will take around four to six hours depending on how often we need to take breaks. It's mostly uphill through thick vegetation."

As the convoy rumbled to life, the trucks began to roll out in a line, the sound of engines filling the air, blending with the whispers of the departing group. Marco, Renée, and Antara exchanged one last look of resolve, knowing that the journey ahead would most likely test their endurance and their unity to the very limit.

TWENTY-NINE

Noah had bought a Kawasaki Z750 from a cluttered motorcycle dealership in Waingapu, using a high-level credit card disguised as a Bank of Sumba card and a fake Indonesian ID. Following that, he'd strapped his rucksack to the back, donned a helmet, and ridden out of the dealership.

The Kawasaki now roared beneath him as he sped through the countryside, driven by an urgency to find the others.

The landscape began to change as Noah approached Kataka, the last known location of Neil and Jenny. The roads became narrower as they worked their way up the hills, and the tranquil countryside gave way to a more populated area with more buildings and people appearing along the roadsides.

The outskirts of the town were dotted with one-story wooden houses, their porches filled with people who stared at him with suspicious eyes as he passed.

This place feels off, Noah thought.

The winding roads led him deeper into the heart of the hillside town, the stares of the villagers following his every move. The sense of unease grew with each passing second. More and more people began lining the road, seemingly warned of his approach, though Noah never spotted anyone speaking into a radio or phone. The coordinated nature of their stares was unsettling, as if they all knew something he did not.

Where are Neil and Jenny? Noah's concern was intensifying.

His eyes scanned the surroundings as he rode farther into Kataka. The mood was eerie, more and more people leaving their houses and lining the road. Noah's heart skipped a beat when he spotted an abandoned coach with its windows smashed out. It matched the description of the one Jenny and Neil had been traveling in.

Noah passed it, working the bike up the hill, his mind racing. The unsettling silence was broken only by the hum of the motorcycle engine. As he ascended, he observed the wreckage of last night's convoy scattered along the road. Abandoned pickups, cars, minivans, SUVs—all with broken windows and busted doors.

What happened here?

As he reached the top of the hill, Noah spotted a commotion up ahead. The two agents from last night were fighting in the street with the villagers. It was obvious that they had been pulled from their car, which lay abandoned—all four of its tires punctured. The scene was chaotic, the mood intense and urgent, the two men fighting for their lives.

Unfortunately, with his eyes fixed to the fight, Noah

wasn't paying attention to the road. Otherwise he would have seen the spike strip crossing it.

His tires let out a sudden hiss, rapidly deflating and sending him skidding to a stop.

Up ahead, the agents were fighting off the mob of villagers. Gunshots rang out. Several villagers fell, but the rest backed off only briefly before advancing again, fearless and relentless.

Noah watched as the taller agent shot another villager, then another, but the wave of attackers kept coming. The shorter agent wasn't smirking anymore. He was bleeding from the neck and shoulder, staggering around the back of their car. He flung open the trunk and pulled out a machine gun, snapping in a magazine. As Harry was getting subdued by the mob, Tom turned the weapon on the crowd, spraying them with bullets.

The villagers scattered, fleeing into the nearby houses. The gunfire ceased momentarily, and the injured Tom almost collapsed, his strength waning. Harry caught him, supporting his weight.

Their eyes narrowed as they noticed Noah, but their attention quickly shifted as the villagers began to emerge from the buildings again, a second wave forming.

Tom fired off more shots, but the gun clicked empty. Frantically, he grabbed another magazine from the trunk and reloaded. But it was no good. There were too many, and they were fearless. The two men, battered and bleeding, took the only option they had. They limped off into the jungle, disappearing down an alley that led away from the road.

At that moment, the villagers began to approach Noah with a menacing determination, their eyes glinting with the same ferocity they had shown for the agents. He didn't hesitate; he drew his pistol and fired, hitting one, then another—head shots. The brief moment of gunfire bought him enough time to dash toward the jungle, heading between two houses.

Knowing he needed to get clear of the local populace, Noah ran downhill, following dirt pathways that wound through the small village. The rural scenery flashed by in a blur—small farmyards with pigs, goats, and chickens. Villagers emerged from the buildings and yards. Some wielded crude weapons, their faces twisted in murderous fury.

Noah ducked and weaved through the pathways, avoiding the villagers who seemed to appear out of nowhere. The air was filled with shouts and the distant echo of gunfire. It sounded like the agents were running out of ammunition.

As Noah reached the edge of the village, he plunged into the jungle, the dense foliage closing in around him. Gunshots rang out to his right, sharp and clear. The agents were still fighting their way down the hill.

I need to stay on their trail. They'll know what's going on here, Noah thought as he propelled himself forward.

Moving deeper into the jungle, the terrain became steeper, the downhill slope making his descent quicker, more perilous. He slid on loose soil and grabbed on to tree trunks for balance.

Soon, Noah no longer heard the sound of gunshots or the shouts of people. He stopped running, listening carefully to the silence that had replaced the mayhem. The jungle around him was thick and oppressive, but he moved cautiously, picking his way through the tangled undergrowth.

Eventually, he stumbled upon a small clearing and spotted a farm nestled in the middle of it. The rustic farmhouse stood out against the wild backdrop, its windows dark and silent. As he approached, Noah noticed a trail of blood drops leading to the door, which was wide open.

He paused, surveying the scene. There was a faint sound of groaning coming from inside, hushed voices, someone moving around. Drawing his pistol, Noah approached the farmhouse door, his eyes scanning the area for any signs of movement.

He crept in, the floorboards creaking softly under his weight as he entered the hallway. The air carried the scent of metallic blood and decay. Cautiously, he followed the sound of groaning, which was coming from upstairs.

Halfway up the stairs, Noah froze. He could see along the landing to the open door at the end. The injured agent sat against the wall, holding a wound in his stomach. Stab wounds marred his chest and neck. He sat facing the open door, his face drained of all color, each breath a struggle.

His eyes flickered with a little life as Noah emerged at the top of the stairs. He made a weak attempt to lift his rifle, but his strength failed him.

The other agent was nowhere to be seen. But Noah had an idea of where he could be.

While Tom died in a puddle of his own blood, Harry was standing beside the doorway, his back to the cracked plaster, his breath shallow as he listened intently. The lock on Tom's face as he breathed his last breath told him that Noah was there.

As the last of the light faded from Tom's eyes, Harry readied himself, pistol in hand, ready to fire it at the stairs where his partner had been looking before he died. With a quick movement, he burst out of the room, expecting to catch Noah off guard, but found the stairs empty.

Confusion flashed across his face. He stepped out farther, his gun held firm, eyes scanning the empty staircase. As he stepped past the doorway on his left, a pistol emerged from the darkness of the room, cocking with a loud click and pressing into his temple.

"Drop it," Noah commanded.

Harry, realizing he was outmaneuvered, complied. Noah disarmed him swiftly and pushed him back into the first room. The agent stumbled to a stop in front of a large window that looked out onto the vast jungle.

The small room was cluttered with old furniture and dusty belongings. Harry's expression was wary, his eyes darting around as if seeking an escape route. Noah stood firm, his pistol trained on the agent.

Harry sneered, "Who are you? Indonesian police? Local intelligence?"

Of course, Noah was in disguise. He saw only a local.

"I'm the one with the gun. I ask the questions," Noah retorted firmly. "That's how this works."

Harry sighed, feigning nonchalance. "Then ask."

"What's with all those people attacking you?" Noah demanded.

"They mustn't like tourists out here," Harry replied sarcastically.

"OK. Then why did you kill the recruiter?" Noah pressed.

"Did I?" Harry shot back, a mocking grin on his face.

"And what the hell did your people pull out of his head?"

The agent began to sweat, his smirk faltering. "Look, whoever you are, you'd better leave this place before you no longer can."

"You've lost control of whatever you and Palmer have been up to, haven't you?" Noah said, his eyes narrowing.

"Lost control? You think we ever had control?" Harry responded.

"Where's Palmer?" Noah asked, stepping closer.

Instead of answering, the agent grinned at him. "Looks like you have no idea what's going on here. Best to keep it that way. Now do whatever you've come to do."

Noah decided on a different tack. He pulled out the Cognitive Harmonizer and powered it up. The agent's eyes fixed on the device, recognition dawning.

"I've heard of those. It's how Noah Wolf escaped from Cuba. Wait. Does that mean *you're* Noah Wolf?" His voice had begun to tremble slightly.

Noah stepped closer, about two feet away. "Hold still."

"You better leave before you end up joining him. The same as the Special Forces team we sent..."

The guy's voice faded in Noah's ears as his attention was drawn to the jungle outside. As Harry continued to warn him about Palmer, something glinted in the sunlight.

Optics on a scope.

"Duck!"

But before he could react, Harry's head exploded, a 6.5 Creedmoor round bursting through the window, then his head. Blood and brain splattered against the wall. One dead agent became two dead agents.

Noah jumped back, diving into a corner of the room. The sound of the shot reverberated in the small space as he shoved himself low and crawled to the window. Positioned below the ledge, he peeked out cautiously, his eyes scanning the dense vegetation. At first, he saw nothing but the jungle where he'd seen the flash before. The shooter had moved.

Then he saw it: another glint of sunlight off the optics of a scope—followed by muzzle flash.

Bullets began pounding through the thin wooden walls of the house. The wood splintered around him, creating a storm of debris. Noah's mind raced, adrenaline surging through his veins.

I need to move, now!

He threw himself out of the room, down the stairs, and darted out of the house, his movements a blur of desperate speed. Bullets whizzed past him, tearing through the air with lethal precision. Noah zigzagged, dodging the hail of bullets as he sprinted toward the jungle. It would at least offer a semblance of cover. He plunged into the underbrush, branches snapping against his body as he ran. The chaos of the sniper attack faded slightly as the thick vegetation absorbed the sound, but Noah knew he couldn't slow down.

The sniper's professionalism was evident in the precision of his shots. This wasn't some local with a hunting rifle. Whoever was shooting was trained and very good. Noah's only advantage was the dense jungle, which made it harder for the sniper to track his movements.

Keep moving. Stay unpredictable, he thought, disappearing deeper into the jungle, the shadows swallowing him up.

THIRTY

Jenny, Neil, Damu, and Kiya moved through the jungle, the three adults slashing through the undergrowth with machetes. A cacophony of sounds surrounded them—chirping insects, distant bird calls, the rhythmic chopping of the machetes, and the rustling of leaves.

Kiya, frightened by the overwhelming environment, stayed close to her father, her small hand gripping his tightly.

With the day drawing on, they came across a dilapidated temple, its ancient stones covered in vines and moss. The structure was partially hidden by the jungle, with only the weathered stone spires and the remnants of carved figures hinting at its former glory. A stream ran nearby, its babbling waters providing a soothing contrast to the cacophonous sounds of their surroundings.

The group paused at the edge of the clearing, their eyes taking in the sight of the ancient temple, the sun hovering just above it. The need for a break was evident in their tired expressions.

Kiya tugged at her father's sleeve. "Papa, can we eat?" she asked.

Damu nodded, looking around the clearing. "Here's as good a place as any, I suppose."

Jenny, wiping sweat from her brow, looked at Damu. "How far are we?"

"Another six or seven hours. That should get us to the edge of their camp," Damu replied.

Neil nodded at the temple. "How old is this temple?"

"Centuries," Damu replied. "Our ancestors used to worship the mountain and the trees. They believed that spirits lived inside the bark and the rocks. It's why it caused such a stir when the foreigners first arrived."

Jenny asked, "When was that?"

Damu looked at her, slightly puzzled. "You don't know? I thought you said you come from Kodi."

"We moved last year from Java," Jenny replied smoothly.

"Oh, right. But you speak Sumbanese instead of Javan," Damu remarked, his curiosity piqued.

Jenny nodded. "We speak both. Our families are originally from Sumba."

Damu seemed to accept this, nodding. "Oh... OK, then... Well, they showed up about two years ago. First, it was just the scientists. They'd take local guides from the villages and venture out for weeks into the thickest parts of the jungle around Mount Wanggameti."

Neil asked, "What were they looking for?"

"Something in the bark of the most ancient trees. That was when the local shamans got involved. Many of the trees they were dissecting were sacred to our ancestors. It caused a lot of problems. That was until the corporation running it all paid off the government. After that, they simply shot the protesters when they tried to stop them cutting the trees down."

Jenny frowned. "Who is the corporation?"

She thought she might already know.

"Nobody knows," Damu told her. "Sometimes they call it one thing, the next it has another name. But whatever it is, it only believes in evil. Because by cutting those trees down, they have released an ancient evil." Damu's voice had dropped to a whisper.

"What do you mean?" Jenny asked.

"The souls of our ancestors are in those trees as well as the dark spirits they protect us from. By cutting them down, it broke the sacred seal."

It was then that Kiya leaned into her father, cupping her hands around his ear and whispering into them.

Damu nodded, placing a reassuring hand on her shoulder. "I must stop. The stories make Kiya scared."

They sat down by the stream, filling their canteens with the cool, clear liquid. The sound of the trickling water was soothing, a gentle background to their conversation. They ate a little longer, sharing what little food they had as the ancient, vine-covered temple stood behind them, silent and watching.

As they rested, Neil turned to Damu. "You said before about scientists coming up here."

Damu nodded. "Yes."

"Did you ever get to see any of them?" Neil asked, leaning forward slightly.

"Not when they were originally here cutting the trees down, but I have since. The one who came back about five months ago. Just before Ayu went off to work for them. I was trading a trailer full of corn with some people over at Kananga. He was living out in a farm there with his giant bodyguard."

Neil reached into his rucksack and pulled out a photo, showing it to Damu. "Is this the man?"

Damu took the photo, his eyes narrowing as he studied it. Recognition flickered in his gaze. "That's him. Palmer. They all worship him now. Call him Lord. Some say that the spirit of the jungle has taken him over. That it is using him for its own means."

As he spoke, Kiya tugged at her father's arm. An angry look crossed her face as she shook her head at him. "Papa, stop," she whispered.

Damu looked at her, his expression softening. He nodded, respecting her wishes. The group then finished their meal in silence, the weight of the conversation settling over them like a lead shroud.

THIRTY-ONE

IT TOOK THEM THREE HOURS TO REACH THE END OF the road.

Marco, Renée, Detective Antara, and the rest of the convoy disembarked from the vehicles, their eyes widening at the sight before them. Across a wide valley, the rise of Mount Wanggameti loomed in the distance. The lush valleys of Sumba stretched out in a verdant expanse, their rolling hillsides blanketed in vibrant green foliage. The landscape was punctuated by deep, winding ravines and the occasional patch of dense forest, creating a patchwork of natural beauty. As the sun cast its golden light, the valleys shimmered with a serene tranquility, offering a breathtaking glimpse into the heart of the island's untouched wilderness.

Father Sanchez and his people moved among the group, handing out water bottles. "You'll need to stay hydrated. The Lord's work is thirsty work," Sanchez said with a smile.

A distant rumble captured the attention of Marco, Renée, and Antara. They looked up to see three CH-47

Chinook helicopters approaching, growing larger as they hovered above the jungle canopy.

"Look at the size of those helicopters," Marco said. "I didn't think we'd be seeing military-grade equipment out here."

"They're certainly not holding back," Renée added, her eyes following the helicopters as they descended.

"Let's stay alert," Antara said, his tone cautious.

The helicopters lowered their winches to unload the equipment from the trailers. Sanchez's followers managed the unloading with practiced efficiency, while Sanchez himself focused on the people he needed to lead into the jungle. The noise and wind generated by the helicopters added to the organized chaos of the scene, the sight of the winches lowering and the equipment being carefully managed evidence of just how big Palmer's operation was.

Sanchez gathered everyone for a final briefing before they headed into the jungle. He stood on a small rise, his voice carrying over the sounds of the jungle and the helicopters.

"Listen up, everyone," the priest began. "We're about to embark on a journey that requires both physical endurance and spiritual fortitude. First and foremost, you must stay hydrated. We cannot afford anyone falling ill due to dehydration."

He paused, letting the importance of his words sink in. "Avoid interacting with wildlife. The creatures of this jungle are God's creation, but they can also be dangerous. If you see any wildlife, keep your distance and inform one of my followers immediately."

Sanchez's eyes scanned the crowd, making sure he had

everyone's attention. "If you feel unwell or need to rest, do not hesitate to speak up. Your health and safety are paramount. We must all arrive at our destination in one piece."

As was typical with him, Sanchez concluded with a prayer. "I am your shepherd," he said, "and it is my duty to bring you to the Lord safely. Now let's move out."

As they began their trek into the jungle, the sounds of their environment enveloped them—the distant calls of birds, the hum of insects. The helicopters' noise faded into the background, leaving only the wilderness.

The group moved forward, the unease among the newcomers obvious, their expressions a mix of curiosity and apprehension. Sanchez's followers, however, moved with an eerie coordination, their actions synchronized as if driven by an unseen force.

THIRTY-TWO

A STRONG WIND NOW CROSSED THE ISLAND, whipping through the trees, causing leaves and branches to thrash violently. Above, bruised, flashing storm clouds spread across the sky.

Noah moved quickly, his senses sharpened. He had already figured out that he was being hunted by more than one man. It was actually four. Four well-armed and highly trained elite operatives. Perhaps the ones the agent was talking about before his head got in the way of a 6.5 Creedmoor. The distinct weapon types and the strategic directions of the gunfire were clear indicators. Using nothing more than the sounds the guns made, Noah had figured out that one operative was carrying an Atchisson AA-12 fully-automatic shotgun. Another was wielding a high-velocity rifle, firing the 6.5 Creedmoors—he was the one who'd shot the agent. The other two had M4A1 carbines, one firing from the east, the other from the west. They were fanned out, trying to outflank him.

With the operatives firing from different directions, Noah was forced to constantly evade and change his path. Another bullet whizzed past him, grazing his arm. The pain was sharp and immediate, and his suit glitched and distorted from the impact.

Despite the pain, he pushed on, skipping down the tall bank of a ravine. As he did, the storm clouds overhead finally unleashed their fury. Roaring thunder cracked the air, followed by flashes of lightning that briefly illuminated the vegetation like a flashbulb. Heavy rain began to pour, drenching the jungle and making visibility difficult.

Still, Noah thought, *if it's hard for me to see, then it'll be equally as hard for them.*

He was right. The rain altered the dynamics of the chase. The heavy drops created a curtain of water that obscured vision and muffled sounds. Noah used this to his advantage, moving stealthily through the thick foliage, his senses heightened by the adrenaline coursing through his veins.

The storm's intensity increased, the wind howling through the trees and driving the rain sideways. Noah could hear the operatives calling out to each other, their voices strained over the din of the storm. The elite weapons they carried were formidable, but the jungle and the weather had become Noah's allies.

Lightning flashed again, illuminating the scene for a brief moment. Glancing over his shoulder, Noah saw the shadowy figures of the operatives, their movements cautious yet determined. He knew he had to keep moving, to stay ahead of them. The rain-soaked jungle was a maze, and he intended to use every bit of it to his advantage.

I need to lead them deeper. Separate them.

Noah dragged himself through a particularly dense thicket, the branches scratching at his suit and skin. The operatives' gunfire was more sporadic now, but the odd gunshot kept him moving along.

Stay focused, stay alive, Noah reminded himself.

Up until now, Noah had put off using the camouflage setting on the suit. For one, he didn't want them to see him disappear. That way, they'd know he was more than some local. But as the storm raged on and he realized he couldn't keep running forever, he stopped and changed his strategy from evasion to confrontation.

Ducking within the tangled roots of a mangrove, he slipped out of his clothing and switched the suit to camouflage mode using the palm control. The suit began changing, blending seamlessly with his surroundings, the roots of the mangrove and the vines of the surrounding vegetation being mimicked by the suit's surface. Sure they hadn't seen it, now he was the predator and they were the prey.

With the suit's surface reflecting the chaotic patterns of the jungle and the storm, Noah moved stealthily, his steps silent against the muddy ground.

Using the dense vegetation to his advantage, he moved in closer as the four men worked their way slowly through the jungle. He could hear them communicating, their voices barely audible over the thrashing weather.

"You see him?" one whispered close by.

"Not a sign," Noah heard come back over the guy's radio.

"Fan out," came a third voice.

They began spreading out. This was Noah's time. He needed to act quickly and decisively.

He crept forward, every step calculated. The jungle around him was a blur of rainswept green and brown. Noah's focus was razor-sharp. He spotted the operative with the AA-12 shotgun moving through the trees, the weapon ready and searching for a target.

Time to strike.

He closed the distance between them. The storm was his ally, the rain masking his approach. He was just a few feet away from the operative when a crack of lightning illuminated the scene in a flash. The operative turned, but it was too late. Noah lunged with his knife, taking him down swiftly and silently, his hand pressed against the guy's mouth as he lay on top, the knife buried in the operative's chest, almost bisecting his heart.

Noah left the shotgun; it wasn't camouflaged and would give him away. He moved back into the cover of the jungle, his mind already focusing on the next target.

The storm raged on, the thunder and lightning creating an almost apocalyptic backdrop. Noah's heart was steady, his movements controlled and deliberate. He was no longer the hunted. He was the hunter.

One down, three to go.

Navigating through the jungle, he could hear the operatives' frustration growing. The storm was making their task difficult, and Noah intended to use that to his full advantage. The rain was his cover, the thunder his distraction, the jungle his battlefield.

"Sanders, status?" the leader, Corporal Hendricks, called

into the comms, his voice strained with the effort to be heard over the storm.

There was no response. The rain continued to hammer down, and the distant rumble of thunder echoed through the trees.

"Sanders, report," Hendricks tried again.

Still nothing. The silence on the other end of the comms tightened the muscles of the three remaining operatives, their eyes scanning the jungle hard.

"Stay sharp. He's close," Hendricks said in a low growl.

Noah moved silently through the jungle, the camouflage of his suit blending seamlessly with the foliage. He watched as the three men moved cautiously, so close he could reach out and touch them.

One of the men, a German named Hasler, scanned the area through the optics of his Remington 700, the scope barely usable in the heavy weather. The third man, a large Ghanian named Kojo, moved with careful precision, his steps deliberate and silent, his grip on his carbine never wavering.

Highly trained and experienced, these men knew full well that it was they who were now being hunted.

"Stay close. He'll come to us," Hendricks instructed.

Merged with the environment, Noah watched the men, his eyes fixing on to his next target. His movements were swift and silent. He was the shadow, the silent force moving through the storm. The operatives were skilled, but this was Noah's territory. He was the spider, and they were the flies.

Hasler advanced cautiously, his eyes darting through the dense foliage. He continually whispered into his comms. "Sanders, come in. Report your status."

But the only response was the relentless sound of the storm, the rain pouring down, the wind howling through the trees. Tension coiled in Hasler's gut as he moved forward, every sense on high alert.

Suddenly, the foliage beside him burst to life as if the jungle itself was attacking him. The assault was swift and silent, a blur of movement in the storm. Hasler barely had time to react before the knife was across his throat. They grappled in a brief, intense struggle, Noah getting ahold of him, keeping him still and silent as he bled out before dropping him to the ground.

Hendricks's voice crackled over the comms. "Sanders? Hasler? Come in, copy."

There was no response. Only the storm's fury.

Noah melted back into the jungle, his camouflage rendering him nearly invisible against the backdrop of leaves and shadows.

Two down, two to go.

Close to a river, the sound of the water roaring over the lashing storm, Noah prepared for his next strike. As Hendricks passed by, Noah peeled himself from a tree, but his camouflage suit glitched slightly, the pattern flashing where the bullet had grazed his arm earlier.

Hendricks saw it. He turned sharply, raising his weapon, but Noah was faster. He disarmed Hendricks, whipping the carbine from his grip by the barrel. But in the struggle he lost it, the gun flying off into the underbrush.

Hendricks drew his knife, coming at Noah with a series of jabs and back-handed swipes, known in Brazilian knife fighting as the 'rabo de arraia' (stingray's tail). Noah quickly blocked with his own knife, coming back with counter moves, each strike and counter-strike executed with lethal intent. The flickering image of the jungle on Noah's suit added a surreal quality to the brutal encounter, making it seem as though Hendricks was fighting the jungle itself.

The ground beneath the fighters was slippery with mud and rain, making each movement treacherous. Hendricks feinted with a 'garra de tigre' (tiger claw), a deceptive upward slash aimed at Noah's midsection. Noah anticipated the move and parried with a swift 'shield' block, deflecting the blade and stepping to the side to maintain his balance.

Hendricks, relentless, transitioned into a 'faca de dente' (tooth knife), a short, sharp jab targeting Noah's hand to disarm him. Noah pulled back, the tip of Hendricks' knife grazing his gloved hand, damaging the suit further.

The two fighters continued to exchange blows, their knives clashing with deadly precision as they moved closer to the banks of the river, Noah's suit unable to keep up with the rapidly changing environment, making him somewhat visible. Hendricks executed a 'lâmina de trovão' (thunder blade), a forceful, downward slash meant to finish the fight. Noah sidestepped, using the momentum to deliver a 'pico do falcão' (falcon's beak), a quick thrust to Hendricks' side that forced him to stagger back.

Hendricks, panting and enraged, lunged with a 'punhal do diabo' (devil's dagger), a lethal thrust aimed at Noah's heart. Noah twisted his body, narrowly avoiding the deadly blade, and countered with a 'rasga-vento' (wind tear), a sweeping slash that caught Hendricks off guard. The force of the blow sent Hendricks sprawling to the ground.

Noah moved quickly, using a 'pé de anjo' (angel's foot) to pin Hendricks' wrist to the muddy ground with his foot. Hendricks struggled, but the slippery terrain betrayed him. Noah, breathing heavily, positioned his knife above Hendricks' chest, ready to deliver the final blow, but before he could strike, a shot rang out.

Kojo emerged from the jungle, his M4A1 aimed at Noah. The barrage of bullets sent Noah sprawling down an embankment into the fast-flowing river. The icy water engulfed him, the current pulling him away from the shore. He struggled to keep his head above the surface, the storm making the river a churning, deadly torrent.

As it dragged him around a bend, the river's speed increased, the roar of the water growing louder. Noah's eyes widened as he saw the edge of a waterfall approaching. The current dragged him faster and faster until he shot off the end, plummeting through the air and into the lake below.

The impact with the water was jarring. He sank beneath the surface, the water enveloping him. Kicking his legs and using his remaining strength, he swam upward, breaking through to the surface with a gasp.

Exhausted, he struggled to the shore. He crawled out of the lake, collapsing on the muddy bank. His hologram suit was busted, glitching and flickering erratically. He pulled off the mask, his chest heaving as he tried to catch his breath.

Turning around and looking up, he saw Hendricks and Kojo standing at the top of the waterfall. Their silhouettes were stark against the stormy sky. One of them raised their weapon and fired a shot, the bullet striking a rock close to Noah and sending debris flying.

Noah hauled himself up, his leg throbbing with pain

where it had received the kiss of a bullet. Ignoring the agony, he forced himself to run into the forest, his breath coming in ragged gasps. The trees closed in around him, their dense canopy providing some cover from the relentless storm. Noah pushed on, his senses sharp. Every step was a struggle, his body screaming in protest, but he couldn't afford to stop.

THIRTY-THREE

JENNY, NEIL, DAMU, AND KIYA PUSHED DEEPER into the jungle, their progress slow and laborious. The relentless rain poured down in sheets, soaking them to the bone. The wind howled through the trees, and thunder rumbled ominously, creating an atmosphere of constant dread. Added to this, it was starting to get dark.

"Are you sure this is the way?" Jenny asked, her voice strained with exhaustion.

"Positive. It's just that this path hasn't been used in years," Damu replied.

The storm's intensity and the physical exertion of pushing through the dense jungle began to take their toll on Jenny's and Neil's hologram suits. Flickers of static briefly distorted their appearances before returning to normal, unnoticed at first but becoming more frequent.

Kiya, ever observant, tugged at her father's sleeve. "Papa, did you see that?"

Damu turned to look at Jenny and Neil, suspicion

clouding his features as their images flickered. "What's happening to you two?"

Jenny quickly attempted to brush it off. "It's nothing. Just a trick of the light."

But despite her words, the suits glitched again, more noticeably this time. Their images shimmered, distorting the semblances of locals.

"No, I saw it. What is it? Who are you?" Damu demanded, his voice becoming tense.

Jenny and Neil exchanged a glance, understanding that they had no choice but to reveal the truth. With a quick motion, they both deactivated their hologram suits. The illusion of their local appearances vanished, revealing their true selves beneath. The suits, now looking like wet suits dotted with innumerable sensors, glistened in the rain. They lifted their full-face masks, showing their real faces to the astonished father and daughter.

Damu's eyes widened in shock. "What kind of technology is that?"

"State of the art and American," Neil replied.

"So you're American, then?" Damu asked, his suspicion giving way to a cautious curiosity.

Neil nodded. "We came here to find out what's happening in this area and stop it."

Damu's expression shifted from confusion to incredulity. "But why are Americans trying to stop it?"

"Because what's happening here is dangerous, not just for Sumba, but for the whole world," Jenny explained.

"So you're here to help us?" Kiya asked, her voice small but hopeful.

"Yes, we are. And we need your help too," Neil said, his tone sincere.

Damu looked at Kiya, seeing the hope in her eyes. He took a deep breath, then nodded, determination setting in. "All right. We'll help you."

A murmur of fresh hope fluttered through the group. But it didn't last.

"What's that?" Jenny whispered, peering into the darkness ahead. The others strained to see what had caught her attention.

A faint, bobbing beam of light pierced the thick underbrush, cutting through the rain. Another beam appeared, then another, until the jungle ahead was filled with the flickering glow of flashlights. The beams swayed and danced as their holders moved.

"It's a search party," Neil hissed.

Damu's face paled. "We need to hide. Now."

The group quickly dove into the underbrush, pressing themselves low to the ground, hearts pounding as the flashlight beams drew closer.

As they lay low among the vines, feet appeared, trampling the vegetation just inches from their hiding spots. The searchers spoke in hushed tones, their voices filled with urgency. The four of them held their breath, tensing their muscles. Damu clutched Kiya tightly in his arms, his eyes wide with fear. As the last of the group passed by, Kiya whimpered softly.

The woman closest to them heard the noise and turned sharply toward their hiding spot. "Over here! I heard something!" she shouted.

Her hawk-like eyes searched the brush until they

widened, homing in on Damu and Kiya. "I found some-one!" she cried.

All at once, the group converged on them. Hands shot into the brush, dragging them both out. Damu put up a fight, but there were too many. Jenny and Neil were forced out of their hiding spots.

"Get off them!" Neil shouted.

He lunged at the attackers, knocking one assailant to the ground with a leg sweep, grabbing the man's machete and using it to fend off others. Jenny sprang into action, her karambit flashing in the dim light as she fought to free Kiya.

Damu fought fiercely to protect his daughter. He delivered a powerful punch to one attacker's face, sending the man reeling back. But another grabbed him from behind, trying to pin his arms. Neil swung the machete, hacking into the attacker's upper arm, forcing him to release Damu.

Jenny reached Kiya and pulled her away from the melee, keeping her close as the girl trembled with fear. "Stay behind me," Jenny instructed.

One by one, more villagers emerged from the under-brush, their faces grim, their machetes raised—too many to fight. Neil and Damu stood back to back, fending off the relentless waves, panic beginning to creep into their efforts as the jungle came alive with attackers.

Jenny needed all her skill. She plunged her karambit into the chest of one attacker, hooking him out of the way, the curved blade slicing through muscle and bone. But as he crumpled to the ground, the knife lodged inside him, another lunged at her from the side. She swiftly drew her pistol from her hip, firing a shot that dropped him instantly.

The jungle writhed with people, flashlight beams

moving in every direction. Jenny fired again and again, each shot finding its mark. But she knew that the ratio of bullets to attackers wasn't in their favor.

"There's too many of them!" she cried out.

In the background, Kiya watched with wide, frightened eyes when a soft, familiar voice called her name. "Kiya? Kiya?"

The little girl turned, her eyes wide with disbelief. "Momma?" she whispered.

Ayu, Kiya's mother, stepped out from the shadows, her eyes glowing with an unnatural light. "Kiya, come to me. Let me get you out of this storm and this jungle. Let me get you to safety. Come with Momma."

Jenny, in the middle of a struggle, glanced over her shoulder and saw Kiya moving toward Ayu. "Kiya, no!" Jenny shouted. "She's infected!"

But it was too late. Kiya's mother wrapped her in a tight embrace, lifted her up, and whisked her away, the little girl's cries for help drowned out by the storm as they disappeared into the depths of the jungle.

"No!" Damu roared. In the rain and chaos, he surged forward, his desperation lending him strength as he ran after them. He managed to strike down one assailant but was quickly overwhelmed as more attackers piled on, dragging him to the ground. "Kiyaaa!" he screamed, struggling against the weight of the villagers pinning him down.

Neil grabbed Jenny's arm and pulled her away. "We have to go! Now!"

"But Kiya..." Jenny protested.

"We're way outnumbered. We have to get out of here and regroup," Neil insisted.

They ran through the jungle, the cries of Damu and Kiya echoing behind them. The storm continued to rage, the sound of their heavy breathing and the weather drowning out their rapid footsteps.

They ducked into a thick cluster of trees. "Switch on your camouflage settings," Neil instructed.

Jenny nodded, fumbling for the control on her suit. With a quick press of her palm, her suit shimmered and then melted into the jungle around her. Neil did the same, his form blending seamlessly with the foliage.

The attackers, confused by their sudden disappearance, stopped in their tracks. "Where did they go?" one of them shouted, swinging his flashlight wildly through the rain-soaked jungle.

Neil and Jenny moved silently away, creeping deeper into the jungle, careful to avoid any movements that might give away their position. The attackers spread out, their flash-lights creating eerie patterns of light and shadow as they searched the dense undergrowth.

"We need to rescue them," Jenny whispered once they were a good distance away.

Neil nodded. "We will. But first, we need to get somewhere safe. Then we can plan our next move."

THIRTY-FOUR

Noah pushed on, the storm continuing to rage. He knew the two remaining soldiers, Hendricks and Kojo, were still hunting him. He just needed to find a place to regroup and set a trap.

As he reached a plateau, he stumbled upon a chainlink fence. On the other side was an abandoned military village. The sight was eerie, the once-active site now overgrown with jungle foliage. Vines crept up the dilapidated brick buildings, their corrugated roofs red with rust.

This will do, Noah thought as he made his way to a large three-story building on the edge of the site. It was a deserted prison. He would use it for cover.

A rusted ladder led to a guard tower. He climbed it, the metal creaking under his weight. From the top, he had a clear view of the village and the surrounding jungle. The fat storm clouds cast a gloomy shadow over the scene, the occasional flash of lightning illuminating the desolate landscape.

Noah's eyes scanned the jungle, the windswept foliage

obscuring his view. He took deep, steady breaths as he searched for any sign of his pursuers.

A flash of lightning exploded across the sky, casting the jungle in a garish, momentary light. In that brief illumination, Noah spotted movement. Hendricks and Kojo were making their way through the dense underbrush, their progress slow and methodical. They were close.

That's it. Come to me.

Noah's heart was steady, like a predator on the hunt, as he watched them approach the chainlink fence. Hendricks, the taller of the two, reached the same hole in the fence that Noah had climbed through moments ago. He gestured to Kojo, and the two men crouched down, examining the area.

"Stay sharp," Hendricks muttered. "He can't be far."

Kojo merely nodded.

Noah had lost his pistol in the scuffle with Hendricks and his knife in the river, making him unarmed. He had to be smart if he was going to win this. He glanced around the guard tower, searching for anything he could use to his advantage. His eyes settled on a pile of old, rusted metal rods that had fallen from the crumbling cement walls. They weren't much, but they could buy him some time.

He grabbed one of the rods and positioned himself at the edge of the tower, waiting for the next flash of lightning. When it came, he hurled the rod at the concrete ground closest to their position.

Hendricks and Kojo snapped to attention, their eyes darting toward the clattering sound. "What was that?" Kojo asked, his grip tightening on his carbine.

"Could be him," Hendricks replied. "Let's check it out."

Noah watched as the two men moved toward the noise,

their attention diverted. He took the opportunity to climb down the ladder, his movements quick and silent.

Armed with another metal pole, he waited for them to reach the edge of the military buildings, where the compound opened up into the prison. Once they were close enough, he waited for the lightning, then the thunder, and threw it. The rod clattered in the space between them, making the two operatives turn toward the prison.

Noah had already slipped into the shadows of the building.

The interior was a maze of cells and corridors, perfect for setting a trap. He moved quickly and quietly, his mind racing with plans and contingencies.

Hendricks and Kojo cautiously arrived at the entrance to the prison. "We need to split up to cover more ground," Hendricks instructed. "I'll head to the cellblock. You check the basement." He gestured with a nod to a stairway leading into darkness.

"Roger that," Kojo replied.

While Hendricks moved onward toward the cellblock, Kojo descended the stone steps to the basement. The air grew damp and musty as he moved deeper underground. He switched on the flashlight mounted on the barrel of his M4A1, the beam cutting through the darkness, illuminating the narrow staircase and the cobwebs that clung to the walls.

The basement was a labyrinth of old storage rooms and maintenance corridors. Kojo moved silently, his eyes adjusting to the dim light. The damp air clung to his skin, the musty smell almost overpowering. He checked each room, each shadow, his flashlight illuminating the damp walls and rusted equipment.

Suddenly, he heard something being knocked over, the noise echoing through the underground space from somewhere farther on.

Kojo whispered into his comms, "I may have something."

He descended deeper into the dark basement, moving toward an underground boiler room. The sound of scratching and scurrying grew louder, echoing ominously in the confined space.

Kojo rounded the corner into the boiler room, his flashlight beam bouncing off the walls. The scratching noise continued, drawing his attention to a dark corner where the boiler stood. As he approached, he spotted a large rat with a piece of string tied to its tail, tethering it to the leg of the boiler. His brow furrowed in confusion as he processed the odd sight.

In that moment of distraction, Noah burst out of the darkness, knocking the carbine from Kojo's grip. The weapon skittered off, the flashlight mounted on it lighting up the dark chamber in strobing flashes.

The two men clashed in an explosion of fighting techniques, each move countered with equal precision—Kojo launched a powerful roundhouse kick, which Noah blocked with a forearm guard before responding with a swift jab to Kojo's ribs. Kojo countered with a spinning backfist, narrowly missing Noah's face as he ducked and delivered a quick uppercut. The confined space forced them into a dance of close-quarters combat, blending martial arts styles seamlessly. Kojo attempted a Muay Thai knee strike, but Noah deflected it with a sharp elbow strike, then used Brazilian jiu-jitsu to attempt a grappling hold. Kojo twisted free, shifting into a Krav Maga stance and throwing a rapid series of punches, which Noah parried with fluid Wing Chun blocks. Finally, with a burst of speed and agility, Noah feinted to the left, then landed a hard sidekick to Kojo's chest, pushing him backwards before sweeping Kojo's legs out from under him and grounding him.

The impact knocked the breath from Kojo, leaving him gasping for air. As he struggled to get back to his feet, Noah took his chance. He ran from the room, up the stairs, and slammed the heavy door shut at the top, trapping Kojo.

Frustrated, Kojo fumbled for his comms. "I'm locked in the basement!"

Hendricks's voice crackled through the earpiece. "Hold on. I'm on my way."

Hendricks moved rapidly through the abandoned prison. As he approached the basement through the cell-block, he could hear Kojo's frustrated pounding and quickened his pace. He reached the thick metal door closing off the basement, the sound of the storm outside muffling the noise from within. But just as he was about to pull the bar to open it, something moved above his head, and when he twisted around to see, Noah was dropping from a ceiling beam right on top of him.

This time, Noah was wielding the cognitive harmonizer. Hendricks's eyes widened as he reached for his knife, but it was too late. The harmonizer hit his temple, the device humming as it activated.

However, if Noah was expecting him to become docile and compliant, that wasn't what happened.

Hendricks immediately screamed as blood poured from his ears. The cries transmitted to Kojo in the basement, the other man screaming loudly in sync, revealing their linkage. And the screams weren't just restricted to the prison. The harrowing sound also echoed outside as more screams ignited around the jungle.

Noah listened to the synchronized cries, discovering the positions of nearby infected.

With Hendricks on his knees, Noah applied the harmonizer again, giving him another burst of its power. Hendricks writhed in pain as the device wreaked havoc on the parasite lodged in his brain. Blood streamed from his ears, nose, and eyes before he finally collapsed. Down in the basement, Kojo experienced the same agony, screaming until he succumbed.

THIRTY-FIVE

MARCO, RENÉE, AND ANTARA MOVED WITH THE
rest of the group. The rain had lessened slightly, but the air
was thick with humidity, and the ground was slick with
mud. The path they followed was barely visible, overgrown
with vines and foliage, but they pressed on, guided by
Sanchez and his people.

With evening beginning to fall, the faint sounds of
distant construction began to be heard, growing louder and
louder. As they broke through the final line of trees, they
were met with a sight that left them speechless. Before them
lay a massive operation transforming the valley. Hordes of
people were leveling the jungle for roads and houses, the
sheer scale of the project overwhelming.

Renée's eyes widened. "There are thousands of people
here."

At the far end of the site, atop a hill, a temple stood
prominently, its intricately carved stone towers and multi-
tiered roofs striking against the lush jungle backdrop.

Father Sanchez stepped forward and raised his arms. "Welcome to Eden!" he announced.

Marco pointed toward the temple. "What's that?" he asked.

Sanchez smiled. "That is Pura Luhur, our spiritual center."

Behind the temple, they could see one of the Chinook helicopters from before lowering a storage container.

Marco shook his head, his eyes scanning it all. "It looks like they're building a city."

Renée nodded. "The priest did say Eden."

The scene before them was a hive of activity. Workers moved in unison, some operating machinery, others digging by hand. At the bottom of the hill they stood on, trenches for a giant sewer were being dug, water systems were being set up, and purification stations were being constructed. Fields of food crops and livestock pens were spread out across the cleared areas, evidence of a self-sustaining community in the making.

As they descended into the place, Father Sanchez walked ahead, guiding them. "This is our Eden, a place of new beginnings and unity. Here, we are building a future for all."

Antara's eyes narrowed as he watched the workers. "What kind of future are you building?"

Sanchez turned, his smile enigmatic. "A future free from the chaos of the outside world. A place where we can live in harmony with nature and each other."

The sensory overload was immense. The constant noise of construction, the oppressive heat, and the sheer scale of the operation created a disorienting effect. Marco, Renée, and Antara exchanged wary glances, fully aware of the magnitude of what they were witnessing.

As they walked amongst the buildings, Father Sanchez began explaining the next steps to the group. "Once you are refreshed, you will be guided to the communal bathrooms where you will wash in preparation for Communion. Once the ceremony has been performed, you will each be given your respective jobs."

"What exactly is Communion?" Antara asked.

Father Sanchez smiled, his expression serene. "It is a short ceremony we perform with new workers. A five-minute prayer to bless you into our community. But first, you will be examined."

Renée's voice trembled slightly. "Medically?"

"Of course," Sanchez replied smoothly. "We must ensure everyone is in good health."

Marco and Renée felt a surge of panic. Their hologram suits would be discovered during a medical examination.

Marco asked, "And what exactly does this examination entail?"

Father Sanchez's smile remained fixed. "A simple physical check-up to ensure you are fit to join our community. Nothing more."

Marco and Renée's anxiety grew. As they exchanged nervous glances, Father Sanchez continued, "Now let us prepare to embrace the new beginning that Eden offers."

THIRTY-SIX

NEIL AND JENNY MOVED CAUTIOUSLY THROUGH the thick maze of greenery. The ground was uneven and muddy from the rain, which was now no more than a light patter. Set to camouflage mode, their suits blended seamlessly into their surroundings. Nevertheless, the humidity still brought the odd flicker and glitch.

Having escaped the immediate danger, Neil and Jenny had decided to turn back and track the searchers. Having caught them up, they now moved stealthily alongside them as they followed the group to a dirt road that cut through the jungle.

They watched as Palmer's people began loading Damu and Kiya into the rear of a canvassed-back military truck. They saw other captured people, bound and helpless, being loaded into trucks as well. The scene was madness, with armed guards shouting orders and the captives looking scared and defeated.

With night beginning to fall, the headlights of the trucks burst to life.

Noticing that the last vehicle in the convoy was unmanned, Neil and Jenny quickly made their way to it. They crept closer to the truck, their hologram suits flickering slightly in the humidity but still providing effective camouflage. With the sounds of the jungle and the activity of the convoy masking their approach, the two of them clambered up the side of the truck, their suits blending in with the green canvas surface. They positioned themselves on the top, lying flat and holding on to the edges.

As the convoy started moving, Jenny whispered, "This is just the beginning."

Neil nodded, his eyes fixed ahead. "We'll get them back. No matter what."

THIRTY-SEVEN

As Noah moved through the jungle, he encountered infected people wandering aimlessly. They were disoriented, with blood running from their ears and noses. Some murmured to themselves or stared blankly ahead, their eyes glazed over. They moved slowly and erratically, creating a gruesome trail on the jungle floor. The surrounding vegetation seemed to lean away from them, as if repulsed by their presence.

"Make it stop... make it stop..." one of the infected mumbled, her voice barely a whisper.

The harmonizer... it must have done this. But how? What went wrong? he wondered.

He observed the infected more closely and realized that the cognitive harmonizer had damaged the parasites inside them, causing them to become disconnected from whatever controlled them. The realization hit Noah amidst the oppressive heat and the unsettling silence of the infected.

"Please... make it stop..." another infected person

murmured in the local dialect, the man's voice filled with despair.

Noah moved closer to him. He needed to understand more about the parasite's damage. *There has to be a way to reverse this*, he thought.

He crouched beside the infected man who was leaning against a tree, his eyes unfocused. Noah could see the end of a tail poking from the blood pooling in the man's ear, writhing as if in agony. The sight was both fascinating and horrifying.

I will find a way to stop this. I will save them, he thought, his eyes narrowing with determination as he stared at the horror of Palmer's science.

THIRTY-EIGHT

INSIDE THE TEMPLE LAB, DR. ANTHONY PALMER was engrossed in his work, his eyes focused on a specimen under the glare of a powerful microscope. The intricate details of the parasite fascinated him, its writhing form a testament to the complexity of his research.

In the background, a lab technician was pulling a trolley of lab equipment toward the dry heat sterilization oven. The technician backed into the oven, arranging the equipment carefully inside.

A follower entered the lab, passing the huge Brennan Krol as he approached Dr. Palmer with a mix of reverence and concern. "It appears, my Lord, that we have lost contact with one of our squads in Sector Eight," the assistant reported.

Palmer did not look up from his microscope. "That's the search party looking for our Council friends, isn't it?"

"Yes. It looks like something has affected them. Specimen 22-8B..."

"That's Corporal Hendricks, isn't it?"

"Yes. Something appears to have affected his module. It's completely blown, the parasite dead. But that's not all. It appears to have sent out a signal that has overloaded the communication modules inside the parasites of all those in his squad. All twenty-eight members. They're now cut off."

Palmer paused, his mind processing the information. "The sheep are loose from the flock," he said after a while. "Better send a couple of engineers out there as well as another squad. See what's happened."

"Yes, my Lord," the assistant replied, bowing slightly before leaving the room to carry out the order.

Dr. Palmer leaned over the microscope, his intense expression illuminated by the soft glow of the instrument. In the background, the technician inside the dry heat sterilization oven was about to step out when another technician, unaware of his presence, shut the door, sealing him inside.

As the technician outside began setting the heat for two hundred and fifty degrees Celsius, the lab was quiet, except for the soft whirring of machines and the occasional beep from monitors. As the technician inside the oven began hammering on the door, the sound absorbed by the lining of the oven, the atmosphere was one of scientific rigor and cold precision.

Such a simple life these organisms lead, Palmer thought, his eyes glued to the wriggling parasite under the lens. *How much simpler it must be without the burden of self-awareness.* The parasite reacted to the enzyme, its movements becoming more frantic before finally subsiding into a state of eerie stillness. Palmer observed the process with a mix of fascination and satisfaction. The quiet of the lab provided a stark back-drop to his deep, almost philosophical reflections.

Consciousness, Palmer's thoughts went on, *a strange quirk of evolution. An experiment by natural selection. A cruel experiment,* he mused, his thoughts wandering as he watched the parasite. He thought about the nature of consciousness and individualism, comparing it to the simplicity of insect life and hive mentality. The contrast was stark and, to him, enlightening. Man, forever cursed by his individualism. But insects, they swarm, they infest, they work as one.

That is the true path. That is what I am creating here. One single unit, Palmer thought, his vision clear and unwavering. *This is the future. No more chaos, no more individualism. Just a perfect, unified organism. And I will be its creator. Insects know their place, their role. They do not question, they do not falter. They simply do as they are meant to do. That is what humanity must become. A perfect, unified organism.*

In the background, the oven reached seventy degrees. As the man inside began to burn, all the lab technicians cried out in unison, their empathy links reacting to the trapped man's agony. Palmer turned sharply at the sound, his calm demeanor fracturing for a moment—then realizing. "Krol, open the oven," he commanded.

The big man strode over, pulling the bar and opening the oven door. He reached in, pulling out the trolley and then the barely conscious technician. The other technicians continued to groan in pain until Palmer disconnected their empathy links, restoring silence to the lab.

The technicians then quickly regained their composure and rushed to the aid of the burned man. They carefully carried him away, their movements efficient and practiced. Palmer watched them go, a satisfied expression on his face as he returned to his microscope, understanding the importance of unity, now more than ever.

THIRTY-NINE

EDEN STRETCHED OUT AROUND THEM, AN ENDLESS array of single-story buildings, dormitory blocks, and narrow passageways weaving in between. The surroundings were utilitarian, designed for maximum efficiency and order. The atmosphere was filled with the sense of regimented activity, every corner seeming to hum with a disciplined purpose. No one sat around doing nothing. Everyone had a purpose.

The newcomers were shown to their dormitories, passing a schoolhouse along the way. Inside, children sat attentively, completely focused on their teacher. There was a palpable silence in the classroom, broken only by the measured cadence of the teacher's voice.

Outside, everyone was busy with work or exercise. There were no smartphones, no leisure activities, no signs of the modern distractions that have become commonplace in the outside world.

Marco leaned closer to Renée and Antara, his voice barely a whisper. "It's like some communist paradise."

Antara nodded. "How does a foreigner end up with so many followers after only six months?"

Renée's face was etched with concern, her eyes lingering on the children moving in unison as they performed their exercises. "This place is unsettling. It's like everyone is part of a machine."

The efficiency of the place was both impressive and disturbing. The sense of individuality was almost nonexistent, replaced by a collective focus on the community's goals.

As they reached their assigned dormitory, the follower leading them stopped and turned. "This will be your home for now. Until you are assigned a house."

Like the rest of the compound, the dormitory was stark and functional. Bunk beds lined the walls, and personal space was minimal. There was a small locker for each person, and a single window provided a limited view of the outside world. On top of each bed, folded neatly, was a white robe.

Antara looked around grimly. "It's like a prison."

Marco nodded in agreement. "A prison dressed up as a utopia."

Renée sat down on one of the bunks, her mind racing with thoughts of the children and the eerie uniformity of the place. She couldn't shake the feeling of dread that had settled over her since they arrived.

A follower stood at the entrance, addressing the newcomers. "The showers are connected to this room," he said, pointing to an open door. "Once everyone is cleaned up and ready, you need to dress in the Communion robes that are on your beds. Then you shall be taken to the medical house for examination. On completion, you will be inducted through Communion."

Renée, Marco, and Antara exchanged uneasy glances as they moved toward a quiet corner of the dorm. The tension was reaching a fever pitch as they leaned their heads in, talking in hushed tones.

Renée's voice was urgent, her eyes wide with worry. "Garin, we need to tell you something. We're not who we said we are."

Antara raised an eyebrow. "What do you mean?"

Marco glanced around to ensure no one was listening. "We're not locals. We're not even Indonesian. We're American agents."

Antara nodded slowly, his expression thoughtful. "You don't look or sound American."

"That's because we're wearing disguises," Marco told him.

He gave a furtive look around before lifting the mask of his hologram suit to reveal his real face. The transformation was startling, his true features emerging from behind the digital façade.

Antara stared, his eyes widening.

"We're using hologram suits and translation devices to communicate," Marco explained. "This is why we seemed local. It's all part of our cover."

Renée nodded. "We're here to investigate what's going on in this place and put a stop to it. But we need your help."

Antara looked between Marco and Renée, then nodded resolutely. "All right, I'm in. If it means protecting my own people and stopping whatever's happening here, I'll do whatever it takes."

Marco felt a surge of relief. "That's good to hear," he said, lowering the mask.

"However," Renée sighed, "we can't have any doctor touching either of us. If they feel the suits, it's all over."

Antara's face hardened with resolve. "Then we should just escape. I really don't like the sound of this Communion thing anyway. I think now we're here, we should drop our cover, hide out in the jungle around the camp, and document what we see. Then I'll take it to my superiors in Jakarta. You can take yours back to America. Get this thing stopped, whatever it is."

Renée nodded. "I agree."

Marco looked determined. "We could make a run for it on the way to the medical house."

Antara nodded, his mind already formulating a plan. "OK. Then we'll get showered and dressed with all the others. Make a break for it after that."

Agreed on the plan, they followed the other recruits into the shower block. The atmosphere was one of certainty as they each got into separate cubicles and turned on the faucets. The warm water was a welcome relief, cascading down over them and washing away the stress and grime of their journey.

However, a few minutes into the showers, something strange happened. The door to the block closed automatically, shutting them in as it locked. The water flow slowed to a drip, then ceased altogether.

"What the...?" Marco muttered.

Suddenly, bursts of air shot from the faucets, sending everyone stumbling back. Renée's and Marco's instincts kicked in, both of them sensing danger.

"We need to get out, now!" Renée shouted, her voice reverberating in the enclosed space.

Gas began to shoot from the faucets, quickly filling the room. The air grew thick and acrid, burning their throats and eyes. There were no windows, and the door was sealed tight—metal and airtight, a detail they had overlooked as they'd walked inside.

Antara's voice cut through the rising panic. "Cover your mouths! Try not to breathe it in!"

Renée's heart pounded in her chest. "We should have known something was wrong," she cried out. "We walked right into a trap."

Everyone scrambled to the door, pounding on it and shouting for help, but their efforts were in vain. The gas filled the room rapidly, its toxic presence quickly overwhelming them. Marco tried to shield his face with his robe, but the gas was relentless, seeping through the fabric.

"Stay together!" Marco shouted, his voice muffled and strained.

The gas was overpowering. Renée's vision blurred, her legs growing weak. She reached for Marco, her fingers brushing his arm before her strength gave out. The room seemed to spin, the gas tightening its grip around her lungs.

Antara stumbled to the door, his hands pressed against it in a futile attempt to force it open. His vision dimmed, the edges going dark. "Hold... on," he gasped, but his voice was faint and desperate.

Marco's knees buckled, and he sank to the floor. His thoughts were a jumbled mess, his mind fighting against the encroaching darkness. He reached out, trying to find Renée, but his limbs felt heavy and unresponsive.

Outside, followers in hazmat suits, their faces hidden behind the protective visors, moved toward the dormitories.

Others monitored the sedation process from a control room filled with screens displaying live feeds from the dormitories' CCTV.

"Sedation process completed in blocks one to ten. Teams six to thirteen, you are cleared to enter," one of the people in the control room spoke into the comms, his voice calm and methodical.

The followers moved with precision, their hazmat suits rustling softly as they entered the dormitories. The bathroom doors were now open, revealing the unconscious bodies lying in piles stacked against the other side. The followers began the process of carrying them out. They laid the newcomers on the beds, dressing them in the white robes that had been laid out. In the showers, they sprayed off any mess, ensuring that everything was in perfect condition—or at least as good as it could be.

The followers handled the bodies vigilantly. Some of the unconscious groaned and murmured as they were moved, but the followers took the utmost care to avoid causing any harm.

When they reached Marco and Renée, however, they recoiled at the strange feel of their skin. This was quickly followed by the discovery of the hologram suits.

"Contact our Lord," one of the followers said. "He needs to know about this immediately."

FORTY

NEIL AND JENNY CLUNG TO THE ROOF OF THE convoy's last vehicle as it rumbled toward Eden. The bumpy ride had been a test of endurance, but their determination kept them focused. As the vehicle came to a stop at the gate to the massive compound, they quietly rolled off the canvas roof.

Eden was another world from the lush jungle outside. As they ran into cover, they passed a mix of training grounds, construction sites, and schoolyards, all meticulously organized and militaristic in atmosphere. Policemen and soldiers moved with purpose among the people, like soldier ants overseeing the drones.

Neil and Jenny climbed onto the roof of a nearby building to get a better view. From their vantage point, they could observe the entire area without being seen. It was night now, so harsh floodlights illuminated everything, bathing the area in an intense, stark light that created an eerie atmosphere. The base was bustling with activity. Prisoners were being unloaded from the convoy, marched off in an orderly fashion, guarded closely by soldiers and police.

"What do we do?" Neil whispered to his wife.

Jenny's eyes narrowed as she watched the prisoners. "There's nothing we can do at the moment. If we go down there, we don't know what could happen. We'll sit back for now."

Just then, they spotted Damu and Kiya being taken away along with the other prisoners. Neil's heart sank in his chest. "There they are."

Jenny placed a hand on his arm. "Let's see where they're taking them."

The prisoners were marched toward a large building at the center of the base. Guards barked orders, and the prisoners moved in a slow, solemn line.

Neil's jaw clenched as he watched Damu and Kiya disappear into the building. "We'll get you out of there. I promise."

Jenny squeezed his arm. "We will. But first, we need to stay safe and gather as much information as we can."

They settled into their hiding spot, and from there they noticed two things of interest. One was the temple, Pura Luhur, which they surmised was where Palmer might be, especially as it was surrounded by a lot of buildings, equipment, and activity.

The second thing was a large communications tower in the distance. Its blinking lights stood out against the night sky, a beacon drawing their attention. Neil pointed it out.

"Look over there, Jenny. That tower might be our way out of this mess."

Jenny squinted, her eyes following the direction of Neil's

finger. "You think we can use it to get past the signal jammer?"

Neil nodded. "It could be where the jam is coming from. If that's the case, then getting close to the source should see us getting around it. It's our best shot. If we can get a message out, we can warn Noah and the others."

The communications tower loomed in the distance, surrounded by security, its lights blinking rhythmically in the darkness. "Then let's go," Jenny whispered, her eyes fixed on the distant tower.

FORTY-ONE

MARCO AND RENÉE WOKE UP GROGGILY, THEIR senses slowly coming back to them. They found themselves bound and sitting inside a vast stone room. Their vision was blurry at first, but it gradually cleared, revealing a vast chamber with a high ceiling and stone walls adorned with ancient symbols and carvings. It was clear they were inside the temple, the cool, damp air carrying the scent of ancient stone and incense.

Renée blinked rapidly, trying to shake off the grogginess. "This isn't... good," she muttered.

"Stay calm, baby. We'll figure this out," Marco replied.

As their vision cleared further, they saw a giant of a man carrying another, quickly surmising it was Krol carrying Palmer.

They came to a stop before them.

It was at that moment, they registered they were no longer in their hologram suits. The realization hit Marco and

Renée hard. The way Palmer looked at them sent a chill up their spines; it was as if he knew everything.

Marco's voice was firm. "You gonna speak?"

Palmer's expression remained calm, almost amused. "Patience. All will be revealed."

Father Sanchez stepped up beside Palmer, holding their now lifeless hologram suits. Palmer examined them, taking a sleeve in his fingers and feeling the advanced material. The suits, now inert, were the complete opposite of their ancient surroundings.

"Very sophisticated," Palmer mused. "You had my friend here convinced there was nothing the matter. That you were both no more harmful than a couple of locals. What is it, some type of holographic layer controlled by an AI?"

Neither Marco nor Renée said a word.

Palmer's probing gaze shifted between them. "This sort of thing makes me think that the both of you are with my former paymasters. Are you?"

They remained silent, their faces set in blank expressions.

"What about what's been happening in Sector Eight? By the old military prison. Was it you who sent twenty-eight followers offline?"

Still, Marco and Renée kept their reticence, silence their only weapon now.

Palmer dismissed it with a wave of his hand. "It doesn't matter. Your silence is a waste. Once you've gone through Communion, you'll willingly tell me everything. Then we shall see who infiltrates whom."

The mention of Communion brought a chilling effect to the room. The cold stone walls seemed to close in.

"Take them away," Palmer ordered. "Place them with the others."

FORTY-TWO

Under darkness, Neil and Jenny made their way to the communications tower. The lattice structure stood tall against the dark sky, its blinking lights creating an eerie yet rhythmic pattern. Security was tight, guards patrolling the perimeter, their flashlights casting beams of light across the base.

Using their suits' camouflage mode, the two of them snuck toward the base of the tower. The night was quiet except for the distant sounds of the base. Something was going on around the temple, all the activity concentrated around it, making their path to the tower fairly clear.

They climbed the structure carefully and methodically, avoiding the guards' watchful eyes. Even though they were wearing the suits, they couldn't afford the sudden glare of a flashlight beam settling on them. The suit would need a few seconds to register the change in lighting before adjusting its imagery to match. This would be enough to give them away.

The tower's metal structure was cool and slippery from the night's dew, but the framework provided plenty of handholds. The blinking lights dotted all along it created a hypnotic effect.

They reached a platform near the top, equipped with various antennas and communication devices. A large box stood out from the rest of the equipment.

"That's the jammer's frequency generator," Neil said to Jenny. "This close to it, we should be able to get a signal out without the jammer catching it."

"Let's set up quickly," Jenny said.

"I'll handle the device. You keep an eye out for any guards," Neil instructed, his hands moving quickly to set up the NLP's communications settings.

Neil began trying to send a message. "Marco, Renée, Noah. We've reached Palmer's base. If you hear this, our coordinates are 9.7783 degrees South latitude and 119.8850 degrees East longitude. Over," he said into his comms, getting nothing but jumbled static back through his earpiece.

"Keep trying," Jenny urged.

The static was punctuated by moments of clarity, but Neil struggled to maintain a clear connection.

"Marco, Renée, Noah. We've reached Palmer's base. Our coordinates are..." Neil repeated.

"We need to keep the signal steady. Try adjusting the frequency," Jenny suggested.

After several attempts, they managed to get a clear moment and send their coordinates through the static. The final successful transmission felt like a victory. The static cleared just long enough for them to hear their message clearly.

"Marco, Renée, Noah. We've reached Palmer's base. Our coordinates are…" Neil said one last time.

"Let's hope one of them gets it," Jenny said, a combination of relief and apprehension in her voice.

FORTY-THREE

BACK AT KIRTLAND, MOLLY HANSON BURST INTO Allison Peterson's office, her face pale, eyes wide with alarm. Allison, seated behind her large oak desk, looked up from her laptop, frowning.

"We've got a major problem," Molly panted, clutching a stack of freshly printed documents. "Intelligence just came in. Council forces are gathering in the Indian Ocean and the Savu Sea. Three submarines, armed with nuclear warheads."

Allison's eyes narrowed. "What? Why?"

Molly took a deep breath. "The intel says something has gone wrong on the island. Palmer has gone rogue, and the Council is prepared to do anything to stop whatever he's developing from leaving Sumba."

Allison leaned back in her chair, ready to act her part as double agent. "They're willing to nuke the island?"

Molly nodded, her voice shaky. "Yes. We have to warn Noah and the others."

Allison shook her head. "We can't. We've lost contact with them. They're stuck on the island."

Molly's eyes widened even more. "Then we need to send an extraction team! We can't just leave them there to die!"

Allison remained calm, her expression resolute. "We don't know that they'll actually fire the warheads on the island."

"My sources think otherwise. We have to get them out of there."

"No, Molly. I trust in Noah's and the others' abilities to get Palmer. Just give them time."

Molly's voice rose in desperation. "Allison, you're asking me to just sit here while they're out there, possibly facing a nuclear strike! We need to do something!"

Allison stood up, her voice firm. "And what do you suggest, Ms. Hanson? That we send another team into a situation we don't fully understand? We have no idea where they are or what exactly is happening. We can't risk more lives without a clear idea of what is happening in the field. We don't have that luxury."

Molly's voice trembled. "These are our people, Allison. Our friends. We owe it to them to try."

Allison softened slightly but remained steadfast. "I know. But we also owe it to them to trust in their skills and judgment. Noah is resourceful. If anyone can find a way out, it's him. Therefore, we already have our best man out there. No need to send anyone else. We can't act rashly."

Molly slumped into a chair. "And what if they can't find a way out?"

Allison walked around her desk and placed a hand on Molly's shoulder. "Then we deal with it when the time comes. But right now, sending an extraction team would only complicate things further. We need to give them the chance to complete their mission."

Molly looked up, her eyes filled with worry. "And if the Council launches those nukes?"

Allison's expression turned grim. "Then we pray that Noah and his team can find Palmer and stop whatever he's doing before it comes to that."

FORTY-FOUR

THE NIGHT HAD DESCENDED FULLY, ENVELOPING the jungle in a thick, impenetrable darkness. Noah huddled in his makeshift camp, the jungle alive with the sounds of insects and distant animal calls. The air was cool, very different to the heat of the day, and the moonlight barely filtered through the overgrown canopy above.

Noah's NLP suddenly crackled to life, breaking the silence with a static-filled message. He leaned closer, straining to hear.

"Marco, Renée, Noah... We've reached Palmer's base... If you hear this, our coordinates are..." came the faint, crackling voice of Neil.

Noah's heart leaped. *Finally, a message.*

He adjusted the communication settings on the NLP, desperately trying to clear up the static and get more information. But despite his efforts, the message remained intermittent, the device crackling and hissing with occasional bursts of clarity.

The jungle around him seemed to hold its breath as he focused on the device, trying to catch every word. Then, through the static, he heard Neil's voice, clearer this time.

"...coordinates are... 9.7783 degrees... South latitude and...119.8850 degrees... East longitude..."

Got it. I know where they are.

Noah moved quickly. He packed up his camp, checking his gear to ensure he had everything he needed. He now had Hendricks's Beretta M9 and his M4A1, though the carbine only had half a magazine left and the Beretta was only loaded with the standard fifteen bullet mag.

The night seemed to grow darker as Noah set off through the jungle, his senses heightened by the urgency of his mission. With the carbine strapped to his back and the Beretta in his underarm holster, he moved forward, his focus entirely on reaching his friends.

Hang on, Jenny and Neil. I'm coming.

FORTY-FIVE

CAMOUFLAGED, NEIL AND JENNY CROUCHED ON the roof of a building. Below, the unconscious bodies of Damu and Kiya were being carried out of a dormitory on stretchers by people in hazmat suits. The scene was a haunting ballet of motion, as the followers moved with eerie precision and silence, their hazmat suits rustling faintly in the night air.

Neil and Jenny watched intently, their eyes following the procession as it made its way to a large concrete structure. The imposing building loomed in the distance, its sterile façade betraying nothing of the horrors within.

"We need to follow them," Jenny whispered.

Neil nodded.

Together, they descended from their vantage point, their suits cloaking them in the night itself as they approached the concrete building. The followers carried the stretchers inside, and Neil and Jenny slipped in behind them, their movements fluid and silent.

Inside was some type of medical facility, the atmosphere clinical and cold. The air was filled with the hum of machinery and the soft beeping of monitors. Lines of unconscious people lay on gurneys, each one undergoing a series of tests. Blood was taken, heart rates checked, teeth examined, and x-rays performed. The followers moved with an unsettling efficiency among the bodies.

Damu and Kiya were on a gurney each, their faces pale and serene in their unconscious state.

"This place is a nightmare," Neil muttered.

As they watched, the followers began dressing the unconscious in robes, carefully slipping the garments over their still forms. Once dressed, the bodies were carried out, ready for the next phase of whatever twisted plan was unfolding.

Neil's eyes fixed to the scene, while Jenny's gaze wandered to her left. Her eyes sharpened as she spotted someone emerging through a thick metal door at the far end of the room. The door opened briefly, revealing a corridor leading deeper into the complex to what must be laboratories. Before the door swung shut, she saw a glimpse of the sterile, forbidding hallway beyond.

"You wanna see what's going on here?" she asked Neil.

Neil glanced at her, a determined glint in his eyes. "Let's do it."

They waited for someone to emerge through the doors again. When a lab technician stepped out, they moved swiftly, slipping in before the door could close.

Inside, the corridor stretched out before them, stark and clinical, the polished walls glowing under the strip lighting. Another door led to a massive, warehouse-sized room filled with towering columns of incubators. Each incubator held large, writhing nematodes, their bodies pulsing with a sickly glow under the sterile lights. The columns stretched out as far as they could see, creating a labyrinthine expanse of biological horror.

"This must be what they're infecting people with," Jenny said.

Neil nodded, his expression bleak. "There are millions of them."

But before they could say anything else, they heard approaching footsteps. They quickly ducked behind a column as a group of followers dressed in ceremonial robes entered the room. Moving with the same mechanical precision they had seen before, the men and women selected several incubators and placed them on gurneys. The low hum of the machines and the soft clicks of their movements filled the room until finally, they left, wheeling the incubators out.

Once the followers were gone, Neil and Jenny emerged from their hiding spot.

"We need to find out more about these things," Neil said, his eyes scanning the room.

Jenny spotted a computer terminal nestled among the incubators. "Over there." She pointed.

They hurried to the terminal, and Neil set to work on the computer, his fingers flying over the keys as he hacked into the system. The screen flickered to life, displaying a series of files and directories. Neil inserted a small USB flash drive, uploading an advanced persistent threat (APT) toolkit to give him deeper access. This sophisticated malware was designed to infiltrate and take control of highly secured systems. As the drive established a connection, the APT began its multi-stage deployment.

"Got it," Neil said, pulling up the main directory. He scrolled through the files until he found one that caught his eye. "'The Eighth Stage: A History of Mankind's Future by Dr. Anthony Palmer.' This has to be about what's happening here."

He clicked on the file, and a video began, showing Dr. Palmer sitting in a lab, facing the camera with a cold expression.

Palmer's ice-blue eyes shone as he began to speak. "The primary aim of our work is to develop a device capable of seizing control of individuals at any given moment, ensuring absolute loyalty and eliminating dissent." Palmer's voice echoed through the lab. "My approach to this goal leverages an already existing parasite. As we know, there are several lifeforms on this planet that have evolved to control a host's behavior for their own benefit.

"For example, consider Toxoplasma gondii, a protozoan parasite that infects many warm-blooded animals, with its definitive host being the cat. In rodents, it can manipulate behavior, reducing their fear of cats and even attracting them to cat urine, thereby increasing the likelihood that the rodent will be eaten by a cat."

"This is insane..." Neil muttered, his eyes glued to the screen.

"Is this what he's doing to people? Infecting them with mind controlling parasites?" Jenny added, her voice trembling with disgust.

"Another is Ophiocordyceps unilateralis," Palmer went on, "a fungus that infects ants, taking over their central nervous system. The infected ants leave their colonies, climb vegetation, and attach themselves to a leaf or stem, where they die. The fungus then grows out of the ant's body, releasing spores to infect more ants.

"Or how about Leucochloridium paradoxum. This parasitic flatworm infects snails and manipulates them to become more visible to birds. The flatworm causes the snail's tentacles to pulsate and resemble caterpillars, attracting birds. When the bird eats the snail, the parasite completes its life cycle inside the bird's digestive system.

"Then there's Dicrocoelium dendriticum. This liver fluke manipulates..."

"All right, we get it," Neil said, forwarding the video.

He resumed it thirty seconds later. "This then brings me to what I and Dr. Taylor discovered in the vast reaches of Sumba, a small island of the Indonesian archipelago. For some years, I had heard of a parasitic nematode that was indigenous to the deep jungle. It infected many species, including mammals, but I had heard that there had been cases of human infection. The parasite would work its way along the subarachnoid space between the brain and the skull before latching to the prefrontal cortex, digging in and trying to do what it does to smaller mammals. Its name is Nematocerebrus dominatus."

Palmer's voice was disturbingly calm as he continued. "In small mammals, it induces them to be picked up by snakes, where it lays its eggs in the snake's gut. However, in humans, its effects are even more devastating. In all but very few cases, the infected are left with brain damage and paralysis. Nematocerebrus dominatus has evolved over the millions of years it's been in existence to corral much smaller brains.

In a human brain, it merely causes terrible damage and obvious pain to the infected. But"—he held up a finger—"it was a start. The problem was that it was too small and weak to influence a human brain in the way it would a smaller creature. It needed to be much bigger. Therefore, I knew that if we could create a mutant strand, then it could be used in symbiosis to latch on to a human brain the same way it does to smaller warm-blooded animals."

"This is worse than I imagined," Jenny whispered, her eyes wide with horror.

They stared at the computer screen, the glow casting eerie shadows on their faces as Palmer was replaced with video footage. Rows of advanced scientific equipment lined a laboratory. Microinjectors, PCR machines, gel electrophoresis setups, bacterial cultures for cloning DNA sequences, CO_2 incubators, laminar flow hoods for sterile work, temperature-controlled incubators, and humidity chambers—all of it designed for one purpose: genetic engineering.

The camera panned left to show Palmer sitting in his wheelchair beside a series of containers similar to the ones towering over Neil and Jenny, each holding mutated nematodes. These worms, once as thin as a human hair and only a few millimeters long, were now grotesque, stretching up to twenty centimeters in length.

"To make a nematode grow to fifty times its normal size, we needed to make a lot of complex changes to its DNA and how its body works," Palmer explained in his clinical tone. "First, we changed the genes that control its size, making sure its cells can grow larger and more numerous. We also boosted its metabolism with protein strands so it can get enough energy and nutrients to support its larger size. Additionally, we strengthened its outer layer and muscles to handle the extra weight."

The camera zoomed in on the writhing, elongated parasites. They looked like something out of a nightmare, their movements slow and deliberate within the containers.

"Now that we have rapidly evolved the parasite," Palmer continued, "it can finally interact fully with a human brain."

The footage changed to a CAT scan of a human head. In real-time, they watched as a squirming parasite was introduced through the ear canal, lodging on to the brain.

"The parasite first targets specific areas of the brain such as the prefrontal cortex, amygdala, and hippocampus, which are involved in decision-making, emotion regulation, and social behavior. It then alters the production of neurotransmitters such as dopamine, serotonin, and glutamate. These changes affect mood and behavior, making people more prone to taking risks and acting impulsively, just as Toxoplasma gondii makes infected rodents less afraid of cats."

Neil's mind flashed back to the events of the previous day and night. "Just like the locals throwing themselves at us," he whispered. "Completely fearless."

Palmer's image filled the screen again, his eyes gleaming with a twisted excitement. "Now imagine being able to directly control the production of dopamine and serotonin in a person. Just imagine it. Being able to control the very things that make them happy or sad. You have the power to make them feel euphoria one moment, then absolute despair the next. You would have the loyalty of the most fervent addict. Or the biggest zealot. You would be worshipped."

Neil and Jenny watched in horrified silence as Palmer's

face remained on the screen, the light flickering across his icy blue eyes. The walls of incubators towering around them felt even more oppressive, the sinister reality of Palmer's machinations sinking in.

"However," Palmer went on, "the parasite in its current state is still its own creature. It will control the human for its own purposes. On its own, it essentially turns the person into a violent zombie."

The footage shifted to a man inside a cell, infected with the mutated parasite. He was in the midst of a violent episode, smashing himself against the walls and attacking the men who tried to control him. The next shot had the same man strapped to a bed, writhing under the confines of leather bindings.

"Tom has been infected with the mutated parasite," Palmer continued in the video. "As you can see, it has turned him into this. Aimless, purposeless. Neither the parasite nor the man seems to know what to do. It would appear that things have reached an impasse. But that is where you are wrong. Because there is one more element of the Mindweaver program that comes into play. Nanotechnology."

Neil and Jenny watched with wide eyes.

"You see," Palmer explained, "if we think of the parasite as an interface, a connection to the parts of the human brain we wish to access for control, then all we need is something to feed information into that interface—or simply to control the parasite's interaction with the subject. This is where we have turned to nanotechnology."

The footage transitioned to microscopic devices being injected into the parasites.

"These tiny devices are designed to fit inside the parasite and stay powered by using the host's electrochemistry. What they are is a device that uses tiny amounts of electrodes to stimulate not only the parasite itself but the human brain, the two working side by side, but the device making all the decisions, communicating to us back here."

The scene shifted to a large laboratory with a huge cabinet of servers surrounded by cooling fans, people in overalls working methodically. Palmer moved through the lab, carried by the huge Brennan Krol.

"This is our communications hub where we run the Mindweaver program. This is where we control the device— and therefore the parasite and the subject."

Krol moved to a computer terminal, where he gently laid Palmer in a chair. On the screen, code scrolled rapidly.

"This merely looks like code," he said, "but what it really is is Mindweaver messaging back and forth with the subjects. It bases them in groups of twenty to fifty, and each group is in full communication, Mindweaver relaying between them. So if one of them sees something, then the others in that group see it. The same with anything they hear. It means that they all act in unison on the same information, getting it in real-time, even if they're miles apart. Imagine a squadron of soldiers that are entirely intoned to one another. Imagine a workforce like that."

Jenny's voice trembled with revulsion. "I don't want to imagine it. I don't want to imagine any of it."

Palmer's eyes gleamed with pride and something else: madness. "Though Mindweaver can organize them into any tasks, we are yet unable to teach them any new skills. In other words, the doctors are still the doctors, the soldiers the soldiers. Nevertheless, their prior knowledge is now in full service of us. These people do as we say, feel pleasure when we allow it, and despair if we should so wish. There is no better way to gain control of society. And it is easy to apply to each subject. Watch."

The footage shifted again, showing a man strapped to a bed, his head clamped sideways to a pillow. He writhed beneath the straps, crying out as a scientist in a hazmat suit approached with a writhing parasite held at the end of a pair of tweezers. Neil and Jenny watched in horror as the scientist carefully placed the Nematocerebrus dominatus parasite into the man's ear. The man squirmed violently for several seconds before becoming completely still. The camera zoomed in on his sweaty, pale, but now unnervingly calm face.

"David?" Palmer's voice echoed in the room, cold and authoritative.

"Yes," the man replied, his voice steady and devoid of emotion.

"Do you know who I am?"

David's eyes fixed on Palmer's face. "Yes. You are my Lord."

Neil's fists clenched in anger. "We have to stop this."

Jenny's face was pale. "This is completely insane."

The camera panned out to reveal Palmer in his wheelchair, observing the scene with a calm, satisfied expression.

"As you can see, he's completely docile," Palmer said to the camera. In the background, assistants removed the bindings around David, who then stood up, waiting for orders.

"The Mindweaver program is running fully integrated. Hence him calling me his Lord. The program is designed to have the subjects recognize the overseer as their lord and master."

Palmer's eyes gleamed with a manic intensity. "Imagine a society that no longer pulls in separate directions. That no longer speaks a thousand different languages all at the same time. That no longer preys on itself but works together. A society of collective will instead of a society of individualistic apathy. We can clean this world up without having to destroy so much of it. Wouldn't it be easier than killing off four-fifths of the world's population if we just gained control of it?"

Just as this chilling question hung in the air, Neil and Jenny heard footsteps approaching. They quickly switched off the terminal and reactivated their suits' camouflage mode, blending into their surroundings before ducking out of sight as two technicians approached the computer terminal. The technicians switched on the computer, their brows furrowing in confusion as they noticed the open files.

"Who left these files open?" one technician asked, glancing around suspiciously.

"I don't know," the other replied, "but we should report this to our Lord."

While the technicians questioned each other, Neil and Jenny slipped out of the room. Once outside, they huddled together in the shadows.

"We need to get to Damu and Kiya before they're infected," Jenny whispered, urgency clear in her voice.

FORTY-SIX

BUT IT WAS TOO LATE.

At that precise moment, Damu and Kiya, along with Marco, Renée, Antara, and about fifty others, were dressed in white robes and fixed to cushioned railings. Their hands were bound to the railing, their heads positioned sideways, their ears facing upward, fixed in kneeling positions and lining the steps of the temple in rows, five per railing. They could do nothing as followers went around with smelling salts to awaken the last of the sleepers. This had to be done while they were conscious.

The participants woke up in this horrifying arrangement. Many cried out, some shouted curse words, and others merely sobbed. The high stone walls of Pura Luhur rose up, the temple's religious and mystical symbols bearing down on them as the night filled with the echoes of their cries.

"Please, let me go! I don't want this!" one participant screamed.

Marco turned his head as much as he could, whispering to Renée beside him. "Stay strong. We'll find a way out of this."

Renée's thoughts were frantic, her heart pounding in her chest. "This can't be happening. We have to get out of here."

As they tried to remain calm, the doors of Pura Luhur swung open, and a group of followers filed out, dressed in ceremonial robes. They moved with a grim determination, carrying trays laden with incubators. Leading them was Father Sanchez.

The priest raised his hands, calling for silence. The participants' cries and sobs gradually diminished.

"Brothers and sisters," Sanchez began, his voice echoing into the night, "you are about to partake in a sacred ritual. This Communion will bind you to our cause, purify your minds, and align your wills with the divine purpose."

Marco and Renée exchanged a worried glance. The words "purify" and "align" sent chills down their spines.

"Today, you will be reborn," Sanchez declared, his eyes scanning the bound participants. "Embrace the unity, the peace that comes with surrender."

The followers moved methodically as they opened the incubators and removed the parasites with tweezers, the nematodes writhing and curling on the ends. They then moved among the participants, their expressions blank and determined as they came to a stop beside each one, preparing to drop the parasites into the ears of the bound individuals.

Sanchez continued his sermon, his voice rising with fervor. "Through Communion, you will join us in a higher state of being. You will become part of something greater, something eternal."

The followers began their dreaded procession along the lines of bound participants, their movements precise and ritualistic. One by one, they dropped the writhing parasites into the ears of those bound to the railings. The reactions were immediate and violent—people screamed, groaned, and writhed against their bindings, the agony clear on their faces.

The steps to the temple filled with a cacophony of sounds: the chanting of the followers, the cries of the participants, the atmosphere heavy with fear and desperation.

"No... no... get it out!" many of them cried.

Sanchez's voice boomed over the chaos, his words unwavering. "Accept the gift of unity. Embrace your new purpose."

It was then that a familiar voice called out.

"I won't let you! I won't!" Antara shouted in a voice filled with defiance.

Marco and Renée tried to turn to see but couldn't. They could only hear him.

Antara's voice carried through the night, cutting through the pleas and the sobs. He struggled against the railing with everything he had, his muscles straining as he pulled at the metal with all his strength. Positioned at the end of it, he looked to the man next to him, desperation in his eyes.

"Help me lift this. We can get it off its end," Antara urged.

The man next to him was Damu, and beside him, Kiya. Damu nodded, shifting his weight to help. Together, they heaved the railing up, inching it off its end.

"We're almost there," Antara grunted, his voice strained. "Keep going!"

Kiya watched, her eyes wide with fear but filled with a glimmer of hope. As the rail finally came free, Antara pulled himself off, tumbling to the ground with a heavy thud.

But before Damu and Kiya could follow, followers rushed in, their movements swift and decisive. They grabbed the railing and forced it back into place, securing it once more—Damu and Kiya's chance at escape brutally cut short.

"Run!" Damu shouted to Antara, who was already scrambling to his feet.

Antara hesitated for a moment, his eyes meeting Damu's. He gave a quick nod of gratitude before turning and bolting into the darkness before the followers could grab him.

Sanchez's face contorted with anger. "Stop him! Don't let him escape!"

Marco's thoughts turned to Antara, silently urging him on. *Run, Garin. Run for all of us.*

Marco and Renée were not so fortunate. As the followers reached them, they struggled and pleaded, their desperation clear in their voices, but it was to no avail. They were held down, the parasites dropped into their ears.

The moment was excruciating. The parasites wriggled their way into their ear canals, a chilling sensation that sent waves of pain through their bodies. Marco's eyes widened in horror, his voice a desperate plea. "Please, don't do this!"

Renée cried out, tears streaming down her face. "No, no, no..."

As the parasites took hold, Marco and Renée screamed in agony, the pain overwhelming, a burning sensation that seemed to consume their minds.

Slowly, their cries diminished, however, replaced by a

haunting silence. Their eyes went blank, and they began to respond to questions mechanically, their voices devoid of emotion.

A follower stepped forward, his voice cold and detached. "What is your purpose?"

Marco's and Renée's replies were hollow, their words devoid of the people they once were. In unison, they said, "To serve my Lord."

FORTY-SEVEN

NOAH REACHED EDEN UNDER THE COVER OF NIGHT.
Crouched on the wide bow of a large Palmyra palm at the
edge, the site sprawled out before him, a mix of low buildings, narrow alleys, and interconnected rooftops. Darkness
cloaked most of the area, but harsh floodlights punctuated
the gloom, casting long, stark shadows. Armed guards
patrolled the entire base, their figures cutting through the
artificial light like specters.

Noah moved as silently as a calm breeze, using the trees
as cover to approach the town. His hologram suit was now
completely inactive. Its only saving grace was its black color,
blending with the night. From the trees, he climbed onto the
rooftops of the low buildings, each movement careful and
deliberate to avoid detection, a black panther in the night.
Below him, followers moved in a synchronized, almost
robotic manner, their work illuminated sporadically by the
floodlights.

Spotting Pura Luhar, he began making his way toward it

via the tightly-packed rooftops, keeping low and out of the way of the patrolling soldiers.

It was then from a vantage point near the temple that Noah froze. His eyes widened as he spotted Marco and Renée. They walked freely among the followers, their hologram suits conspicuously absent. The sight of them, unbound yet moving with a compliance that set his nerves on edge, was deeply unsettling.

They must be infected.

And with this thought, a chill ran down his spine.

Noah crept away, keeping low as he crawled across the rooftops. The night was alive with tension. He moved with deliberate care, his every sense alert. As he neared the edge of a building in the center of the compound, he peered down into a narrow alley, and that was when he spotted a figure frantically searching for a hiding place.

It was Antara.

Though Noah didn't know who the man was, he could easily identify the desperation in his movements. A crowd, led by an armed guard, was methodically searching the nearby buildings.

The alley became a cauldron of anxiety, the sounds of the searching crowd bouncing off the walls. Noah pressed himself flat against the roof, remaining perfectly still.

Antara's hands were still bound, and his eyes darted around, searching for an escape. On the opposite alleyway, the crowd had split into two groups, each heading in opposite directions around the building, ready to outflank him. His options were limited: he could either climb up or break into the building. As the crowd closed in, he made his decision and darted into a small construction site nearby.

He hurriedly approached a workbench, his eyes catching sight of an electrical band saw. With frantic determination, he began rubbing the bindings against the blade's toothed edge. The crowd's voices grew louder, their footsteps echoing in the alleys. Sweat trickled down Antara's forehead as he worked, his heart pounding in his chest.

Finally, the bindings snapped, freeing his hands. Relief washed over him, but it was short-lived. As he turned to escape, a follower spotted him.

"Here! He's here!" shouted the follower, pointing toward him.

The response was immediate. People dropped their tools, mothers left their children, and everyone within a thirty-meter radius converged on Antara. Noah watched in silent horror as the entire community moved with a single purpose.

They're going to get him. He needs to move fast, Noah thought, his muscles tensing.

As the crowd closed in, Antara sprang up to a window sill, climbing onto the roof of a building as hands snatched at his feet. The detective then began clambering across the rooftops, jumping the short distances between the buildings. People climbed after him. A gunshot cracked through the night, the bullet narrowly missing Antara as he leapt from one roof to another.

Noah knew he had to act. He got up off his belly and began moving like a cat from one roof to the next, catching up with Antara, who lacked Noah's skills in parkour.

An armed guard knelt on a nearby rooftop, his rifle trained on Antara, following his every move, readying the shot. Noah moved silently, approaching the guard from behind. Focused entirely on his target, the guard was unaware of Noah's presence. In a swift, fluid motion, Noah disarmed him, wrenching the rifle from his hands. The guard barely had time to react before Noah shoved him off the roof, sending him tumbling into the crowd below.

Noah then sprinted and leaped across the buildings, making his way toward Antara. The situation was dire, but he was determined to help the man escape.

Noah reached the same rooftop as the detective. His eyes locked on Antara, who was just ahead. "Hey! Hey!" he shouted, trying to get the man's attention.

Antara glanced over his shoulder, his eyes widening with fear. He must have mistaken Noah for another follower. Panicked, Antara quickened his pace, misjudging his next jump. He slipped, plummeting into the narrow alley below.

Within seconds, the followers were upon him. Antara, despite the odds, fought back with skill, his movements a blur of powerful strikes and fluid defenses. His mastery of the Indonesian martial art pencak silat was evident as he deftly parried blows and countered with devastating efficiency as one after another came at him.

The alley became a battleground. The sound of fists meeting flesh and the grunts of combatants filled the claustrophobic space. Antara moved like a whirlwind, his fists and feet striking out with deadly accuracy. He took down one follower after another, but their sheer numbers were overwhelming.

Noah knew he had to act quickly. He positioned himself on a nearby rooftop, the M4A1 carbine he had taken from Hendricks ready in his hands. He took aim and began firing at the attackers, each shot precise and calculated. One by one, the followers fell, giving Antara a momentary respite.

But, with the carbine's magazine only half full, it quickly ran out. The click of the empty chamber was deafening in the midst of the chaos. Noah pulled out the Beretta.

He continued firing, the pistol barking sharply in the night. He took down several more attackers, but the followers kept coming, their relentless advance unyielding. The Beretta soon clicked empty as well, leaving Noah weaponless once more.

"Hold on! I'm coming!" he shouted, leaping down into the fray.

Just as Antara was about to be overwhelmed, Noah activated the cognitive harmonizer, jamming it into the temple of the man nearest the detective. Immediately, a wave of agony rippled through the crowd. The followers screamed and writhed in unison, clutching their heads as if in immense pain.

Noah seized the opportunity, rushing to Antara's side and helping him to his feet. "Come on, we need to move now!" he urged.

Antara, still dazed from the fight, looked around at the writhing followers in horror. "What did you do? They're all..."

"There's no time," Noah shouted. "Come on!"

They climbed up onto a nearby building, their movements swift and desperate. As they reached the roof, the screams of the affected followers resonated through the night, adding to the chaotic and disturbing atmosphere below.

"You must be with Marco and Renée," Antara panted, finally catching his breath.

"That's right. You've been with them?" Noah replied, glancing around to ensure they were not followed.

"Yes. But they have been infected with whatever it is that is making these people like this," Antara explained.

From their vantage point, they could see more of the followers converging on their location, the floodlights illuminating the sea of faces. The sound of their footsteps and shouts filled the air, a rising tide of impending doom.

Noah's heart sank at the sight. "We are in a lot of trouble."

FORTY-EIGHT

MARCO AND RENÉE WERE LED INTO PALMER'S private quarters. A stark contrast to the utilitarian feel of the rest of Eden, the rooms of the wooden house exuded understated luxury, with tasteful decorations that spoke of quiet wealth. A large table dominated the dining room, set meticulously for dinner. At the head of the table sat Dr. Palmer, his demeanor calm and composed. In a corner, Father Sanchez sat in a meditative state, his eyes closed and body perfectly still, though his lips moved as if he were silently speaking.

"Welcome. Please, have a seat," Palmer said, gesturing to the chairs opposite him.

Marco and Renée took their seats, and Palmer was about to speak when Sanchez's eyes snapped open, his voice breaking the stillness. "There has been another instance of a blowout," he said blankly. "We've lost contact with fifty subjects inside Eden."

The suddenness of Sanchez's report sent a ripple through the room.

"Not to worry," Palmer replied smoothly. "Send out the engineers. If it's the same as what happened at the prison, it shouldn't take long to get them back online."

Sanchez's eyes closed once more, his lips twitching as he sent the message.

"Nevertheless," Palmer said as he turned his attention to Marco and Renée, his blue eyes sharp and calculating, "I would like to know why this keeps happening." He leaned forward slightly, his voice calm but probing. "How many of you are there?"

Marco answered without hesitation. "Five."

Palmer's gaze didn't waver. "Who? Starting with yourselves."

"We are Marco and Renée Turin."

Palmer nodded. "And the others?"

"Jenny and Neil Blessing and Noah Wolf."

At the mention of Noah's name, Palmer's eyes widened, a flicker of recognition and surprise crossing his face. The room seemed to close in on him, the air thick with tension.

"As in *the* Noah Wolf?" Palmer's voice was almost a whisper, but the words hung heavily in the air.

"Yes" came Marco's reply.

FORTY-NINE

As Neil and Jenny exited the lab, they were immediately struck by the commotion on the other side of the compound. Crowds of people moved purposefully in one direction.

"What's going on?" Neil asked.

"Let's find somewhere higher so we can see," Jenny replied.

They climbed a nearby building, using field glasses to scan the area. The chaotic scene below came into sharp focus. The crowd was dense, moving with purpose and urgency. Amidst the throng, they spotted two men being chased across the rooftops.

"There! It's Noah," Neil said, handing the field glasses to his wife. "It's just like him to be in the middle of the action already."

"We need to get to him," Jenny replied, gazing at the scene through the binoculars. "He's going to need our help."

FIFTY

BACK IN PALMER'S QUARTERS, THE DOCTOR'S VOICE cut through the room like a knife.

"So you're E & E?" he asked, his eyes boring into Marco.

"Yes, my Lord," Marco replied.

"When did you arrive?"

"Two days ago."

Palmer leaned forward slightly, his curiosity piqued. "How, and where did you land?"

"Submarine then dinghy," Marco answered, each word measured. "The two of us arrived at Lalindi. Neil and Jenny arrived at Waitabula. Noah at Waingapu."

"And you were all wearing these hologram suits?"

"Yes."

"And looking for me?"

"Yes."

"Do you know where your companions are now?" Palmer's eyes narrowed.

"No. We lost contact one day ago. Right before we came here," Marco admitted.

"Yes. That'll be my jammer. It works at least. So you're not with the Council," Palmer said, a satisfied smirk playing on his lips.

"No. We are against the Council. Our intelligence stated that you are with them," Marco stated.

Palmer's eyes narrowed further, his suspicion turning into a calculated interest. "Would any of your people be armed with something that could disrupt electromagnetic signals?"

Marco and Renée exchanged a glance, thinking for a moment.

"Yes, my Lord," Renée answered.

"What?" Palmer demanded.

"Cognitive harmonizers. Noah has one," Renée replied.

"A cognitive harmonizer, of course," Palmer mused. "I heard about this. It makes sense. It would disrupt the implants." He turned his attention back to Marco and Renée, his tone taking on a chilling calmness. "So Noah Wolf has one, then?"

"Yes, my Lord," Renée said.

"Then he has already arrived at Eden," Palmer mused.

His eyes gleamed with a predatory glint as he leaned back in his chair, his fingers steepling together thoughtfully. "Marco, I have a job for you," he said, his voice dripping with calculated intent.

"What kind of job, my Lord?" Marco asked.

Palmer's smile was devoid of warmth. "I need you to eliminate Noah Wolf."

Marco's expression remained stoic. "Understood," he replied.

Turning his attention next to Renée, Palmer's smile widened, but there was no mirth in his eyes. "And as for you, Renée, I have another job. Something equally important."

Renée met his gaze. "What is it, my Lord?" she asked.

"You're going on a little journey," Palmer said, his tone almost casual.

FIFTY-ONE

NOAH AND ANTARA FOUND THEMSELVES PURSUED by a relentless tide of humanity, a sea of followers moving after them from every angle. The gaps between the buildings were filled with surging bodies, all eyes fixed on the two fugitives as they jumped from rooftop to rooftop.

"We can't get surrounded," Noah shouted above the din.

"They're everywhere," Antara shouted back, his eyes darting around for any possible escape route.

The scene was frenetic, a human maze surrounding them. The floodlights cast harsh shadows, creating a surreal, almost nightmarish atmosphere. The followers moved as one, their actions synchronized. They helped each other scale walls and clamber onto rooftops, their eyes never leaving Noah and Antara. They were all part of a single organism, a collective mind bent on capture.

"They're closing in," Noah yelled.

They came to a wide street, its dirt ground carved out of the flattened jungle. Floodlights illuminated the area in garish light. From both ends of the street, people surged toward them, their cries merging into a deafening roar.

Jumping down into the mud, they sprinted to a large schoolhouse on the other side, the only structure that offered any semblance of refuge.

"Quick!" Noah urged as they reached the building.

Noah helped Antara up the wall, boosting him to a balcony. As Antara reached safety, Noah turned to face the oncoming wave.

They were right there.

Noah immediately had to fight off several followers. He jabbed at one with the cognitive harmonizer, but the man ducked under it, and as he went to strike a second time with it, another follower coming in from behind knocked the device from Noah's hand, sending it skittering away on the ground.

Panic surged through Noah as he watched the harmonizer bounce and roll out of reach. The device wasn't just a piece of technology; it was his only real weapon against the infected. Without it, he was as vulnerable as anyone else.

More followers closed in as Noah fought to keep his footing. He ducked under a wild swing from another attacker, then moved his body through the crowd. Desperation fueling his movements, he punched, kicked, and dodged with a fierce determination, trying to get to the fallen harmonizer before he was overpowered. But it was no good; it was gone.

As he fought off two men, a woman picked it up out of the mud and ran off, the people closing in her wake, forming a human barrier between them.

Noah had no other choice. He felled one man and, using

the guy's back as a springboard, launched himself up to the balcony. Antara grabbed his arm, pulling him up with a swift, strong tug. Together, they climbed higher to the roof of the school's main hall as more people flooded up the building from below.

As they reached the flat rooftop, it quickly turned into a battleground. Attackers came from all sides, their numbers seemingly endless.

"We're surrounded!" Antara shouted.

As he watched more and more people climb up onto the roof, the usually cool Noah Wolf began to feel panic creep into him. It was like standing in the middle of the fifty-yard line at the Michigan Big House and having everyone in the entire stadium running at you.

But he couldn't give up.

Noah's breath came in ragged gasps as he fought his way through the mass of bodies, his mind racing to find a way out of this nightmare. The rooftop was crowded, and there was no time to think, only react. He threw a powerful elbow into the ribs of one follower, then spun to kick another in the knee, sending him crashing to the ground. But for every one he knocked down, two more seemed to take their place.

"Move!" Noah yelled at Antara, his voice almost lost in the cacophony of the crowd.

He saw it then—the edge of the roof, just a few feet away. If they could reach it, there was a lower building just beyond. It wasn't much, but it was a chance. Without hesitation, Noah surged forward, muscles burning with exertion, and cleared a path with a desperate burst of energy.

He reached the edge and, with one final glance at Antara, he leaped. The world seemed to slow as he flew through the air, the chaos fading into the background. His feet struck the roof of the lower building with a jarring thud, and he rolled to absorb the impact, coming up in a crouch.

"Noah!" Antara's voice rang out.

Noah twisted around just in time to see Antara fighting his way toward the edge. But as he reached it, the tide of followers overwhelmed him. Noah's heart sank as he saw Antara's figure struggling, barely visible in the tangle of limbs. Then, in an instant, Antara was gone, pulled back into the sea of bodies and dragged into the darkness of the night.

"Hey!" Noah shouted, his voice hoarse.

But it was too late. The spot where Antara had disappeared was now just a void, the followers moving with eerie precision as they turned their attention back to Noah. He knew he had only moments before they came for him again.

Jumping down from the lower building, Noah dashed toward the perimeter and the relative freedom that the jungle offered. The deafening roar of the crowd right behind him made him run with everything he had, his legs burning, lungs aching. The edge of the jungle loomed ahead; a tidal wave of humans trailed behind.

But as Noah reached the edge of the site, something happened. Hands burst from the shadows of a building, grabbing him. He tensed, ready to fight, but before he could react, he was pulled into an alcove, two people pressing him into a wall as their bodies covered him.

"Who—?" he started, but then he saw the faces of Jenny and Neil. They worked quickly, standing over him, camouflaging him against the wall. Their hologram suits shimmered, blending them seamlessly into the building.

The crowd surged past, oblivious to the ruse, their pounding feet vibrating the ground beneath them. The air was thick with dust and the smell of sweat, the sounds of the crowd gradually fading as they disappeared into the jungle.

For a few tense moments, the three of them remained perfectly still, hidden in plain sight. Then, as the last of the followers vanished into the trees, Jenny turned to Noah with a wry smile. "Hello, Mr. Wolf."

Noah let out a breath he hadn't realized he was holding. "Thank God," he said. "I don't think I've ever been happier to see you two."

FIFTY-TWO

At the back of Palmer's residence, the helipad was a hive of activity. The helicopter's lights cut through the darkness and the rotors' deafening roar created a sense of urgency.

Renée, dressed in casual traveling clothes and carrying a metal case, boarded the aircraft. The helicopter then ascended, its lights flickering as it climbed higher. Gradually, it became a flashing speck against the backdrop of the dark sky, the noise of the rotors slowly fading, leaving an eerie silence in its wake.

Dr. Anthony Palmer sat in his wheelchair, his eyes fixed on the departing helicopter. The huge figure of Krol stood behind him while Father Sanchez stood beside him, the priest's face as serene and composed as it always was. The three men watched as the helicopter lights faded until they flickered out of sight.

Palmer then broke the silence. "Godspeed, Renée Turin," he murmured. "Godspeed."

FIFTY-THREE

THE DEAD OF NIGHT IN EDEN WAS ANYTHING BUT quiet. More and more people arrived from the surrounding areas, creating a constant bustle. Search parties, their flash-light beams bobbing in the darkness, scoured the vegetation with barking dogs in tow. Helicopters hovered overhead, their blades slicing through the thick air. And if that wasn't bad enough, in the sky, another tropical storm brewed, rolling in from the ocean, its ominous presence adding to the sense of impending doom.

Noah, Jenny, and Neil were hiding inside a recently constructed underground sewage channel. The channel was dark and damp, the walls slick with moisture, the air almost solid with humidity. Above their heads, the people roamed the streets, the sounds of their movement reaching them in the sewers below.

"Go on," Noah whispered. "Tell me how you both ended up here. What happened when you reached Kataka?"

Over the next few minutes, Neil and Jenny recounted

the events surrounding the convoy attack. They described the father and daughter, Damu and Kiya, who had essentially rescued them during the chaos. They then detailed the harrowing moments when Damu and Kiya were taken, their escape, and the journey that ultimately led them to Eden.

"We arrived with the convoy that brought Damu and Kiya," Neil explained.

"And how have you found this place since you arrived?" Noah asked.

Neil and Jenny looked at each other.

"We found a lab," Jenny said.

Huddled together, the darkness of the sewer tunnel seemed to grow around them as Neil and Jenny told Noah about the warehouse full of incubators and the film they'd watched.

Noah nodded, his expression troubled. "I saw something similar on a Council research boat. Two scientists removed a parasite from a man's head."

He then recounted his experience, telling them about the two agents he'd encountered. "It didn't look like they were working with Palmer but were looking for him. One of Palmer's followers—a Special Forces soldier—shot the agent in the head before he and his team came after me."

Jenny and Neil listened intently, their expressions growing more serious.

"I take it said Special Forces guy is now dead," Jenny put to him.

"He is. And that brings me to my next point. I used the cognitive harmonizer on him. Whatever it did, it disrupted the signal between the parasite and the host's brain, effectively breaking the mind control Palmer exerts over the infected. It also spread to all the infected in the area, disorientating them."

Jenny and Neil were nodding. "That's awesome," Neil said. "So where is your cognitive harmonizer?"

"I lost it," Noah told him. "Where's yours?"

Neil looked uncomfortable. "I didn't bring mine."

Noah's eyebrows shot up. "Why not?"

Neil shrugged. "I don't think it's ethical."

Noah's eyes narrowed in disbelief. "Is that sarcasm? I can't tell."

Neil shook his head. "No. Do you know how many trials Wally has done into that thing about long-term brain damage? None."

Noah sighed loudly. "We're assassins, Neil. The very name of our organization is Elimination and Extraction. Elimination. What does it matter if we're a little unethical?"

"I don't think it's right is all," Neil countered.

Noah rolled his eyes and turned to Jenny. "Where's yours?"

Jenny's response was calm but unsettling. "I didn't bring mine either."

"Why not? Ethics?" Noah asked, exasperated.

Jenny's eyes gleamed. "No. I just prefer good old-fashioned physical torture to make my prisoners compliant."

Noah sighed a second time. "Great. Then it looks like we're back to just sneaking around."

Neil tried to lighten the mood. "It's worked so far."

There was a brief pause, the gloom of their situation settling over them. Jenny broke the silence. "First, before we do anything, though," she said, "we need to rest. None of us has slept for days. We need to conserve our strength if we're to get to Palmer."

They all nodded in agreement, the need for rest undeniable. The storm outside continued to grow in wrath, its intensity reverberating through the underground channel.

Noah spoke up, his voice firm. "I'll take the first watch."

FIFTY-FOUR

ALLISON PETERSON, DOC PARKER, AND MOLLY Hanson stood in Kirtland's operations room, the atmosphere tense, the room dimly lit by the glow from the various monitors. Two operators sat at desks in front of them, wearing headphones and communicating with a ground team.

At the front of the room, a large screen displayed satellite images of Sumba and its surrounding waters. The three nuclear-armed Council vessels were clearly delineated, their ominous presence a constant reminder of the stakes at play. The possible site of Palmer's lab was highlighted around the foothills of Mount Wanggameti, its exact location still a mystery.

The screen also showed footage of the ground team: four men waiting in a small boat off the coastline of Lalindi. They were armed and ready, their expressions taut as they awaited word from Noah. The plan was for them to receive the signal and move in for extraction at Lalindi marina. From there, they would travel to Denpasar, Bali and catch a plane to safety—with or without Dr. Anthony Palmer.

Molly leaned in, her voice barely above a whisper. "Those submarines could fire at any moment," she said, her eyes never leaving the screen. "Are you sure you don't want to send someone onto the island? Find out what's happening?"

Allison's face was set in stern determination. "I'll tell you what's happening, Ms. Hanson. Noah's getting us Palmer is what's happening."

"But he may need help," Molly pressed.

"No," Allison responded firmly.

"Why not?" Molly demanded, frustration creeping into her voice.

Allison turned to face her, her expression hard. "Because if they know that Noah Wolf is on that island, and that he might get to Palmer before them, they might just nuke it out of principle."

It was a long shot, but Allison was desperate to deflect away from the fact that she was being held back by the Council's orders. Of course, in any normal circumstance those four men would be wading through the jungle in search of them. But Seven had told her that under no circumstances was she to rescue him. He either got Palmer off the island or perished beneath a mushroom cloud.

Molly's shoulders slumped, and she gave in, returning her attention to the screen.

Doc Parker's phone rang, breaking the strained silence. He answered it quickly, his face growing more serious with each passing second. When he got off the phone, he turned to Allison, his expression dire.

"Vice President Brown won't give the go-ahead to send American submarines into the area," he said, his voice heavy with frustration. "Says it could start a nuclear war. They really are on their own."

Gazing at the screen, Allison's eyes flickered with a mix of hope and fear. "Then let's hope Noah and the others complete their mission," she said softly, the weight of her words hanging grimly in the air.

FIFTY-FIVE

DAWN BROKE, BUT THE RISING SUN WAS OBSCURED by a raging storm. The sky was blackened, and the jungle trees were swept sideways by gale-force winds. Rain, which had been building all night, now reached its deafening crescendo.

Inside his villa, Palmer sat in his study, seemingly oblivious to the tempest outside. The wind howled, and rain drummed against the windows, but his focus was on a framed picture of his wife and daughter. He gazed at it, the weight of their absence heavy on his shoulders.

"Soon I will have rid the world of the true parasites," he whispered to the picture. "I will have avenged you and destroyed the one thing feeding off of mankind: the Council."

In the corner of the room, Krol stood silently, a towering, vigilant presence. The storm outside grew fiercer, but inside, the atmosphere was thick with Palmer's introspection and grief.

Father Sanchez entered the study. "My Lord, there is still no sign of Wolf," he reported. "He must have escaped into the jungle, and the storm makes it practically impossible to find him. Security advises suspending the search and creating a perimeter around Eden."

"Yes. Do that," Palmer replied, his tone decisive. "But also, summon Marco."

"Yes, my Lord."

"And what about the Special Forces soldier Wolf didn't kill?" Palmer inquired, stopping Sanchez as the priest was about to enter his fugue state. "The one the engineers found locked in the prison basement. Has he been fixed?"

"Yes, my Lord," Sanchez affirmed.

"Then summon him, too," Palmer ordered.

Sanchez complied, entering his fugue state to summon Marco and the soldier Kojo.

Moments later, Marco arrived at the villa, drenched from the relentless storm outside, his long black hair plastered to his face. As he entered the study, Palmer's gaze was piercing, his eyes narrowing as he regarded Marco. "Noah Wolf has disappeared. Where do you think he will be?"

Marco took a deep breath and replied, "Whatever has happened, Noah Wolf will do everything he can to complete his mission. That is always his number one priority."

"And that mission is to extract me," Palmer stated.

"Yes," Marco confirmed. "He will not go far from you— the target. He will not quit or leave the area until your extraction is achieved."

Palmer leaned back in his chair, considering Marco's words. "Do you think you can find him?"

"Yes," Marco replied.

At that moment, the door opened, and Kojo entered the room. He was a formidable figure, standing at 6'3" with a muscular and athletic build honed by years of rigorous training. His dark skin was marked by a few scars, testament to his experience in combat.

Palmer turned to Marco, his voice commanding. "Take this man with you. He is a skilled operative like you. Go find Noah Wolf and the others. Use whatever weapons you find in the armory and take whoever you need."

Marco nodded, sizing up Kojo. "Me and him will do. Just get everyone else out of the way."

FIFTY-SIX

INSIDE THE SEWER TUNNEL HIDEOUT, NOAH, NEIL, and Jenny had just woken up after a couple of hours of much-needed rest, having been awake for more than 48. They gathered around what was left of their supplies, their faces drawn with fatigue but their eyes sharp with determination.

"We've got two flash bangs," Jenny said, her voice barely above a whisper, "one and a half mags for the carbine, and one each for the two pistols we have, only one of which is full."

"So not much ammo," Neil remarked, stony-faced.

"Not enough to fight our way out of here. That's for sure," Jenny replied, her tone matter-of-fact.

The three of them looked at each other, the lingering weariness from their previous sleepless hours bloating their features.

"Our only hope," Noah whispered, "is to get to Falmer

and his lab. Shut down Mindweaver from where it's run centrally."

Neil nodded. "That'll be the one he runs from the temple. Jenny and I took a look earlier on. It's where his AI is set up."

"Then that's where he controls them," Noah said. "If we break that, we break his hold. Then it'll just be us and Palmer."

Neil glanced at him, a concerned look on his face. "What do you think will happen to them when we unplug it?"

"I don't know," Noah admitted.

Jenny's voice was firm. "Whatever it is, it's better than being a zombie."

Noah suddenly raised his hand. "Shh!"

They heard movement outside and quietly moved to the edge of the sewer. The grills of the storm drains, now flowing with water, gave them narrow views of the street outside.

They saw followers moving in unison into the buildings, shutting doors, closing blinds, and locking up. The storm raged, lightning illuminating the street intermittently, casting eerie shadows as the followers retreated inside with unsettling synchronization.

"What do you think is happening?" Neil asked.

"Nothing good," Noah replied, his eyes narrowing as he watched.

"Then we should move," Jenny said.

They gathered their supplies quickly. Thunder rumbled ominously as they prepared to make their way to Palmer's lab. Each of them knew the risks, but their mission was clear: shut down Palmer's operation and stop Mindweaver.

FIFTY-SEVEN

THE ARMORY WAS FILLED WITH WEAPONS TAKEN from local army and police forces. The metallic scent of gun oil hung heavy in the air. Metal racks and tables were covered with various firearms, knives, and tactical gear, all waiting to be used.

Marco and Kojo moved purposefully through the armory, selecting their weapons with care. Marco picked up a Beretta pistol, an M16 carbine, and a machete, feeling the cold steel in his hands. Kojo chose an M110 Semi-Automatic Sniper System, coating himself in camouflage gear, ready to take up a covering position.

As they inspected the weapons, a follower entered the armory, carrying an engineering map of Eden, including the sewage tunnels. Marco spread it out on a table, the map illuminated by a single overhead light.

"Which of these are accessible and which aren't?" Marco asked.

The follower pointed out the accessible tunnels on the

map. "These ones lead from the river to the cooling units for the reactor. So that it can be flooded in case the fusion reaction becomes unstable."

Marco's eyes narrowed as he studied the map. "Do any of them lead directly to our Lord's laboratory?"

The follower pointed again, the lines and notes on the map clear and detailed. "Here," he said.

"They'll be somewhere in there," Marco mused. "If you don't see them above ground, they'll be below it. And they'll want access to that lab. Can we get water down there?"

The follower nodded. "Yes. We have pumps and enough hosing to get down to the river. If we close off the lab, it will flood the whole sewer."

Marco's expression hardened as the plan took shape. "Then make it done. Let's flush them out. Get them onto the streets."

FIFTY-EIGHT

THE BUSTLING DUBAI AIRPORT WAS A HIVE OF activity, filled with travelers from around the world. People hurried to their next destinations, announcements echoed through the terminals, and the air buzzed with the energy of travelers.

Renée stepped off her flight from Jakarta and made her way through the crowded terminals, weaving through the throngs of people.

She headed toward the baggage claim area, the sound of luggage rolling and people calling out to each other filling the air. Conveyor belts hummed as they delivered bags to the waiting passengers.

Renée spotted her case easily. It was the only one that was reinforced titanium.

With the case in hand, she joined the line for customs. The area was busy, customs agents scrutinizing documents and x-ray images, the air filled with the quiet murmur of travelers waiting their turn.

An agent called her forward, his eyes narrowing as he examined her documents. "What's inside the case?"

"Samples of nematodes for the college I work for," Renée replied calmly, handing over a permit.

The agents at the x-ray machine recoiled slightly at the images of the parasites inside the case.

"These look... unusual," the customs agent remarked.

"They're for educational purposes. Here's the permit," Renée replied.

After a moment of scrutiny, the agent nodded and waved her through, Renée continuing toward the gate for her connecting flight to Chicago, the ten incubated parasites ready for implantation.

FIFTY-NINE

NOAH, JENNY, AND NEIL MOVED CAUTIOUSLY through the dark sewers, the rising rainwater splashing around their feet. The storm's muffled roar was ever-present, adding to the urgency of the situation.

"We should almost be at the edge of the temple," Neil stated, his voice bouncing off the wet concrete walls.

They trudged through the cold, damp sewers, the smell of wet concrete and stagnant water permeating the air. The narrow passageways seemed to close in around them, every step reverberating against the backdrop of the storm.

Finally, they reached a series of venting shafts that ran along the sewer. The air grew colder, a sign that they were closing in on the lab's cooling units.

"We're almost there," Noah said. "Stay close and be ready for anything."

That was when the ground beneath their feet began to vibrate, the tremors growing stronger by the second. The water around them began to rise steadily. Within seconds, it was halfway to their knees as a loud noise, like the roar of a distant avalanche, grew louder.

"What is that?" Jenny asked.

Noah's eyes widened as realization struck. "Run."

Without hesitation, the three of them turned and began running and splashing through the rising water. The roar of rushing water filled their ears. Then they saw it. Hundreds of tons of water surged after them, a tidal wave in the confined space of the sewers.

"There's a vent! Head for it!" Noah yelled, pointing to a grate in the ceiling.

The water caught up with them, slamming into their bodies with brutal force. They fought against the current, their movements frantic, uncoordinated. Noah reached for the grate, his fingers slipping on the wet metal. He managed to grab hold and pulled himself up. Neil caught it next, reaching out and taking hold of Jenny, pulling her to the grate so that she too could cling on.

The three of them clutched the bars, debris hitting them and threatening to knock them off. The force of the water was immense. They struggled to hold on, their knuckles white with the effort, the water rising rapidly.

"Lift it! We have to get it open!" Noah shouted, his voice barely audible over the deafening roar.

They pushed against the grate, their muscles straining as the water surged around them, making every movement a battle. The grate was heavy and reluctant to budge. The rising water now covered their shoulders, and panic began to set in. They couldn't afford to fail.

"Come on, push!" Neil urged.

They redoubled their efforts, their fingers slipping and

finding purchase on the slick metal, pressing their feet against the walls for purchase. With a monumental effort, the grate finally gave way, the hinges protesting as they forced it open.

One by one, they hauled themselves through the opening, their bodies aching from the exertion. Lying on the muddy ground, panting and soaked, they took a second to review things. All their weapons except Jenny's karambit and Noah's fighting knife were gone, washed away. As for their suits, the debris had torn them in several places, and the electronics were completely soaked.

Neil fiddled with the control pad on his palm, frustration etched on his face. "Come on, work," he muttered, pressing the buttons more forcefully.

Jenny watched him, pressing her own control pad. She tried activating her hologram suit, but it did no more than flicker and die. On the back of it was a large gash, the material hanging down where a piece of debris had ripped it. "It's no use, Neil. The water must have short-circuited the electronics," she said. "Plus, mine's torn real bad."

Neil sighed, shaking his head. "Great. Without the suits, we're exposed."

"Looks like it's just us now," Noah said breathlessly.

The street they'd emerged into was an abandoned stretch of mud, the storm lashing rain and sweeping wind around them. Flaming torches lined the houses, casting flickering light on the locked doors and shutters.

The temple loomed ahead, rising above the streets of the newly built town, a dark silhouette against the stormy sky.

"What now?" Neil put to the others.

"We need to find shelter and regroup," Noah replied.

"We're exposed out here," Jenny added, her eyes scanning the darkened street for any sign of movement.

With no time to lose, they began moving toward the temple.

———

MARCO AND KOJO stood atop a building, surveying the storm-lashed streets below through thermal imaging binoculars. Both were armed and ready for a fight. Kojo held an M110 Semi-Automatic Sniper System, a Beretta M9 in an underarm holster, and an M7 bayonet strapped to his hip. Marco was equipped with a Benelli M4 combat shotgun, another M9, and a Gerber compact clearpath machete with a serrated edge.

The streets below were deserted, the storm's fury crashing down on it all. Water poured from vents, and the wind howled, making it the perfect setting for an ambush.

"There! I see them," Kojo said, his voice cutting through the noise of the storm.

Marco grinned, his eyes narrowing as he spotted Noah, Jenny, and Neil about two blocks away. "Warriors, come out to play-e-ay!" he called out mockingly, removing a grenade from his belt.

The two men jumped down into the street, then split up, each taking a different route to close in on their targets.

———

THE HEAVY RAIN and strong winds whipped through the mud-slick streets. Lightning flashed, illuminating the scene in garish bursts. Amid this pandemonium, Noah, Jenny, and Neil were moving with caution when Noah spotted something flying through the air, coming over the top of the building next to them.

It landed in the mud with a splash.

"Grenade!" Noah shouted.

They all dove for cover as the grenade exploded, the blast showering them with dirt and debris. The sound was deafening, a violent crack that reverberated through the storm.

In the aftermath, they peeked out from their cover, their faces streaked with mud.

"We need to split up and find cover," Noah said urgently.

With a quick nod, they each ran in separate directions, their movements careful but swift. The storm's fury continued unabated, the rain lashing at them, the wind howling like some angry god. They knew whoever was coming after them would try to outflank them, and their only chance was to spread out and find better positions.

Noah dashed down a narrow alley, the muddy ground slippery under his boots. Lightning flashed overhead, casting jagged shadows on the walls. He pressed on, determined to stay ahead of their pursuers.

Jenny darted through a series of abandoned market stalls, her mind racing. The storm made it hard to see, but she kept her focus.

Taking a different route, Neil weaved through a street strewn with construction materials and lined by half-built buildings. The rain soaked through his clothes, making his bones ache. He glanced over his shoulder, aware that their pursuers could be anywhere.

Rounding the corner of a building, Neil immediately came face to face with Kojo, the Special Forces soldier standing on the other side of a square no more than thirty feet away.

Kojo raised his rifle and opened fire, forcing Neil to flee from cover to cover, diving behind the stacks of building materials.

Bullets whizzed past him as he dashed behind a large bulldozer. He crouched low, pinned down as Kojo continued to fire from his vantage point on top of a rooftop. The metallic ping of bullets ricocheting off the dozer's surface rang in his ears as he frantically searched for a way to escape or retaliate.

Then, suddenly, he felt a touch on his shoulder. Neil's blood turned to ice, and he spun around, expecting to face an enemy. But instead, he found Jenny crouching behind him.

"Jesus, Jenny!" he whispered harshly. "You scared the life out of me!"

Jenny managed a grim smile, her eyes scanning the area. "Baby, I have an idea. You draw his fire, and I'll go get him," she said.

"You mean go be bait?" Neil replied, an eyebrow raised.

"Yes, baby. Go be bait," Jenny confirmed.

Neil let out a sigh. "OK. I'll draw his fire."

"Be careful," Jenny said, leaning forward and kissing him on the lips.

After that, Neil took a deep breath, then sprinted from behind the bulldozer, the bullets following him as he dove behind the cover of some concrete piping.

While he did, Jenny peeked out from the other end of

the dozer, looking to see if she could spot Kojo's muzzle flash within the storm.

Neil zigzagged from one piece of cover to the next, using every bit of plant machinery, building, and vehicle he could find. He ducked behind a rusted excavator, the metal echoing with the impact of bullets. He sprinted to a parked truck, its windows shattering as shots pelted it. He dove behind a stack of metal beams, the sound of the storm and gunfire merging into a cacophony around him.

I need to stay alive long enough for her to get the drop on him, Neil thought. *Come on, baby.*

He sprinted to another piece of cover, this time a large forklift, its tires providing scant protection as Kojo's bullets kicked up mud and debris around him.

Jenny moved quickly and silently, using the storm to mask her approach. She could see Neil's precarious situation, the danger he was in, and knew she had to act fast.

Neil made a break for a small shed, the onslaught of bullets following him all the way.

Come on, Jenny flashed through his mind as he huddled behind the shed.

Jenny snuck up behind the building Kojo was on, carefully climbing up the back. The rain slicked the tiles, making her ascent treacherous. She crouched behind a chimney stack, her breathing steady. She could see Kojo, his back turned as he fired at Neil.

Crawling down the tiles, she readied her karambit. But just as she was about to strike, Kojo noticed her presence— seeing her reflection on the wet tiles as lightning exploded nearby. He whipped around, blocking her knife attack with his M7 bayonet, the two face to face.

Jenny had the higher ground, but Kojo had the weight.

He flung her off him, Jenny doing well to regain her footing as Kojo went for his rifle. Using the sleek tiles, Jenny threw herself into a skid, beating Kojo to the rifle with a kick as he reached for it, sending it off the edge. The big man went for his Beretta, pulling it from his underarm holster, but Jenny's foot was just as quick. Her kick collided with the pistol and the hand, sending the Beretta to the same place as the rifle.

Kojo pulled his bayonet, a cold, deadly glint in his eyes. Jenny had her karambit, its curved blade gleaming in the intermittent flashes of lightning.

I need to get him off balance, she thought, her mind focused on the fight ahead. *He's stronger, but I'm faster.*

They exploded at one another, their blades flashing in the storm like lightning bolts. Kojo lunged with his bayonet, Jenny deflecting the strike with her karambit, twisting her body to avoid his follow-up attack. She countered with a series of quick, slicing motions, aiming for his flanks and ribs, moves the big man was quick to avoid, her knife cutting into no more than his body armor.

They jumped from roof to roof, their fight turning into a dance amid the storm. The slippery tiles forced them to rely on their balance and skill. Lightning provided brief, stark illumination, disorientating both fighters as they clashed.

Kojo swung his bayonet in a wide arc, but Jenny ducked under it, rolling to the side and coming up with a quick slash at his legs. He stepped back just in time. The blade missed, barely.

Jenny leaped to another roof, Kojo close behind. She

landed and immediately spun to face him, the karambit ready. He was on her in a heartbeat, their blades meeting with a metallic clang. She pushed him back with a series of rapid strikes, forcing him to defend himself as they dropped into the abandoned streets, separating momentarily, catching their breath before clashing once more. Jenny feinted to the left, then spun to the right, her blade cutting a shallow line across Kojo's arm, drawing blood. He grunted in pain but retaliated with a powerful thrust, barely missing the underside of her ribcage.

The battle raged on, as did the storm, a relentless backdrop. Jenny's speed and agility allowed her to keep Kojo on the defensive, but his strength and endurance made him a formidable opponent.

———

NOAH CREPT through the rain-lashed streets. It poured down in a curtain of water, making visibility poor and the footing treacherous. Suddenly, Marco appeared at the other end of the passage, his figure emerging from the shadows like a specter. He fired off a shot from his Benelli M4, the roar of the shotgun mingling with the thunder.

Noah dove out of the way, narrowly avoiding the blast, and scrambling behind a building.

Marco cocked the pump-action, the shell ejecting into the storm with a hollow clink. Noah knew he had to move quickly.

Just as Marco was approaching the building, Noah rounded the corner and positioned himself on the opposite side. Determined to gain the upper hand, he scrambled up the slippery wall of the building. As he reached the roof, he heard Marco's footsteps approaching. Without hesitation, Noah crossed the roof and dropped down on top of him, disarming him of the shotgun with a vicious kick, the weapon clattering away into the storm.

Noah then grabbed Marco's pistol, ripping it from his holster and tossing it aside, leaving both of them weaponless. He then backed off, the two men facing each other in the driving rain, the streets around them a mess of water and mud.

Marco reached for the machete at his belt, the blade catching the flash from a sudden bolt of lightning. Noah responded by drawing his Ka-Bar USMC fighting knife, the seven-inch steel blade gleaming in the intermittent light.

"Marco, you need to snap out of it," Noah shouted over the storm. "This isn't you. This is that thing they've put inside your head."

Marco said nothing, his eyes empty. Then, with a sudden burst of aggression, he attacked.

The two engaged in a brutal knife fight, their combat skills on full display. Marco's attacks were relentless and lethal, his infected mind driving him to kill. Noah, on the other hand, fought defensively, trying to incapacitate his friend without causing permanent harm.

Marco lunged forward, the machete aimed at Noah's chest. Noah sidestepped, grabbing Marco's wrist and twisting it, forcing the machete from his grip. Marco retaliated with an elbow to Noah's ribs, knocking the wind out of him. Noah stumbled back, barely managing to keep his footing on the slippery ground.

The fight continued, each man driven by his own desperate need. Marco, controlled by Palmer's Mindweaver, fought with a single-minded ferocity. Noah, driven by his determination to save his friend, fought with both skill and restraint.

KOJO AND JENNY engaged in a brutal dance, their blades flashing in the storm's chaotic light. Rain hammered down as they circled each other warily, eyes locked.

Jenny lunged, her karambit aiming for Kojo's midsection. He parried the strike with a swift, practiced motion, their blades clashing with a sharp metallic ring. She spun on her heel, aiming a low sweep at his legs. Kojo leapt back, narrowly avoiding her blade, and countered with a vicious slash toward her face. Jenny ducked, the bayonet slicing through the space where her head had been mere moments before.

Jenny was starting to feel the fight, the last few days, and the relentless march of the mission. She managed to parry the next few strikes, but Kojo's incessant assault left her little room to counterattack. Knocking her knife hand aside with a powerful swipe, Kojo used his free hand to twist her wrist, forcing her to drop the blade. It fell into the mud with a dull thud.

With a swift motion, Kojo grabbed Jenny by the shoulders and drove her to the muddy ground, coming down on top of her, straddling and pinning her. Jenny struggled, her hands grasping at his wrists, trying to push him off. Kojo's grip was like iron, his face a mask of grim determination.

Rain poured down on them, mingling with the sweat, the blood, and the mud.

Kojo raised his knife, his eyes locked on to Jenny's. Her heart pounded in her chest as she fought against his overwhelming strength. In a desperate move, she twisted her body, trying to throw him off balance, but Kojo's position was solid.

"Any last words?" he growled.

Jenny's eyes blazed with defiance. "Not today."

With a final, desperate effort, she managed to grab a handful of mud and fling it into Kojo's face. The mud splattered across his eyes, momentarily blinding him.

But it wasn't enough.

While the mud dripped from his face, he began to drive the knife toward her chest. Jenny had ahold of his wrists with both hands, her arms straining to hold off the blade. The tip of the bayonet pressed into her hologram suit, the material beginning to tear. The whole time, Kojo's face remained emotionless, his eyes blank, devoid of humanity.

Jenny felt the cold steel of the blade begin to cut into her flesh, a searing pain spreading through her chest. She gritted her teeth, using every ounce of strength to hold off the inevitable.

Then, suddenly, there was a gunshot.

Kojo's body jerked. Another shot and he became a dead weight, the knife slipping from his grasp.

Jenny, gasping for breath, managed to push him off, rolling to the side. She looked up to see Neil standing at the other end of the street, holding Kojo's fallen Beretta.

He rushed over to his wife, dropping the gun as he lifted

her from the ground, taking her in his arms and embracing her tightly.

"That was close," Jenny whispered, her voice trembling from the intensity of the encounter.

"I'm sorry," Neil said as he held her close. "It took me all this time to find the gun."

The violent storm was all around them, but for a moment, the world seemed to pause. He kissed her forehead and held her tightly, his relief palpable.

———

NOAH AND MARCO'S fight continued, their movements fierce, every strike a struggle against the elements and each other.

They separated in the middle of an open area filled with construction materials and scaffolding. The storm's fury made it a warzone, the wind howling, the lightning illuminating the sky in sharp, brief flashes.

"Marco, please. Just wake up out of this," Noah shouted over the din.

Marco's eyes were empty, his face set in a macabre, unnatural determination. "I *am* awake, Noah."

"Then put the machete down," Noah responded.

When Marco answered, his voice was cold and detached. "Of course, Noah," he said. "But first you must give yourself to our Lord. Join him in Communion."

Noah shook his head. "That what you did?"

"Yes. And now I am complete. Join us and you too can be complete."

"Nah. I'm good," Noah retorted.

"Then you die," Marco declared, charging at Noah with the machete raised.

Noah turned and sprinted to a bamboo scaffold, climbing up it with the agility of a cat. Marco followed, but he was slower, more cumbersome on the scaffolding.

"You never were as good as me at climbing, Marco," Noah taunted, moving swiftly along the scaffold. "Looks like having that worm in your head doesn't change that fact."

Marco lost his footing briefly, his hands slipping on the wet bamboo. He managed to stay hanging on, but his progress was labored and clumsy. Noah scaled another part of the scaffolding with ease, his movements fluid and precise despite the rain and wind.

The storm intensified, the thunder rumbling louder and the wind whipping around them with greater force. The bamboo scaffold swayed under their weight.

Noah reached the top and looked down at Marco, who was still struggling to keep up. He knew he had to find a way to end this without killing his friend, but Marco's relentless pursuit left him with few options.

"Marco, you don't have to do this. Fight it!" Noah shouted down at him, hoping against hope that his words would reach through the haze of control clouding Marco's mind.

But Marco's eyes remained vacant. "Join us... Noah," he said breathlessly as he climbed.

He clambered onto a platform—a pair of boards tied precariously to the bamboo scaffolding. The structure clung to a half-built stone building, the storm making it creak and groan as it swayed against its bindings.

It was as high as the scaffold went, so Noah had to be here somewhere.

Marco moved cautiously along the platform, his eyes scanning the unfinished windows of the building for any sign of Noah, the slick boards bowing under his weight. The constant rumble of thunder and the intermittent flashes of lightning created an eerie, strobe-like effect.

"Noah!" Marco called out.

A flash of lightning illuminated the scene, casting stark shadows against the stone walls. In that sudden burst of light, Noah emerged from behind Marco, climbing silently up from a lower level, where he had been hanging in wait.

Marco felt the boards bow underfoot. He twisted around, but it was too late. Noah swung a piece of timber, the force of the blow knocking Marco unconscious. He crumpled to the platform, his body limp and lifeless.

Noah took a moment to catch his breath, the piece of timber still clutched in his hand. He looked down at Marco, his heart heavy with the weight of what he had just done.

He knelt beside him, checking to ensure that his friend was still breathing. Satisfied that he was only unconscious, Noah lifted him onto his shoulder. With careful, deliberate steps, he then began to make his way down the scaffolding, Marco draped over him.

The rain continued to pour, the wind continued to howl, and the lightning continued to flash, but Noah pressed on, driven by a singular purpose: to save his friend and complete their mission. The storm might rage on, but so would he.

SIXTY

Renée arrived at Chicago O'Hare International Airport. She navigated through the bustling terminal, making her way to E & E's private hangar.

"ID, please," a security personnel requested.

Renée handed over her ID. "Here you go."

They scanned her retinas and let her through, a private chauffeur shuttling her across the runway. The bustling atmosphere of the airport gave way to the quiet, controlled environment of the private hangar. It was a secure, well-lit space with sleek, private aircraft ready for departure.

A hangar attendant approached her. "Welcome, Agent Turin. Your flight is ready."

"Thank you," Renée replied.

An E & E flight direct from Jakarta would have been quicker, but it would have raised too many questions. This way, they wouldn't see her coming. She'd catch them by surprise.

Renée boarded a Gulfstream G450, the sleek black jet

standing ready. On her way to her seat, she crossed paths with the pilot. He took one look at the case Renée was carrying and asked, "What's in the case?"

"None of your business," Renée snapped back.

The pilot, accustomed to the brusque behavior of E & E agents, thought to himself, *Typical, always curt and to the point*, and said no more. He prepared for takeoff as the staircase folded back into the Gulfstream.

Settling into her seat, Renée looked out the window as the plane began taxiing to the runway. This was it. The final leg of the journey. Inside her case, the parasites writhed in their tanks, as if sensing the proximity of their destination.

SIXTY-ONE

ALL ALONG THE STREETS OF EDEN, THE DOORS unlocked and swung open, releasing a flood of people into the stormy streets. The controlled, synchronized movements of the infected transformed into a chaotic search as they hunted for Noah and his team.

Noah, carrying an unconscious Marco over his shoulder, sprinted through the rain-slicked streets. His eyes scanned the shadows, alert for any sign of the pursuing mob. The sounds of their movement, their feet splashing through the puddles, was all around him. Then another sound: a diesel engine.

Noah spun around to see a bulldozer approaching him along the street, Neil at the controls and Jenny perched in the bucket. She was gripping Marco's Benelli shotgun, a belt of shells over her shoulder.

"Get in!" Neil shouted over the roar of the storm.

Noah reached the bulldozer, lifting Marco into the lowered bucket with Jenny's help. Noah then climbed into the cab, where he took up a position at the back of the driver's seat. Neil raised the bucket, flooring the pedal. The bulldozer let out a plume of black smoke as it powered forward, heading toward the towering communications structure in the distance.

At that moment, the streets erupted into a frenzy as people surged toward them from every direction. Neil's hands tightened on the controls. The bulldozer barreled forward, forcing those in its path to leap aside or be crushed beneath its massive treads.

"I've got a plan!" Neil shouted over his shoulder as he handed Noah Kojo's Beretta M9.

"What?" Noah yelled back, immediately shooting an attacker as the man began climbing the back of the dozer.

"Your experiences—"

He was cut off when someone jumped from the roof of the building they were passing, landing right at the side of the open cab. The man began trying to pull Neil off it, tugging at him until Noah shot him, knocking him off.

From the rooftops, figures leaped onto the dozer like shadowy phantoms. The Benelli barked thunderously in Jenny's hands, each deafening blast sending a spray of rain and blood into the air, the boom briefly drowning out the storm. One attacker climbed up the bucket and was then propelled backward by the force of Jenny's shot, landing with a wet thud on the sodden ground below before being run over by the wheel.

With the coast relatively clear, Neil continued, "Your experiences with the cognitive harmonizer gave me an idea. I think we can replicate it using the jammer on the communications tower."

Noah's brow furrowed in concentration as he processed Neil's words. "How's that going to work?"

Neil took a deep breath, focusing on navigating the bulldozer through the narrow streets. "The cognitive harmonizer works by—"

Two loud blasts of the Benelli interrupted him.

"It works by disrupting the communication between Palmer's Mindweaver program and the parasites controlling the infected. It emits a specific frequency that scrambles the signals, cutting off Palmer's control."

Noah nodded, his mind racing. "OK, so how do we—"

A man had just clambered up the back, grabbing on to Noah's leg. He kicked viciously, his boot colliding with the attacker's face, sending him tumbling off the dozer, disappearing into the mud below.

Coming back beside Neil, Noah shouted, "So how do we use the jammer to do the same thing?"

"When Jenny and I were up there yesterday, I spotted the jammer's frequency generator and its PLL. If we modified the jammer to emit the same frequency as the harmonizer, we could boost its output to cover a wider area, ensuring that it reaches all the infected within range. This would create a blanket signal that disrupts Palmer's control over everyone here. It would cut them off."

Noah's eyes widened as he grasped the implications. "Neil, you're a genius."

"I know," Neil confirmed with a grim smile. "Once we—"

He was abruptly interrupted by another burst of the Benelli. Jenny fired the shotgun again. An attacker clinging to the side of the bulldozer was thrown back, disappearing under the rear wheels.

"Once we activate it," Neil went on, "the infected will lose their synchronized behavior. They'll be disoriented, and it'll break their coordinated attacks. It'll be our chance to take them down and rescue everyone they've got under control."

"Neil, that's..."

"Oh crap," Neil let out.

Noah followed the direction of his grim look. Up ahead, a blockade of vehicles had been set up to halt their progress. The followers had placed a series of vehicles—pickup trucks, dozers, a small crane, diggers—across the road to trap them.

Neil brought the bulldozer to a screeching halt, the massive machine hissing as it settled. Noah jumped off as Neil lowered the bucket. All around, infected ran at them, Jenny letting off more blasts from the Benelli to force them back, the shotgun acting as crowd control.

"We need to get on the rooftops!" Noah said.

As they prepared to go, Marco began to stir in the bucket, his eyes fluttering open. Noah noticed immediately, unsure what to do as the roar of the approaching crowd intensified.

"They're coming!" Jenny yelled, firing off another round from the Benelli.

Neil glanced at Marco, then at the horde closing in on them. "We don't have time! We have to move, now!"

"No, we can't leave him!" Noah shouted back.

Neil's expression was resolute, his mind already calculating their chances. "We have no choice, Noah. If we don't break the connection at the tower, there'll be no saving any of us—including Marco. He's still under their influence."

Marco groaned, trying to push himself up, but he was too weak, his limbs trembling. Noah's heart wrenched at the sight of his friend in such a state, but Neil was right. They couldn't save him now—not while he was still connected to Palmer's control.

Jenny's eyes met Noah's. "He's right, Noah. Once we break the connection, we can come back for him. But if we stay here, we're all dead."

A guttural roar rose from the approaching mob, and it was clear they were out of time. With a heavy heart, Noah nodded, his decision made. He turned to Neil. "Let's go."

The Benelli got them some clearance and they hauled themselves up onto the roof of a building, darting across the rooftops, their feet slipping on the wet tiles as they moved. The communications tower loomed just a little bit farther.

As she stopped at the edge of a rooftop to fire back at their pursuers, Jenny's Benelli shotgun fired its last round, the deafening boom echoing through the storm. She reached for more ammunition from the belt, but it was empty. As she did, a wave of hands grabbed her, pulling her down into the street below.

"Jenny!" Neil cried out, but Noah grabbed him, yanking him away.

"Just get to that tower," Noah commanded, his voice fierce. "We can't lose you too!"

Jenny's screams filled the air as she fought valiantly, kicking and thrashing against the overwhelming tide of bodies. The infected held her down, binding her hands and feet with rough ropes, intent on bringing her to Communion rather than killing her.

Neil's eyes burned with fury and fear, but he forced himself to focus. Together with Noah, he sprinted toward the communications tower, the ocean of people closing in around them.

As they reached the base of the tower, the crowd surged even more fiercely. Noah and Neil began climbing, their fingers slipping on the wet metal rungs. Neil climbed ahead, his mind laser-focused on reaching the jammer's frequency generator.

"Noah, hurry!" Neil shouted, glancing down as he continued to ascend.

Noah fought off attackers who tried to pull him down, hands grabbing his boots as the infected climbed after them. But the sheer number of followers was too much. More and more hands grabbed Noah's legs, arms, and shoulders, dragging him away from the tower.

"Noah!" Neil cried, panic rising in his chest.

"Get to the jammer!" Noah roared as he was pulled down into the throng, swallowed whole, his body disappearing into the mass of people.

Neil's heart pounded as he scrambled up the tower, his fingers raw from the climb. The infected scaled the tower after him, their relentless pursuit driving him to move faster. He reached the frequency generator, breaking open the box with trembling hands.

With almost the whole of Eden climbing up toward him, Neil worked frantically, pulling out wires and adjusting the PLL. His fingers moved with practiced skill, but time was running out. Hands reached for him, clawing at his legs and arms, Neil kicking back.

"Come on, come on," he muttered, yanking out more wires and switching fuses. He fought against those pulling him away, reaching for the final wires, his fingers brushing against them just as the hands dragged him back. He turned to his attackers, batting them off with his ebbing strength, and, then, with a last desperate effort, he snapped the wires together. The signal went out, a powerful pulse radiating from the tower.

Instantly, the followers released their grip on Jenny, Noah, and Neil, dropping to the ground in convulsions, those climbing the tower falling away. The streets of Eden were filled with writhing bodies, their movements erratic and disjointed. Then, as quickly as it began, the movement ceased. Silence fell over the town, broken only by the distant rumble of thunder.

Neil collapsed against the tower, his breath coming in ragged gasps. He had done it. The signal had disrupted Palmer's control.

Jenny, freed from her bonds, staggered to her feet, her eyes wide with relief. She looked around, spotting Neil high up on the tower, and gave a weak wave.

Noah, shaking off the hands that had dragged him down, stood among the fallen.

"We did it," Neil whispered to himself. "We actually did it."

SIXTY-TWO

THE OPERATIONS ROOM AT KIRTLAND BUZZED with a rabid energy. Allison, Doc Parker, and Molly stood around the central console, their eyes glued to the monitors displaying the movements of the three nuclear submarines.

"They're going into attack mode," Doc Parker said.

"They're running their jammers," Molly added.

The submarines disappeared from the screens, a typical maneuver for nuclear subs about to attack. The room fell silent, everyone holding their breath as they tried to anticipate the next move.

"We can't risk losing more people than we should." Molly said, her voice shaking slightly. "Do we get the extraction team out of there?"

Doc Parker's face was lined with worry. "If we pull them out now, we might save them. But if we do, we lose any chance of extracting Palmer or saving Noah and the others."

"This is real bad," Molly continued, glancing at Allison. "What do we do?"

Allison felt the weight of the world pressing down on her, slowly squashing her to pulp. Her mind raced as she tried to think of a solution, but nothing except a despairing blankness came back to her. So instead of answering Molly, Allison made her excuses and stepped out of the room, her heart pounding.

The second she was out of the building, she took out her phone, dialing a number with trembling fingers.

Seven answered on the first ring. "You said three days," Allison said the second he did, her voice sharp with anxiety.

"And it's almost been three days," came Seven's cool reply.

"No, it hasn't," Allison snapped back. "It was less than two days ago when we met."

"Yes. But it's three days since Noah and the others arrived on Sumba," Seven replied calmly. "That is the three days I meant. And those end in a matter of minutes. I do like to be precise with these things."

"Give him time!" Allison demanded, her voice rising.

"He still has time. Seventeen minutes, to be exact."

Allison felt a surge of helplessness and anger. "This isn't a game, Seven!"

"I am well aware of that, Eleven," Seven replied, his voice infuriatingly composed. "But precision is key. Trust in the process."

Allison took a deep breath, trying to steady herself. "Just make sure they have the time they need."

"Of course. I never intended otherwise. Seventeen minutes, Eleven. Let's hope he makes them count."

———

NOAH, Jenny, and Neil moved cautiously through a field of disoriented people, their once-synchronized movements now erratic and confused. The disruption caused by the modified jammer had severed their connection to the hive mind and the Mindweaver program, leaving them adrift.

"We need to stay alert," Noah whispered. "They might still be dangerous."

Jenny nodded, gripping the Benelli shotgun tightly, even though it was out of ammunition. Neil kept close, his body steeled, ready for any sudden threats.

They moved up the steps to Pura Luhar, the temple towering over them. The vine-ridden, greened stone was littered with stunned, aimless men and women. Just moments ago, these same people had been relentlessly pursuing them. The shift was jarring, the eerie quiet adding to their unease as they approached the entrance to Dr. Anthony Palmer's lab.

Inside, the temple felt even more unsettling. The once-bustling hub of activity was now only filled with the occasional mutterings of disoriented lab technicians and assistants. Some wandered aimlessly, while others lay on the ground, all of them trapped in a fugue state.

Noah, Neil, and Jenny hoped to free them entirely. All they needed to do was find Palmer.

"Almost there," Noah murmured, leading the way through the dimly lit corridors.

As they ventured deeper into the temple, they finally reached Palmer's main lab—the heart of Eden. The room was filled with advanced equipment, screens displaying complex data, and various scientific instruments.

At the center of it all, Dr. Anthony Palmer sat in his wheelchair, his eyes filled with a spiteful rage.

"Welcome," he said in a voice dripping with venom. "I see you've managed to disrupt my work. But you won't stop it."

Noah stepped forward, his expression hard. "It's over, Palmer. Your control is broken. We've freed your followers."

Palmer's lips curled into a bitter smile. "They're not free. Merely stunned until I fix the connection. Only I have the means to release them permanently."

"Then I suggest you do that," Noah said, stepping forward, a fist curled at his side.

Instead of complying, Palmer merely smiled. It was an unsettling sight.

Just as Noah took another step forward, a massive figure emerged from behind the dry heat sterilization oven. Brennan Krol, an imposing seven-and-a-half-foot, 600-pound giant, a mountain of rippled muscle, stepped between them and Palmer, blocking their path to both the scientist and the servers running Mindweaver.

"Krol isn't connected to the same system as the others," Palmer said with a smug look. "He's the prototype. On an entirely different system altogether."

The three of them had no other choice. They squared off against Krol, their muscles tensing as the giant advanced with slow, deliberate steps.

"Get ready," Noah muttered, his fists tightening.

———

ALLISON RETURNED to the operations room, her heart pounding in her chest. Coming through the door, she found Doc Parker standing at the console, his voice tense as he spoke into the microphone.

"Extraction team, this is an order. Get the boat as far away from the island as you can. Do not wait. Repeat, do not wait. Get clear immediately."

Allison's eyes widened in shock. She rushed over, snatching the microphone from Doc Parker's hand. "Belay that order!" she commanded. "Under no circumstances are you to leave the area. Stay in position."

The room fell silent, everyone staring at Allison. Doc Parker opened his mouth to protest, but Allison cut him off with a fierce glare.

"He'll make it off the island," she said. "We have to trust him."

Doc Parker and Molly exchanged uneasy glances but said nothing. The tension in the room was palpable, everyone turning their eyes to the screens, hoping for any sign of Noah and the team.

Allison discreetly checked her watch, noting the count-down. It was already down to fourteen minutes. Each second ticked by with agonizing slowness, the moment pressing in on her and everyone around her. They were like the crew of a submarine trapped at the bottom of an abyss, being slowly crushed by the water pressure.

———

KROL LUNGED, his massive fist swinging at Noah like a wrecking ball. Noah ducked and rolled to the side, barely avoiding the crushing blow. Jenny swung the empty Benelli at the back of Krol's knees, but the giant barely flinched as it crashed against him.

In fact, Jenny felt more pain coming back up her arms than the giant did in his joints.

Neil circled around, looking for an opening. He grabbed a metal tray from a nearby table and flung it at Krol's head, hoping to distract him. The tray clanged off Krol's skull, and the giant turned his attention to Neil with a low growl.

"Spread out!" Noah shouted.

Krol charged at Neil, but Jenny intercepted him, swinging the butt of the shotgun into Krol's ribcage. The blow landed with a dull thud, but Krol swatted Jenny away with a backhanded strike, sending her sprawling across the lab floor.

Noah found himself at the open door of the dry heat sterilization oven. Just inside was a shelved cart with various metal implements ready for sterilization. On it, Noah found a scalpel.

He seized the moment, darting in to slash at Krol's Achilles tendon with the knife just as the giant was cornering Neil. The blade cut deep, and Krol roared in pain, his massive frame staggering slightly. Neil took advantage of the distraction, grabbing a fire extinguisher from the wall and spraying it directly into Krol's face.

The foam blinded Krol momentarily, and Jenny scrambled back to her feet, grabbing a heavy metal pipe from a workbench. She swung it at Krol's head with all her strength, the impact causing the giant to stumble backward.

"Now!" Noah shouted. "Get him to the oven!"

They coordinated their attacks, driving Krol back

toward the dry heat sterilization oven. Neil swung the fire extinguisher at Krol's midsection while Jenny struck at his legs and Noah slashed at any exposed flesh he could reach. The giant roared and thrashed, but the combined assault was too much.

Step by step, they forced Krol back until he was standing in front of the oven. With a final coordinated effort, Noah kicked Krol's legs to destabilize him, and Jenny and Neil shoved him into the open oven. The giant tumbled inside, his massive frame barely fitting into the confined space.

"Close it!" Neil yelled, and they slammed the heavy door shut.

Krol pounded on the inside of the oven, his fists denting the metal as he tried to break free. Noah reached for the control panel, his fingers flying over the buttons.

"Are you sure about this?" Jenny asked, her voice strained.

Noah nodded grimly. "It's the only way."

He activated the oven, and the machine roared to life, the dry heat rapidly increasing in temperature. Krol's pounding grew more frantic, but the reinforced door held firm.

The lab filled with the sound of the oven's machinery and the muffled roars of Krol inside. The three of them stood back, their breathing heavy and their bodies bruised but victorious.

SIXTY-THREE

Like Krol, Renée remained perfectly under the control of Mindweaver. She sat in the plush leather seat of the Gulfstream G450, staring out of the window, watching the clouds pass by as the plane soared through the sky. The case was beside her, a hand clutching its handle, keeping it secure.

The intercom crackled to life, and the captain's voice filled the cabin. "For those onboard, this is your captain speaking. We will be landing in Kirtland in approximately fifteen minutes. Please fasten your seatbelts and prepare for our descent."

As Renée clicked her seatbelt into place, she glanced at the case once more, knowing inwardly that it held horror and the end of the world but being absolutely powerless to stop the urge to unleash it.

SIXTY-FOUR

NOAH, NEIL, AND JENNY STOOD IN FRONT OF THE massive servers, their hearts pounding, muscles straining from the recent battle. The sounds of Krol trying to beat his way out of the oven had finally ceased, leaving an eerie silence in its wake—as well as the stench of burned flesh.

Dr. Anthony Palmer was now their prisoner. He lay on the floor in the background, his hands bound behind his back with cables they'd ripped from one of the computers.

Before them, the servers loomed like mechanical giants —interwoven cables snaking around cooling units, fans whirring softly and terminals blinking with cold, indifferent light. They took up half the room, a testament to the amount of storage needed to keep thousands of people under control.

"Where do we even start?" Neil asked.

Jenny didn't hesitate. She picked up a metal chair and charged at the nearest server. The impact of the chair against the metal casing reverberated through the room, a satisfying crunch that spurred the others into action.

"Just smash everything!" Jenny shouted.

Neil nodded and began ripping up cables, the wires snapping and sparking as he tore them from their connections. Noah spotted an emergency fire axe mounted on the wall and grabbed it. He swung it with force, the blade biting deep into the metal and plastic, sending shards flying.

The room was filled with the sounds of destruction. Metal clanged against metal, wires snapped and crackled, and the servers' hum turned into a high-pitched whine as they began to fail.

On the floor, Palmer watched them with a twisted smile, his eyes gleaming with malevolent amusement. Despite his position, he seemed entirely at ease, his laughter cutting through the cacophony.

"You think I don't know about the three nuclear submarines?" Palmer called out, his voice drowned out by their noise.

Unable to hear him over the chaos they were creating, the others continued their frenzied assault on the servers.

Palmer's laughter grew louder. "You don't think I have a plan for that, too? Oh, and by the way, those servers only attend to Sumba. They have nothing to do with those operating outside the island."

His words were lost in the din, the trio too focused on their task to notice his taunts. Palmer's laughter continued to echo through the room, a chilling sound that mocked their efforts.

———

ALLISON NERVOUSLY CHECKED HER WATCH, her pulse quickening as she saw the time. The countdown was down to the last few minutes. Her hands trembled, and a cold sweat broke out on her forehead. The reality of the situation settled over her like a suffocating weight. This was probably it.

"OK," she said, her voice barely more than a whisper. Clearing her throat, she forced herself to speak more clearly. "Get the extraction team out of there."

Doc Parker nodded. He picked up the microphone. "Extraction team, this is Parker. Pull out immediately. Get clear of the island. I repeat, get clear of the island."

Allison stood there, her whole body shaking. The room closed in around her, the murmurs of the equipment and the people around her fading into a distant hum. She stared at the screens, the images of Sumba blurring as tears welled up in her eyes. The thought that Noah Wolf and the others were likely dead was almost too much to bear.

Doc Parker turned to her. "Allison..."

She shook her head, unable to speak. She felt the crushing pressure of her recent choices and was struggling to keep her composure. The extraction team's boat began to pull away from the island.

Molly placed a comforting hand on Allison's shoulder. "We did everything we could."

Allison nodded, but the words offered little comfort. She felt a deep, gnawing pain in her chest, a hollow emptiness that seemed to grow with each passing second. The clock continued to tick down, each moment dragging them closer to the end.

As they smashed the servers, Palmer's laughter turned into desperate shouts. "If you destroy those servers, you'll kill them all!"

The three of them paused, turning to face the scientist. His eyes were wide with gravity.

"What do you mean?" Noah demanded, stepping closer.

"Just what I said. Most of what you've destroyed already is no more than spare storage. Nothing to do with the people here. But if you finish the job, destroy the whole thing, and sever them like that, you'll be killing them," Palmer insisted.

Noah marched over to him, lifting him by the scruff of his shirt. "How do we stop it?" he growled.

Palmer's lips curled into a bitter smile. "By ending the program and ejecting the parasite. It will hurt them, but it's fairly harmless in the long run."

"Then how do we do that?" Noah growled.

Palmer's smile widened slightly. "Do you know something, Noah Wolf?"

"We haven't got time for this. How do we shut it off?"

But Palmer wasn't listening. "We're after the same thing, you and I."

"And what is that?" Noah asked, his grip tightening.

"The Council. We both want an end to them," Palmer replied.

Noah's eyes narrowed. "What happened between you and them?"

Palmer's eyes went blank as he whispered, "They took the last of my humanity away."

It was then that Noah spotted a framed photograph sitting on one of the desks. He picked it up and held it in front of Palmer. The picture showed a woman and a teenage girl. Palmer gazed at it, tears welling in his eyes.

"That's your family?" Noah asked, his voice softening.

Palmer looked at him from the picture, his eyes red. He nodded. "The Council took them," he spat bitterly.

"Then come with me. Help us at E & E. End this nightmare here on Sumba and come help fight the Council for good, not evil."

Palmer looked at the photo again, his eyes reflecting a blend of sorrow and resolve. He nodded again. "Get me to a terminal."

Noah placed Palmer at a terminal. The doctor's fingers flew over the keyboard. As he initiated the program to end Mindweaver on the island, the screens lit up with diagnostic data and progress bars.

"This will end it," Palmer said quietly, his eyes fixed on the screen.

The program executed, sending a signal throughout Sumba. Almost immediately, the parasites began to eject themselves from their hosts. The people jerked in pain as the parasites emerged from their ear canals, the nematodes dropping to the ground and writhing in their dying throes. The sight was horrifying, the parasites' slick, pale bodies squirming on the ground, leaving their human hosts gasping for breath and clutching their heads.

In the streets of Eden, Marco lay beside the bulldozer bucket, the parasite sliding out of his ear and wriggling away, his body convulsing from the pain before going still, his breathing becoming more even.

Detective Antara, who had gone through communion not long after capture, dropped to his knees as the parasite left his body. He gasped, clutching at his ear as the worm emerged, the pain etched on his face turning to relief as the control over him was severed.

Damu and Kiya, huddled together in a corner of the village, experienced the same agonizing release. The parasites exited their bodies, and they clung to each other, tears of pain and relief mingling as they realized they were free.

Throughout the island, people collapsed as the parasites were expelled, the ground littered with the writhing creatures. The once synchronized movements of the infected gave way to disordered chaos, but it was the chaos of freedom, the first steps toward reclaiming their lives.

In the lab, Palmer watched the screens as the program completed its execution. He slumped back in his chair.

"It's done," he said quietly.

Noah placed a hand on Palmer's shoulder. "Thank you," he said. "Now. Do you think you can switch that jammer off?"

———

ALLISON STARED INTENTLY at her watch, the numbers on the countdown clocking into the final two minutes. The others had their eyes glued to the screen, the tension in the room almost suffocating.

Suddenly, the piercing ring of an incoming call broke the silence. The operator, glancing over his shoulder with an expression of disbelief and joy, turned to Allison. "It's Noah Wolf, ma'am," he said, a huge smile spreading across his face.

"Patch him through," Allison commanded, her heart leaping in her chest.

Noah's voice filled the room, strong and clear. "I'm en route with our good friend the doctor. Is the extraction team in place off Lalindi?"

Molly Hanson couldn't contain her emotions and hugged a blushing and rather flustered Doc Parker, who returned the gesture awkwardly but warmly.

Allison, tears of relief welling in her eyes, answered, "Not at the moment, but we can get it back there. It's only a few minutes away."

Molly, her voice trembling, interjected, "But you need to be quick, Noah. There's..."

Allison stopped her with a shake of her head, signaling to keep the crucial information under wraps. "You need to be quick," she repeated to Noah, her voice steady. "Time is of the essence. The extraction team will be waiting at the harbor. What's your ETA?"

"ETA less than an hour. We've commandeered a chopper."

Allison's heart pounded with hope. "We? Does that mean that the others are with you?"

There was a brief pause before Noah's voice, tinged with sadness, replied, "No. We've lost Renée. But everyone else is present."

Everyone in the operations room exchanged looks of concern.

"Do you have an idea where she could be?" Allison asked.

"Marco is sure she's not on the island," Noah replied.

"He saw her leave in a helicopter. She was due to go to Sumatra. We'll get Palmer out, then head that way."

Allison checked her watch again; the countdown was entering the final minute. She took a deep breath, focusing on the task at hand. "Look, get yourself to Lalindi. Godspeed."

She nodded at the operator, who ended the call.

"Why didn't you tell him about the nukes?" Molly asked.

Allison waved her away, a determined look on her face. She left the room briskly and, once outside the door, pulled out her phone. Dialing quickly, she brought it to her ear. "Stop them!" she snapped into the phone. "Stop the submarines. He's got him."

Seven's voice, calm and slightly amused, came through the line. "Ooh, and with seconds to spare, too. Good. I'll give you instructions later on for Palmer's handover."

The call ended abruptly, leaving Allison standing in the hallway, her heart pounding. She took a few moments to compose herself, leaning against the wall as she felt her body trembling. Her hands were shaking uncontrollably. The weight of her double agent role, the near loss of Noah, and the immense pressure of their mission were almost too much to bear. She reached into her pocket, fumbling for the small bottle of pills she kept for moments like this. Her fingers managed to unscrew the cap, and she quickly popped a few into her mouth, swallowing them dry.

Taking a deep breath, she willed herself to steady. It had to be done. It was the only way. She couldn't afford to fall apart now.

After a few more deep breaths, Allison straightened her posture and returned to the operations room. Molly and Doc Parker looked up as she entered, relief evident on their faces.

"Allison," Doc Parker said. "The submarines—they've switched their jammers off and are leaving the area."

Molly nodded, a hint of a smile on her lips. "It looks like the immediate threat is over."

Allison allowed herself a second of relief. "Good. That's one less thing to worry about."

Just then, one of the operators looked up from his console, his expression puzzled. "We're getting a call from someone claiming to be Renée Turin."

Allison's heart skipped a beat. "Patch her through," she said.

The operator nodded and made the connection. A moment later, Renée's voice came through the speakers.

"Hello, this is Renée."

Allison, Molly, and Doc Parker exchanged shocked glances.

"Renée," Allison said, stepping closer to the microphone. "Where are you? We thought you were in Sumatra."

"Sumatra? No, I'm not in Sumatra," Renée replied. "I've just arrived at Kirtland. I need to meet you all at R&D. I have something very important to show you."

Molly's eyes widened. "You're at Kirtland? Right now?"

"Yes," Renée confirmed. "Please, it's urgent. I'll explain everything when we meet."

"All right, Renée," Allison said. "We'll meet you at R&D immediately."

The call ended, and Allison turned to the others. "Doc, you stay here, keep liaising with Noah. Molly, you come with me. Let's see what Renée has."

SIXTY-FIVE

THE CHINOOK HELICOPTER ROARED THROUGH THE sky, its massive blades slicing through the air with relentless force. Jenny sat at the controls, her focus intense as she piloted the craft. Beside her in the co-pilot's seat, Neil monitored the instruments, making sure everything was running smoothly.

In the back, Noah sat with Marco and Dr. Anthony Palmer. The doctor was strapped into his seat, his hands bound, his glazed eyes staring off into the distance. A half-smile played on his lips, as if he knew something they didn't.

Noah leaned over to check on Marco, who was rubbing his temple with a pained expression. "You good, buddy?"

Marco looked up, managing a weak grin. "My head really hurts, boss man," he replied. "Did you really have to hit me so hard with that piece of wood?"

Noah chuckled softly. "You were trying to kill me. You understand that, right?"

Marco's smile faded, replaced by a look of sadness.

Noah noticed the shift and gently probed. "What was it like?"

Marco shook his head slowly. "It was insane. I knew I was just doing someone else's will, but I couldn't stop it. And do you know what?"

Noah shook his head.

"I didn't want to stop."

"What do you mean?" Noah asked, leaning closer.

Marco met his gaze, his eyes haunted. "I didn't want to stop because it felt good. Felt good to do as I was told, to do his will. It was like I was being rewarded with this feeling of peace. That I didn't have to worry anymore. Everything would be fine so long as I complied. And do you know what the worst thing is?"

"What?" Noah asked.

Marco's eyes shone with an unsettling light. "The worst thing is I really wanted to kill you out there. Felt it with every part of me. Isn't that insane?"

Noah and Marco stared at each other, the weight of Marco's words hanging between them. Noah was about to respond when Palmer's voice cut through the tension.

"No, Marco, it isn't insane," the scientist said, his tone matter-of-fact. "It is the warm safety of the herd. Of belonging to something much bigger than oneself. Of being guided by the unseen hand. You feel colder now, don't you?"

Marco shivered involuntarily, the truth of Palmer's words resonating deeply.

"Colder now that you're out on your own," Palmer continued, his voice almost soothing.

"Shut up," Noah snapped, his eyes flashing with anger.

He turned his attention back to Marco, his expression softening. "You're free now, Marco. That's what matters."

The flight continued in tense silence, the coastline gradually coming into view. Jenny adjusted their course slightly, her eyes fixed on the horizon.

"We're almost there," Neil called into the back. "Should be at the extraction point in a few minutes."

Noah nodded, grateful for the progress. He glanced at Palmer, who still wore that infuriating half-smile. "You're going to answer for everything you've done," he said quietly.

Palmer's smile widened, but he said nothing. The coastline grew clearer, and the helicopter began its descent.

"Get ready," Jenny called out. "We'll be on the ground soon."

Noah tightened his grip on Marco's shoulder. "Stay strong, buddy. We're almost home."

———

The front of the R&D facility was a hive of activity as Renée pulled up in her car, having retrieved it from the airport. Allison and Molly stood at the entrance to the science labs, their expressions tight, bodies filled with anticipation. As Renée got out of her car, carrying the metal case, both women rushed forward.

"Renée, thank God you're here!" Allison said. "What's going on? Why aren't you with Noah and the others?"

Molly joined in, her voice edged with worry. "Are you OK? We've been getting fragmented updates. Noah said that you'd been taken."

Renée took a deep breath, steadying herself. "There isn't

enough time to explain," she began. "What I hold in this case is much more important. We need to get inside a lab so I can show it to you."

The gravity in Renée's voice left no room for further questions. Allison and Molly exchanged a glance, then nodded.

"All right, let's go," Allison said, leading the way into the R&D building.

———

THE CHINOOK HELICOPTER touched down on the edge of a small marina on the outskirts of Lalindi, Sumba. The blades continued to spin, kicking up a whirlwind of dust and debris. Jenny powered down the engines while Neil and Noah unstrapped Dr. Anthony Palmer from his seat. The scientist remained eerily calm, his half-smile never wavering.

"Let's get him off," Noah shouted over the dying roar of the engines.

Neil nodded, and together they lifted the paraplegic scientist, carrying him between them as they moved toward the waiting boat. The leader of the extraction team, a tall, muscular man named Captain Harris, stood at the dock.

"Good to see you made it," Harris called out as they neared. "We've got everything ready to go."

"Thanks, Captain," Noah replied. "Let's get him loaded up."

They carefully took Palmer into the boat, strapping him securely to one of the seats. The doctor remained calm the whole time, his expression serene.

Captain Harris glanced at Palmer and then back at Noah. "Is he sedated or something?"

"No," Neil said, shaking his head. "He's just... resigned, I guess."

Jenny leaned into Noah, her voice low. "You get the impression he's just a little too calm?"

Noah frowned. "What do you mean?"

"Like this is all part of some plan. I mean, we just busted down his whole enterprise. You'd expect him to be pissed," Jenny explained.

"And where's Renée?" Marco added, rubbing his still aching head.

Noah looked at Palmer, who met his gaze with that same enigmatic smile. "We'll figure it out. For now, let's just get off this island."

The boat, a Cranchi Z35 powerboat designed for speed, was ready. The extraction team finished their final preparations as Noah, Neil, Jenny, and Marco took their seats.

Captain Harris took the wheel. "Everyone secure?"

"Yeah," Noah confirmed. "Let's go."

The engines roared to life, and the boat shot forward, cutting across the ocean toward Bali, Sumba gradually fading behind them. The nightmare was over. For now.

———

THE STERILE WHITE walls of R&D's lab gleamed under the fluorescent lights as Renée, Molly, and Allison gathered around a gurney. Renée placed the metal case on the surface with a clink.

She then opened it, revealing ten incubated and writhing

specimens. She carefully extracted one of the containers, holding it up for the others to see.

"What is it?" Molly asked.

"It's a nematode," Renée replied, opening the container that held the parasite.

"Should you be doing that?" Allison asked, her tone laced with concern.

Renée gently lifted the nematode from the container, the worm playing between her fingers. "It's OK," she said reassuringly. "It's perfectly harmless."

She held the nematode up for them to see, its pale, wriggling form stretching out as if sensing its surroundings. Molly leaned forward, fascinated despite herself. The nematode seemed to react to her proximity, elongating and moving toward her.

"Molly, be careful," Allison warned, an uneasy feeling creeping up her spine.

In an instant, Renée's demeanor shifted. With a swift motion, she grabbed Molly and forced the nematode toward her ear. The parasite latched on immediately, its tiny, gripping mouthparts burrowing into Molly's ear canal.

"Molly, no!" Allison cried out, horror and disbelief mixing in her voice as she watched her struggle.

Molly's hands flew to her ear, her face contorting in pain and fear as the parasite sank deeper. Renée turned to Allison, her expression cold and determined. Allison backed up toward the door, her heart pounding.

"Renée, what are you doing?" Allison demanded.

Renée advanced on her, her movements swift and purposeful. Allison made a dash for the alarm by the door, but Renée, much younger and fitter, beat her to it. She grabbed Allison, subduing her with ease.

As Allison struggled against Renée's grip, she looked over to see Molly standing still, her eyes glazed over with a blank expression. The transformation had been swift and unsettling.

"Take one of the other ones from the case," Renée instructed Molly as she held Allison. "And bring it over."

Molly, now under the parasite's control, moved mechanically to the case. She reached in and extracted another nematode, its writhing form held delicately between her fingers.

Allison's struggles intensified, panic surging through her veins. "Molly, don't! Fight it!" she pleaded, her voice desperate.

But Molly moved with the eerie precision of someone no longer in control of their own body. She approached slowly, the parasite extending toward Allison.

"No! Please, don't do this!" Allison cried, her voice breaking.

Renée tightened her grip, holding Allison firmly on the floor. Molly knelt beside them, the nematode wriggling eagerly in her hand.

————

THE BOAT SPED across the calm waters, the sun lowering in the sky and casting a golden glow over the waves. The storm clouds had all but disappeared, leaving a tranquil scene in their wake. Noah sat opposite Dr. Anthony Palmer, who was securely strapped to his seat. The rhythmic hum of the powerful engines filled the silence between them.

"You know, Noah Wolf," Palmer said, breaking the silence, "I've heard so much about you. An apex killer, they say. And as a scientist, it is always good to meet nature's best examples. Of course, seeing you in action, I can only say that your tenacious reputation is not understated."

Noah met Palmer's gaze, his expression unreadable. "I'm not sure if I should feel flattered about that."

Palmer gave another of his half-smiles, his eyes drifting to the horizon where the sun's rays danced on the water. "Your boss is Allison Peterson, isn't she?"

"Yes," Noah replied, his voice steady.

"The Dragon Lady," Palmer said, turning back to Noah, his cold blue eyes glinting in the sunset. The look sent a shiver down Noah's spine, but he remained silent.

Still staring right at Noah, Palmer asked, "Do you ever wonder what they did with her those three months they had her?" His words hung in the air, heavy and loaded with implications before he turned back to the view.

THE DOOR to the lab burst open, and Wally Lawson stormed in, flanked by two armed security guards. Allison was just getting up from the ground, dusting herself off. Renée and Molly stood on either side of her, their faces tense.

Wally looked from one to the next, his eyes wide with concern. "Esmeralda alerted me. On the surveillance cameras, you were fighting."

Allison forced a smile, trying to appear calm. "A slight disagreement between ladies," she said smoothly.

"It looked like a lot more than that," Wally countered. "They were holding you down."

In the background, Molly quietly packed up the case containing the parasites.

"It's OK," Allison repeated, her tone soothing. "It's been a hard day."

Wally's gaze shifted to Renée and Molly. "Renée, aren't you supposed to be in Sumba? And Ms. Hanson, you've got blood coming out of your ear."

Molly touched her ear, feeling the dampness there. "A little too eager with cleaning them," she said, offering a weak smile.

Allison stepped forward, laying a reassuring hand on Wally's shoulder. "It's OK, Wally. We're OK."

Wally frowned, clearly not convinced. "Are you sure? This doesn't seem right."

Allison's grip tightened slightly. "Trust me. It's under control."

———

THE BOAT JOURNEY was long—five hours and bumpy. They were now at Denpasar airport. The Boeing C-17 Globemaster III loomed large on the tarmac, its cargo ramp lowered and ready for boarding. Noah, Jenny, Neil, and Marco moved quickly across the tarmac. The extraction team followed closely, Captain Harris pushing the bound Dr. Anthony Palmer in a wheelchair.

As they climbed into the cavernous interior of the C-17, one of the pilots approached Noah, a satellite phone in his hand. "This is for you," he said, handing over the device.

Noah took the phone, pressing it to his ear. "Noah here."

Allison's voice came through, clear and steady. "Noah, just to let you know, Renée is back."

"Where was she?" Noah asked, his eyes narrowing as he glanced over at Palmer, who was being secured to a seat by the extraction team.

"She was on her way back to Kirtland when the parasite ejected from her," Allison explained. "It happened in mid-flight."

"Is she OK?"

"She will be," Allison assured him. "It's a lot to process, but she's stable now."

"Can Marco speak with her?" Noah asked, looking over at Marco, who was rubbing his head, still recovering from his own ordeal.

"Not at the moment," Allison replied. "Just get back to Kirtland. We'll debrief then."

The entire time Noah spoke, Palmer sat watching him with a cold, calculating gaze. The scientist's eyes never left Noah, as if he were studying him, measuring him.

"See you soon, Allison," Noah said, ending the call.

He handed the satellite phone back to the pilot and took a deep breath, trying to shake off the unsettling feeling that Palmer's stare gave him. He walked over to Marco, placing a reassuring hand on his shoulder. "Renée's back. She's safe."

Marco managed a weak smile. "That's so good to hear," he breathed.

The engines of the C-17 began to hum, growing louder as they prepared for takeoff. The extraction team made final checks, securing the cargo and ensuring that everyone was strapped in. Noah took a seat across from Palmer, meeting the scientist's icy gaze with one of his own.

Noah leaned forward. "Renée was on her way to Kirtland," he said. "You wanted to take us over?"

Palmer tilted his head slightly, raising his shackled hands with a nonchalant gesture. "Guilty as charged," he replied, his tone almost playful. "But of course, you quashed that when you made me stop the program. So que sera sera."

The words hung in the air, and Palmer turned away, his eyes drifting off into the distance as if lost in thought. The half-smile returned to his lips, but it held no warmth, only a sense of resigned amusement.

Noah felt a shiver run down his spine. There was something deeply unsettling about Palmer's demeanor, as if the scientist still held cards they didn't yet know about.

SIXTY-SIX

ALMOST SEVENTEEN HOURS LATER, THE BOEING C-17 Globemaster III touched down at Kirtland Airport. It was early morning, and the Colorado air was crisp with a noticeable chill. The mountains gleamed in the background, as though cloaked in fire by the first light of dawn. The aircraft came to a halt, and the ramp lowered, revealing the figures of Noah, Jenny, Neil, Marco, and Dr. Anthony Palmer in his wheelchair.

Waiting at the bottom of the ramp were Allison, Molly, and Renée, their faces marked with both relief and anticipation. Jenny and Neil, visibly exhausted, clung to each other for support, their steps faltering slightly from the epic battle they had endured. Marco, his head bandaged and looking sheepish, descended the ramp, his eyes lighting up as he saw his wife waiting for him.

Renée rushed forward, wrapping her arms around him. "You OK, baby?" she asked, her voice filled with concern.

"I think so," Marco replied, his relief evident as he held her close.

Renée's gaze shifted to Palmer, who was being wheeled off the plane by Noah. Her eyes blazed with hatred. "And that's the bastard that had us calling him Lord," she spat venomously.

"Come on," Marco said softly. "Let's just get home."

Noah wheeled Palmer over to Allison, who stood with an unreadable expression on her face. Palmer's cold blue eyes met hers, and he smirked.

"Dragon Lady," Palmer said mockingly. "We meet at last."

"We do," Allison replied blankly before turning to Captain Harris and his team. "Take him to the cells. After that, he's going to Guantanamo."

Noah frowned, stepping forward. "What? I thought he was going to stay here with us. He knows things. Has access to things. He can be useful."

"I'm afraid President Brown has insisted we hand him straight over. The CIA has their own plans for him."

Noah turned to Palmer, who was smiling smugly from his wheelchair. Captain Harris began to wheel him away, but Noah couldn't shake the feeling of unease growing in his gut.

"You did a good job, Noah," Allison said, placing a hand on his shoulder. "But the CIA are more equipped to get the information we need from him."

"But he's more than just intel," Noah argued. "The guy's a genius. An evil one, granted, but still a genius. He could be invaluable for R&D. We should have him working with Wally, utilizing every weapon against the Council. And he hates the Council. They killed his family."

Allison squeezed his shoulder, giving him an earnest look. "But he's also insane, Noah. The type of work Palmer is into is not the sort of thing we need."

Noah sighed, knowing she was right but still feeling conflicted. He watched as the extraction team loaded Palmer into the back of a minivan.

Just then, Jenny and Neil approached, practically holding each other up. They had slept most of the ride, and Noah didn't blame them. Their exhaustion was evident in their limping steps and bleary eyes.

"We're gonna head home," Neil said, his voice hoarse. "Get showered, get some Vicodin, and get some more sleep."

"Sure," Noah said, managing a small smile. "We'll do the debrief tomorrow."

Neil nodded, and he and Jenny made their way to their car, their bodies visibly sagging with relief at the thought of rest.

"Go see Sarah and Norah," Allison told him gently. "We'll settle up here. You did well out there. Go see your family."

She smiled at him before walking away. Molly came over and hugged him tightly. "Good to have you back, Noah," she said warmly before joining Allison.

Noah stood there for a moment, watching as the extraction team finished securing Palmer. The minivan's ramp lifted, and Palmer's eyes met his one last time, the same smug smile playing on his lips.

SIXTY-SEVEN

Noah drove along the familiar winding road to his home. As he pulled into the driveway, the sight of the cozy farmhouse reflected on the waves of Temple Lake brought a wave of relief that washed over him.

As he stepped through the door, the smell of blueberry pancakes wafted through the air, filling his senses with warmth and comfort. He walked into the kitchen to find Sarah at the stove, flipping the pancakes. Norah was perched on a stool at the breakfast bar, swinging her legs back and forth as she waited. That was until she spotted her father standing in the doorway.

"Daddy!" Norah cried out, jumping off the stool and running to him. Noah scooped her up into his arms, holding her tightly.

"Hey, princess," he said. "I missed you so much."

Sarah turned from the stove, a smile lighting up her face. "Welcome home," she said softly, coming over to hug him and Norah together. "I'm so glad you're back."

Noah kissed his wife gently, then set Norah down. While Sarah went back to the pancakes, he took a seat at the breakfast bar, pulling his daughter onto his lap. "So what have you been up to while I was away?" he asked.

Norah's eyes sparkled with excitement. "I made a new friend at school, Daddy! Her name is Emily, and she has a cat named Whiskers. And Mommy and I went to the park, and I got to feed the ducks!"

Noah smiled, listening intently. "That sounds wonderful, sweetheart. Did you and Mommy have lots of fun?"

Norah nodded vigorously. "Yes! And I painted a picture for you. It's in my room! Can you come see it later?"

"Of course," Noah said, his heart swelling with love. "I can't wait."

As he sat there in the warmth of his home, watching Sarah cook pancakes and listening to Norah's cheerful chatter, his thoughts drifted back to the recent horrors he had witnessed. He remembered the infected, their blank eyes and mechanical movements. He thought about Kiya, the little girl Neil and Jenny had told him about. She was the same age as Norah, innocent and full of life, until the parasite took over.

The thought of his own family being taken over by those vile creatures filled him with horror. He imagined Sarah and Norah with those vacant, lifeless eyes, their bodies controlled by some malevolent force. The fear and helplessness he had felt during the mission resurfaced, gripping his heart with icy fingers.

"Noah." Sarah's voice broke through his macabre reverie. She was standing in front of him, holding a plate of blueberry pancakes. She placed it on the counter and lifted his chin with soft fingers, smiling at him. "It's OK," she whispered. "You're home now."

Noah looked into her loving eyes and felt a sense of grounding. He leaned forward, and they kissed, the warmth of her lips melting away the darkness that had crept into his thoughts.

As they kissed, however, a knock at the door interrupted them. Sarah pulled back, a puzzled expression on her face. "I wonder who that could be," she said.

"I'll get it," Noah replied, getting up from his stool. He walked to the door, the peaceful moment with his family still lingering in his mind. When he opened it, he found Wally standing there, his expression grave and worried.

"Wally," Noah greeted him, a sense of foreboding returning. "What's going on?"

"I have to show you something," Wally said, his tone urgent.

MARCO AND RENÉE returned home to their cozy apartment overlooking the center of Kirtland. The events of the past days had left them both exhausted, but being home brought a sense of normalcy. They went straight to their bedroom, shedding their clothes and crawling into bed, holding each other close.

Marco took a sip from a bottle of beer, the cool liquid soothing his parched throat. "It's good to be home," he said. "I can't believe we made it through all that."

Renée nestled closer to him, her head resting on his

chest. "I know," she murmured, her voice soft and warm. "It's a miracle we're here."

They lay in silence for a moment, their experiences casting a heavy shadow upon them. Marco broke the silence. "What was it like for you?" he asked, his tone tentative. "Being infected?"

Renée's eyes closed for a moment, a serene smile spreading across her face. "It was magical," she said, her voice almost dreamy. "To just let go and allow yourself to become something more. It felt like... like being part of a grand design. Everything had a purpose, and all you had to do was follow the path."

Marco's brow furrowed at her words, a sense of unease creeping over him. "But it was horrific, right?" he said, his voice rising slightly. "Having no choice."

Renée opened her eyes and looked up at him, her gaze calm and steady. "It wasn't like that," she said softly. "It felt right. It felt like everything was as it should be."

Marco felt a chill run down him. The warmth in her speech, the calm acceptance, made him suspicious. He finished his beer and gently dislodged himself from her embrace. "I'm going to get another beer," he said.

———

ON HIS DOORSTEP, Noah was just finishing watching the tablet Wally had handed him, the screen displaying security footage from one of R&D's labs. Noah's eyes widened as he watched Allison being held down by Renée and Molly. His heart sank, and a cold dread settled over him as they administered the parasite.

"Oh my God," Noah murmured, his voice barely above a whisper. "We need to find them. Fast."

Noah turned back inside. Sarah was still in the kitchen, Norah at the breakfast bar.

"Sarah," Noah said, his voice steady but urgent. "I need you to take Norah to the safe room. Do not answer any calls from Allison, Renée, or Molly. In fact, just stay in there until I call you."

Sarah's eyes widened with concern. "What's happened?"

"I'm not entirely sure yet," Noah replied, trying to keep his voice calm. "But I think E & E is compromised. Stay in the safe room."

Sarah nodded, her face pale but resolute. She quickly gathered Norah in her arms. "Come on, sweetheart, we're going to play a game in the special room."

Norah looked up with wide, curious eyes. "OK, Mommy."

Noah leaned forward, kissing Sarah on the lips, then his daughter on the top of the head. "I'll be back soon. Just stay safe."

Sarah gave him a brave smile. "We will. Be careful, Noah."

Noah watched as they headed to the safe room, then turned and hurried back to Wally. The urgency of the situation pressed down on him like a physical weight.

"Let's go," Noah said.

Wally nodded, and they quickly made their way to the car.

MARCO WALKED INTO THE KITCHEN, his mind stuck on his wife's odd behavior. Opening the fridge, he reached for another bottle, but something caught his eye. An empty glass container sat on the top shelf, its shape unmistakably similar to the small incubators used for the parasites. His heart skipped a beat, and a sense of dread washed over him.

He turned around to find Renée standing there, her eyes cold and focused. In her hand, she held something that turned Marco's blood to ice. It was one of the long, writhing parasites.

"Renée," Marco whispered, his voice trembling. "What are you doing?"

She stepped forward, her expression blank. "Join me, Marco," she said softly, her voice almost hypnotic. "It's time to become something more than just yourself."

Before he could react, she lunged at him, the parasite poised to strike.

———

NEIL AND JENNY were in a hot tub on their decking, the warm water soothing their tired muscles. They were both high on Vicodin, the tension of the past days melting away in the relaxing bubbles, and drug haze. The sun was setting, casting a warm glow over their peaceful retreat.

Jenny leaned back, her eyes half-closed, a content smile on her lips. "This is heaven," she murmured, the water rippling around her.

Neil nodded, sinking deeper into the water. "We deserve this," he replied, closing his eyes.

Suddenly, the doorbell rang, followed by a fist

hammering at their door. The abrupt intrusion shattered their tranquility.

"Who could that be?" Neil muttered, reluctantly pulling himself out of the hot tub. He wrapped a towel around his waist and went to answer the door, his movements slow and lethargic from the Vicodin.

The second he opened the door, Noah and Wally pushed their way in, grim and urgent looks on their faces.

"We've got trouble," Noah said.

Jenny, still in the hot tub, heard the commotion and climbed out, wrapping a towel around herself. Her eyes glazed over, bubbles still clinging to her skin, she walked into the living room, a lazy smile on her face. "Hey, Noah. How are you?" she drawled, swaying slightly.

"Look," Noah said, showing them the tablet with the footage from the lab.

Neil and Jenny's expressions shifted instantly as they watched the video. The sight of Allison being held down by Renée and Molly snapped them out of their drug-induced haze.

"This isn't good," Neil remarked, his voice suddenly clear and serious.

Jenny's eyes widened, the reality of the situation hitting her hard. "What do we do?" she asked.

Noah's face was set with determination. "We need to get to them before they infect anyone else."

———

"Please, baby, no," Marco pleaded, his voice strained as he struggled to hold Renée off. She had him leaned over the kitchen worktop, her body pressing down on him, his hand gripping her wrist tightly. The parasite writhed violently in her fingers, its movements erratic and terrifying as it reached for him. "Please, baby. I don't want to go back into that. You have to wake up. Please."

For several agonizing minutes, Marco had been wrestling with Renée around their kitchen, trying to figure out how to end this nightmare. But there was no way he could think of that didn't involve severe violence—and how could he knock out the woman he loved, the woman he'd married? He couldn't bring himself to hurt her. All he could do was hold her back.

But under the control of Mindweaver, her strength seemed inexhaustible. He didn't know how much longer he could hold her off. "Please, baby," he pleaded. "Please, wake up. Please—"

There was a loud crash. Just as Renée was about to get the parasite to him, the front door was kicked in. Noah, Neil, Jenny, and Wally rushed in, their faces set with determination.

Noah and Neil grabbed ahold of Renée, pulling her away from Marco. Jenny tore the parasite from her fingers. It immediately wrapped itself around her hand. She looked around frantically for something to kill it, her eyes landing on the microwave.

"Hold on," she muttered, opening the microwave door. She ripped the parasite from her hand, flung it into the microwave, slammed the door shut, and pressed cook. The parasite writhed and squirmed before it finally popped.

Meanwhile, Noah and Neil held Renée down while

Wally administered a sedative. Slowly, her struggles ceased, and she went limp in their arms.

Marco, breathless and shaken, looked down at his unconscious wife. "I thought... you guys switched it off," he said.

"It looks like it was only on Sumba," Noah replied grimly.

"Which means," Neil added, "Palmer must have another server somewhere on US soil, running the program and controlling them."

Noah's expression hardened. "Then we need to get to it." He turned to Wally, his eyes intense. "Wally, do you think you can use Renée to source where the signal is coming from?"

Wally looked down at Renée. "I can try."

"Good," Noah said. "You and Marco take her to the lab."

Marco looked at Noah, his face filled with concern. "What about you guys?"

"We need to get to Allison and Molly," Noah replied.

———

NOAH, Neil, and Jenny arrived at the Kirtland detention unit in Noah's Dodge. Jenny got out of the car a bit unsteadily.

"I still feel a little woozy from the Vicodin," she admitted, rubbing her temples.

"Just stay with me, Jen," Noah said, giving her a reassuring look.

All of them were carrying cognitive harmonizers, the

small devices tucked into their pockets, ready to be used. As they reached the entrance of the detention unit, they noticed the four members of the extraction crew leaving.

"Hey, Noah," the leader, Captain Harris, greeted as they met outside the glass doors. "Jenny, Neil," he added with a nod. "I thought you guys were getting some well-deserved R & R."

"Where's the Dragon Lady?" Noah asked.

"Oh, they're gone. They got a call from Washington. Things were brought forward. She left with Palmer about twenty minutes ago." Harris checked his wristwatch. "Their plane should be leaving Kirtland any moment now."

Right on cue, a Gulfstream roared over their heads, everyone craning their necks to see it glide past.

"There she goes," Harris remarked, pointing skyward.

"Was Molly with her?" Neil asked.

"Oh, yes. The three of them left. We offered our help, but they said they didn't need it. I guess the doc being a paraplegic, he won't give them no trouble."

But Jenny, Neil, and Noah weren't listening. They were already jogging back to the car, their minds reeling with the implications. They jumped into the Dodge, the engine roaring to life as Noah floored the accelerator, the tires screeching against the asphalt as they sped away.

SIXTY-EIGHT

THE LUXURIOUS INTERIOR OF THE GULFSTREAM G450 hummed with a sense of calm and purpose. In the back, Dr. Anthony Palmer reclined in his chair, free from his shackles, his demeanor one of relaxed confidence. Opposite him sat Allison, her face a mask. In another part of the plane, Molly sat facing forward, her expression vacant, locked in the same fugue state that Father Sanchez had once inhabited.

"So they have it right underneath Central Park," Palmer was saying, his tone casual as if discussing a mere trifle.

Allison opened her mouth to reply, but Palmer held up a finger, signaling her to wait as Molly approached.

"Ms. Hanson," Palmer said. "What is it?"

"My Lord," Molly replied in a flat, monotone voice, "Renée has been taken."

Palmer's eyes gleamed with mild amusement. "Our resourceful Mr. Wolf, no doubt. Oh, well. Not to worry. I've gotten a little bored with world domination. Really, all I want is for the end of my former paymasters. So onward with this mission."

Molly nodded and moved away, returning to her seat and the fugue state.

Palmer turned his attention back to Allison. "Now, Number Seven. Where is he?"

"He's in charge of New York," Allison confirmed.

"Well, then, that means that soon we will be in charge of New York," Palmer mused, a hint of a smile playing on his lips. "I shall take them a piece at a time. Just like in chess."

———

INSIDE ONE OF the labs at R&D, Renée lay on a medical bed, her wrists and ankles secured with restraints. Wally and two of his assistants moved around her, dressed in hazmat suits. Advanced monitoring equipment surrounded the bed, ready to track the parasite's activity and Renée's brain function.

In an observation room adjacent to the lab, Noah, Jenny, and Marco watched anxiously. Marco looked terrible, his face pale with worry as he stared at his wife through the glass.

Wally's team was busy setting up the necessary equipment. "We need a full neural scan," he instructed his assistant. "Let's see what we're dealing with."

One of the assistants connected sensors to Renée's head, her movements precise and careful. "Scanners online," she said after a moment. "We're getting readings."

The door to the observation room opened, and Neil entered, his expression stern. Noah and Jenny turned to him immediately.

"They switched their tracking off over Pennsylvania," Neil reported.

"So they never went to Washington, then," Noah pointed out, a frown creasing his brow.

"How is she?" Neil asked, nodding toward the operating theater on the other side of the window.

"As well as can be expected," Jenny replied glumly before turning back to watch the ongoing procedure.

The team in the lab analyzed the initial data, focusing on the parasite's interaction with Renée's brain. Wally's eyes scanned the images on the monitors intently.

"The parasite is integrated deeply," Wally said. "It's manipulating all major brain functions."

Noah pressed the intercom button and spoke into it. "Can you remove it?"

Wally looked up, his expression serious. "We'll need to run a few more tests," he said, "but it's possible. The key will be isolating the parasite's neural pathways and the link with Mindweaver without damaging Renée's brain."

He pointed at the CCT image of the parasite displayed on a nearby screen. "You see the dark spot inside it?" he asked.

It was the nano device that used the parasite as an interface to run Mindweaver.

"Yeah," Noah said.

"Well, inside are tiny communication nodes. If we can disrupt the signal between there and wherever Palmer is controlling it, we might be able to trace its origin. But we'll need more equipment for that."

Noah nodded. "Do whatever you need to. The best way

to get it out of her safely is to find out where he's running it. Shut it down from the source."

Wally gave a determined nod and turned back to his team. They continued their work, connecting more sensors and calibrating the equipment to ensure they could accurately map and analyze the parasite's influence over Renée's brain.

Marco watched every movement with an intensity born of desperation. He leaned closer to the glass, his fists clenched at his sides. "Please, Wally," he whispered, though no one in the lab could hear him. "Save her."

Jenny put a comforting hand on Marco's shoulder. "They'll do everything they can," she assured him.

———

THE GULFSTREAM STOOD MAJESTICALLY in the background of E & E's private hangar at Kennedy Airport, its engines now silent. Allison and Molly were busy loading Palmer into a blacked-out minivan, with Molly pushing his wheelchair up a ramp into the back. Allison had the case containing the parasites, her movements delicate and deliberate, as though her own child was inside that case.

Once Palmer was securely inside, Allison joined him in the back, holding the case tightly in her lap. Molly took the driver's seat, her expression focused as she started the engine. The minivan hummed to life, the engine's sound breaking the afternoon quiet.

Palmer clapped his hands together, the sound sharp and jarring in the enclosed space. "Aren't you excited, ladies?" he said gleefully, his eyes glinting with manic enthusiasm.

"Yes, my Lord." Allison and Molly replied in unison.

"Then full steam ahead," Palmer said, a satisfied smile spreading across his face.

The minivan began to move, smoothly taxiing off the runway and heading toward the Belt Parkway.

———

THE LAB AT R&D was a flurry of activity. Noah, Neil, Jenny, and Marco were still inside the observation room. On the other side of the glass, Renée lay unconscious on a medical bed, her head secured in a specialized frame designed to keep her still while the team worked. Wally stood at the center, directing the operation with a calm but focused demeanor.

"We need to be extremely careful," he said in a steady voice. "The parasite inside Renée's head is still active, and we're going to use it to trace the signal back to its source."

"Are you sure this will work?" Neil asked, pressing the intercom.

Wally nodded confidently. "Yes. The nano device is still receiving commands. If we can amplify and trace the signal, we can find out where it's coming from."

Various sensors and electrodes were connected to Renée's head, linking her to a series of monitors and a signal tracing device.

Adjusting an electrode, Wally looked up at Marco, who was watching anxiously. "This is our best shot."

"Just make sure she's safe," Marco said, his voice thick with worry. "I can't lose her."

"She'll be fine," Wally reassured him. "The restraints and monitoring systems are in place. Let's get started."

Wally initiated the trace, and the monitors began displaying complex waveforms and data streams. The room fell silent except for the soft beeps of the machines and the occasional click of a keyboard.

"We're picking up the parasite's neural activity," Wally said, his eyes glued to the screen. "Amplifying the signal now."

The monitors showed a visual representation of the signal's path, a complex web of lines and junctions. Wally used the equipment to triangulate the source, his fingers flying over the controls.

"The signal is bouncing off multiple relay points," he told them. "We need to narrow it down."

Inside the observation room, Neil was sitting at a laptop, checking a screen with a map on it, colors indicating where the signal could be coming from, the area getting smaller and smaller by the second. "Looks like it's coming from a central hub here in the US," he said.

"That's good," Noah said. "That means we won't have to go far."

"There," Jenny said, pointing at the map. "Where is that?"

Neil checked the coordinates, his face lighting up with realization. "I got it."

"OK, let's go," Noah said sharply.

On his way out, he pressed the intercom and said, "Thanks, Wally. You're the best."

Wally smiled, a hint of pride in his eyes. "Just make sure you come back in one piece."

As they headed for the door, Marco moved to follow, but Noah stopped him with a firm hand on his shoulder.

"Stay here with your wife," Noah told him, his voice gentle but resolute.

Marco looked torn but nodded, his eyes filled with gratitude and worry. "Bring them back safe," he said.

Noah gave him a reassuring nod before following Neil and Jenny out of the lab.

SIXTY-NINE

THE MIDDAY SUN SHONE BRIGHTLY OVER CENTRAL Park, bathing the landscape in a crisp, clear light. The park was alive with activity: joggers pounded the paths, dog walkers chatted amiably as their pets frolicked, picnickers spread out blankets, frisbee throwers laughed and shouted, and romantic couples snuggled on benches. It was a typical bustling March day in New York, with the trees just beginning to show the first signs of spring.

Molly pushed Palmer's wheelchair along the winding paths, Allison walking beside them, clutching the case tightly. Palmer's eyes roamed over the scenes around them, a faint smile playing on his lips.

"My, aren't they crafty, our friends the Council," he mused, his gaze shifting from one group of park-goers to another. "To build a base right beneath the feet of one of the most populous cities in the world. Just like them, really. To burrow themselves deep beneath the rest of us, like ticks on a dog."

They continued through the park, moving closer to the Inscope Arch. The air was filled with the scent of fresh grass and the distant sound of traffic, mingling with the chatter and laughter of the park's visitors.

A little farther on, Palmer asked Molly to stop. He turned to her, his expression serious. "Now, Ms. Hanson," he said softly. "You must stay here. They won't like it if they see you with us. They might suspect something. Best you stay behind. OK?"

"Yes, my Lord," Molly replied obediently.

Allison took over, pushing Palmer the rest of the way, the case resting on his lap. They reached the Inscope Arch, a grand structure that blended seamlessly with the natural beauty of the park. Like before, Allison used a card to open a discreet door, and they moved through it into a narrow tunnel.

They eventually reached a small, secure room, where Allison used her retinas to gain access. The door slid open silently, revealing a very small room with stark, metallic walls.

Palmer raised his hands. "Better put the handcuffs back on," he said calmly. "Make it look real."

Allison nodded and reapplied the handcuffs, securing them around Palmer's wrists. Then she pressed a button on the wall, and the floor beneath them began to descend.

"Isn't this splendid?" Palmer said, his voice filled with a twisted sense of wonder as they dropped into a vast chamber.

Lights flickered on, illuminating a walkway that stretched across the floor of the immense, empty room as they descended through the middle of it. As the elevator dropped into the very center, a door at the far end opened, and out stepped Seven, flanked by two armed guards.

"So here he is," Seven announced, his voice echoing inside the vast space. "The great Dr. Anthony Palmer. Good work, Eleven." Gesturing to the case on Palmer's lap, the scientist's cuffed hands resting on top, Seven asked, "What's that?"

"His research," Allison replied.

"Oh good. Then let us go inside," Seven said, satisfaction evident in his tone.

The two guards moved forward, taking over the task of pushing Palmer's wheelchair. Allison and Seven led the way, their footsteps reverberating in the immense, empty space.

As they walked, Palmer's eyes gleamed with a mixture of anticipation and satisfaction. He knew that the next phase of his plan was about to unfold, and he relished the thought of the chaos it would bring.

———

NOAH HAD CALLED in a favor with the nearby US Airforce base, securing two F-22 Raptors and a pilot. The two fighter jets now streaked across the sky, slicing through the atmosphere with incredible speed as the United States of America rolled by underneath. Noah sat in the back seat of one of the Raptors, his mind focused and ready. The pilot in front of him, a seasoned Air Force veteran, expertly guided the aircraft as they rocketed toward their destination.

In the other Raptor, Jenny piloted with skill and determination, her eyes locked on the horizon. Neil sat behind her, monitoring their instruments and communications, ensuring that they stayed on course. The sleek jets were traveling at almost Mach 1.6, being that their mission required speed.

The source of Palmer's American signal was their target, and they were closing in fast.

"How are we doing, Lieutenant?" Noah asked through the headset.

"ETA five minutes, sir," the pilot responded. "We're making good time."

Noah nodded, glancing out of the canopy at the blurred landscape below. They were flying low and fast, the ground a mere blur beneath them. He could see the other Raptor keeping pace beside them—a symbol of their united front.

In the other jet, Jenny's hands were steady on the controls. "Almost there," she said, her voice crackling through the comms.

"We're right on target, baby," Neil replied, double-checking their coordinates.

The two Raptors roared over the landscape, their sleek forms cutting through the air with unmatched efficiency. Below them, the cityscape gave way to more rural areas, their destination drawing ever closer.

———

DEEP within the hidden base beneath Central Park, Seven, Allison and Dr. Anthony Palmer were inside a secure conference room. The guards stationed outside the door ensured that their meeting would remain undisturbed. The room was stark and utilitarian, the walls lined with soundproofing panels and the lighting subdued.

The three of them sat around a large conference table, the case containing the parasites resting ominously in the center. Seven's eyes were fixed on it, his curiosity barely contained.

"So this contains working samples that can be linked to the Mindweaver program he was running?" Seven asked, his voice filled with fascination.

"Yes," Allison replied. "And now they are yours."

Seven nodded slowly, a gleam of excitement in his eyes. "Open it up."

Allison stood, moving to the windows and closing the blinds, plunging the room into near darkness. The only light now came from the overhead fixtures, casting a sterile glow over the table. She returned to her seat, and then, with deliberate and meticulous movements, opened the case, revealing the parasites writhing inside their incubation containers.

Seven's eyes widened in awe as he gazed at the creatures. Their movements were eerie, almost hypnotic, as they squirmed within their confines.

"Would you like to see one in practice?" Allison asked.

All the while, Palmer watched from the edge of the table, a satisfied smile playing on his lips. His eyes flickered between Allison and Seven, a glint of amusement and anticipation in his gaze.

"Yes, show me," Seven said, his voice barely a whisper.

Allison carefully reached into the case, extracting one of the incubation containers. She placed it gently on the table, the parasite within reacting to the change in environment, its movements becoming more agitated.

THE F-22S HAD GOTTEN them as far as the airport, where they'd jumped into a waiting Dodge Durango. The SUV was now skidding to a halt outside a suburban house on the edge of Seattle, Washington.

The house was marked with old police tape fluttering in the breeze, a reminder of the tragedy that had occurred six months ago. Noah, Jenny, and Neil exited the vehicle in a hurry.

A neighbor, who had been mowing his lawn, stopped and approached them as they marched down the driveway toward the house.

"Hey, what are you doing?" the neighbor asked, concern etched on his face.

"It's OK," Neil said, flashing a quick, reassuring smile. "We're with the American government."

"Oh. You know the guy killed his family, right?" the neighbor continued.

"We do, sir. Yes. Now go back to your mowing," Neil replied, trying to keep the exchange brief.

"His wife and daughter were real nice. But he was real up himself. Too clever to talk to his neighbors..." the man rambled on.

"Please, sir," Neil interrupted, his patience wearing thin.

With the neighbor reluctantly returning to his lawn, the team picked the lock of the front door and rushed inside. The house was eerily quiet, the remnants of a once-normal life scattered about in disarray. They quickly located the entrance to the basement and descended into the dimly lit space, where they found the sealed door of Palmer's lab.

"That's why I brought this," Jenny said, unslinging a rucksack and pulling out a tube of plastic explosive.

Seconds later, they were upstairs, crouched in anticipation. Jenny held out her phone, her thumb hovering over the detonation button. "Fire in the hole," she called out, pressing down.

The explosion shook the house, the sound reverberating through the quiet neighborhood. Smoke billowed up the basement stairs as they rushed back down.

In the basement lab, they found the terminal, half-hidden among the debris, the room filled with the acrid smell of burnt electronics and the haze of smoke.

"Shut it off," Noah instructed Neil, who immediately took a seat at the terminal.

"OK," Neil said, his fingers flying over the keyboard. He quickly assessed the security measures in place and pulled out a USB stick from Jenny's rucksack, linking it up to the terminal to download malware designed to breach the system.

"This may take some time," Neil warned, his eyes focused intently on the screen.

———

DEEP within the underground Council base, the atmosphere in the conference room was charged with anticipation. Allison stood by the table, opening a container. Inside, the parasite wriggled and writhed. Seven sat across from her, his eyes fixed on the nematode, fascination evident on his face.

"So tell me, Doc," Seven said, his voice tinged with curiosity, "how does it work?"

Palmer, seated beside Allison, began to explain, his tone measured and authoritative. "Nematocerebrus dominatus, our little friend here, latches on to the brain of a human host. Once attached, it gives our Mindweaver device access to the human brain, allowing us to control neural pathways and influence behavior."

Allison carefully lifted the parasite, holding it between her fingers. The creature squirmed, its body reacting to the air. As she brought it closer to Seven, it began to move more vigorously, as though sensing the presence of a potential host.

Palmer continued, his voice steady, "The parasite integrates itself with the host's nervous system, establishing a link that allows for precise control and manipulation."

Allison brought the parasite even closer, her eyes fixed on Seven. The parasite writhed more energetically, its instinct driving it toward Seven's ear.

"Incredible," Seven said, his eyes fixed to the parasite as Allison brought it closer.

Without warning, she grabbed Seven by the back of the head, forcing the worm to his ear, the parasite latching on to him.

Seven stood up abruptly, his hands clawing at his ear as the parasite burrowed deeper. His thrashing became frantic, his face contorted with pain and fear. At the same time, Allison moved to Palmer and released him from his handcuffs.

"Thank you, my dear," Palmer said, rubbing his wrists, a satisfied smile on his face.

Seven's movements slowed, and then he stopped altogether, his body going rigid. For a moment, the room was silent, the only sound the faint hum of the base's ventilation system.

"Are you OK there, Seven?" Palmer asked, his tone almost mocking.

Seven turned around slowly, his eyes glassy and his movements robotic. "Yes, my Lord," he replied in a flat voice.

Palmer's smile widened, a look of triumph in his eyes. "Excellent. Now we will proceed with the next phase of our plan."

———

BACK IN THE basement of Anthony Palmer's former suburban home, the heat was rising. Neil sat at the terminal, his fingers flying over the keyboard as he worked to break into Palmer's system.

"Come on, Neil," Jenny urged her husband. She stood on his left shoulder, her eyes darting between the screen and the basement door, half-expecting trouble at any moment.

"I'm working as hard as I can," Neil replied, his voice strained. Sweat beaded on his forehead as he continued to type furiously, plotting a course through layers of security protocols.

Noah stood on Neil's right, a hand resting on his shoulder, offering silent support. "You've got this, Neil. Just a little more," he said.

Neil's fingers never stopped moving, each keystroke bringing them closer to shutting down the system.

"Almost there," Neil muttered, his eyes narrowing as he hit another barrier.

SEVEN WHEELED Palmer into the vast operations room of the underground base, Allison walking beside them. The walls were lined with monitors displaying images from around the world: inside palaces, government buildings, military facilities—all the activities that the Council was currently controlling and watching.

"The world right there at your fingertips," Palmer said, his gaze sweeping across the monitors.

Council members worked diligently at their stations, the hum of activity filling the room. They kept to their tasks as Seven guided Palmer to the center.

"And now it is all mine," Palmer declared, his smile widening as he took in the scene. The power and control before him were intoxicating. He would defeat the Council using its own weapons, its own people.

He was on the cusp of getting exactly what he wanted.

INSIDE PALMER'S BASEMENT LAB, Neil's face lit up with triumph. "Got it!" he cried out.

He pressed the final key, ending the program and shutting it down. The screens flickered and then went dark, signaling the end of the control Mindweaver had over their hosts.

Jenny let out a breath she didn't realize she had been

holding. She threw her arms around Neil, hugging him tightly. "You did it, baby! You did it!" she exclaimed in a voice brimming with pride and relief.

Noah stepped forward, a broad smile spreading across his face. "Good man," he said, clapping a hand on Neil's shoulder.

As Dr. Anthony Palmer's smile grew, an unexpected horror began to unfold. Seven and Allison, standing beside him, suddenly began jerking and coughing, their bodies convulsing as the parasites inside them started to eject.

Palmer's eyes widened in shock and disbelief as he watched the nematodes, previously so firmly integrated, begin to burrow their way out of Seven's and Allison's ears. The scene was grotesque, the parasites writhing and pushing their way free, leaving a trail of blood in their wake.

Around them, the Council members stopped their work, their faces masks of horror and confusion. The room, once buzzing with controlled activity, descended into an unsettling silence.

"Sir," one of the Council members said, rushing to Seven's side, "are you OK?"

Seven's body continued to convulse, his eyes rolling back as the parasite finally freed itself and dropped to the floor, twitching and writhing. Allison was no better, collapsing to her knees as her parasite completed its violent exit.

She gasped, her hand instinctively reaching up to touch her ear, feeling the warm trickle of blood. Catching her breath, she was disoriented but quickly came back to her senses.

Seven, meanwhile, gathered himself, the shock of the sudden freedom from control replaced by a surge of fury. His eyes locked on to Palmer, who sat in his wheelchair, looking both horrified and incredulous.

"Get him!" Seven shouted at the armed guards stationed at the edge of the room. "I want him hung in a cell!"

SEVENTY

NOAH, JENNY, AND NEIL WALKED OUT OF THE house into the fresh Seattle air. As they moved toward the Dodge Durango, Noah's phone buzzed. It was Molly.

"Molly, where are you?" Noah asked the second he answered the call.

"Noah, I'm... I'm at Central Park," Molly's voice came through, slightly shaky. "And... oh my God, it's Allison! She's here!"

Noah's heart skipped a beat. "Allison? Is she okay?"

Molly's voice grew louder as she approached Allison. "She's staggering toward me. Noah, she looks... exhausted."

There was a pause, and then another voice came on the line. "Noah, it's me," Allison said, her voice weak but clear. "I lost Palmer. I don't know where he is. I came to not far from here, under the Inscope Arch. He was gone when I woke up."

"You're safe now, that's what matters," Noah replied. "We'll regroup and find him. Just stay there with Molly."

Jenny and Neil exchanged relieved glances as Noah continued, "We're on our way to get you. We'll figure out our next move together."

He ended the call, turning to Jenny and Neil with a determined expression. "She's safe. Palmer's on the loose, but we'll find him. Let's go."

They quickly climbed into the Dodge Durango, driving off with renewed focus. The hunt for Palmer wasn't over, but now they had Allison and Molly back—and that was a victory in itself.

EPILOGUE

A WEEK LATER, NOAH STOOD ON THE VERANDA OF his lakeside farmhouse, gazing out at the reflection of the mountains on the still, serene lake. The sun was setting, casting a golden hue over the landscape. The tranquility surrounding him was very different than the turmoil roiling away inside of him.

He took a deep breath, the crisp air filling his lungs, but it did little to ease his mind. His thoughts were consumed by the horror he'd witnessed on Sumba, and the ever-present threat of Palmer's next move. The weight of it all felt crushing.

As he stood lost in thought, he felt a gentle hand on his shoulder. He turned to find his wife, Sarah, her eyes filled with concern and love. Beside her was Norah, her innocent eyes wide as she looked up at her father.

"Daddy," Norah said softly, reaching up to hug him.

Noah knelt down, scooping her into his arms. "Hey, princess," he said. "How's my girl?"

"I'm good, Daddy. Mommy and I made cookies. Do you want one?"

Noah managed a smile, holding her close. "I'd love one, sweetheart. But maybe later."

Sarah moved closer, wrapping her arms around both of them. "We're here for you, Noah," she whispered, her voice soothing. "Whatever happens, we're in this together."

———

DETECTIVE GORAN ANTARA stood with his superiors at Pura Luhur, the temple site, a place now crawling with Indonesian CSIs meticulously combing through every inch. The once-sacred ground had become a scene of intense scrutiny, with photographers snapping pictures and forensics gathering evidence. The world's media clustered at the edges of Eden, their cameras and microphones ready to capture any detail.

Antara explained to his superiors, "The steps over there were where Palmer's people would infect new arrivals. It was a systematic process."

One of his superiors, a stern-looking man with graying hair, nodded gravely. "We need to ensure that every corner of this place is examined."

Just as Antara was about to continue, a voice called out from behind him. "Detective Antara, there's someone here for you."

He turned to see one of his colleagues waving him over. Antara excused himself and walked briskly toward the perimeter of the site. As he approached, his heart skipped a beat. There, standing amidst the clamor, were Renée and Marco.

Antara's face broke into a wide smile, and he quickened his pace. Renée and Marco did the same, and they met in a tight, emotional embrace.

"I'm so glad you made it out," Antara said. "It's so good to see you both."

"It's good to see you too, Goran," Renée replied. "It was pretty close out there."

Marco nodded, clapping Antara on the back. "We never thought we'd all be standing here together again. It's a miracle."

The three of them stood there for a moment, taking in the gravity of their reunion. The world around them seemed to fade as they reminisced about their time together.

After a while, Antara's superior approached, a curious look on his face. "Detective, are these friends of yours?"

"Yes, sir," Antara replied. "This is Renée and Marco. They're the ones I told you about. Renée and Marco, this is Detective Bintang. He was the one I was looking for on Sumba."

The second Detective Bintang heard who they were, a grateful expression came over his countenance. He stepped forward, shaking both their hands vigorously. "Then I owe you my thanks," Bintang said. "Because you saved my life from this nightmare. You saved all our lives from this nightmare."

As the sun began to set, casting a golden glow over the temple, the reunited friends stood together, their resolve strengthening under the weight of their shared experiences and the gratitude of those they had saved, ready to face whatever challenges lay ahead.

———

NEIL AND JENNY stepped out of their car onto the familiar streets of Kataka, Sumba. The pleasant hillside town, surrounded by lush greenery and small one-story wooden houses, was a stark contrast to the chaos they had recently endured on these very same streets.

As they walked through the village, they were greeted by friendly faces and warm smiles. The community had endured much, but the strength and resilience of its people were evident in every interaction. Neil and Jenny followed a winding path to a small, cozy house at the edge of the village.

Damu was waiting for them at the gate, a broad smile lighting up his face. "Neil, Jenny, it's so good to see you!" he called out, waving them over.

"Damu!" Neil replied, his voice filled with genuine happiness. "It's great to see you, too."

As they approached, Kiya ran out from the house. "Jenny! Neil! You came!" she exclaimed, hugging them both tightly.

"Of course we did," Jenny said, her eyes sparkling with joy. "We wouldn't miss this for the world."

Sama, Damu's wife and Kiya's mother, appeared at the doorway, wiping her hands on a cloth. "Welcome, welcome," she said warmly. "Please, come in. We've prepared a meal for you."

Inside, the house was filled with the delicious aromas of home-cooked food. The table was set with an array of traditional dishes, each one a testament to Sama's culinary skills. They all sat down together, the atmosphere relaxed and filled with a sense of family and belonging.

As they began to eat, the conversation flowed easily. Neil and Jenny shared stories from their recent adventures, careful to keep the more frightening details to themselves. Damu, Kiya, and Sama talked about how life had slowly returned to normal, their gratitude for the peace that had finally settled over the island evident in every word.

"I'm just glad to see you all safe and happy," Neil said, lifting his glass in a toast. "To family, friends and to better days ahead."

"To family and friends," everyone echoed, clinking their glasses together.

———

DEEP beneath the Earth's surface, in the cold, sterile confines of an underground lab, Dr. Anthony Palmer sat hunched over a terminal, his fingers moving mechanically across the keyboard.

Palmer's blue eyes, once sharp and full of ambition, now stared vacantly at the screen before him. The Mindweaver program, his creation, was running countless simulations, each more complex than the last. Yet, despite the monumental work being done, Palmer seemed detached, as if the man who once commanded respect and fear was now only a shell of his former self.

The hours bled together in the windowless lab. The only indication of time's passage was the slow, methodical work he continued to perform, not out of passion, but obligation.

His thoughts were a jumbled mess, memories of the past and the realities of his present merging into one continuous, exhausting loop.

As he worked, a small bead of blood formed at the corner of his ear. It lingered there for a moment before gravity took hold, pulling it down his face until it finally dropped onto the cold metal surface of his desk. The crimson droplet stood out starkly against the sterile environment, unnoticed by Palmer as he continued to work.

A fellow scientist, passing by, caught sight of the blood. He quickly approached, concern etched on his face. "Oh, Tony," the scientist said, his voice gentle yet tinged with pity. He reached into his lab coat and pulled out a tissue, carefully wiping the blood from Palmer's face and the desk. "That thing inside you has made a mess."

Palmer paused, his hands stilling on the keyboard as he slowly turned to look at the scientist. His eyes, devoid of emotion, met the man's concerned gaze. "Thank you," he replied, his voice flat, almost robotic.

The scientist studied Palmer for a moment longer, the hollowness in the man before him a stark contrast to the vibrant, driven individual he once knew. With a sigh, the scientist patted Palmer on the shoulder, a futile gesture of comfort, before moving on to attend to his own work.

Palmer watched him go, then turned back to the terminal. The Mindweaver program continued to run, the screens filled with data that once would have excited him. Now they were nothing more than numbers and figures, part of a machine he was no longer in control of.

Don't miss WOLVES IN THE DARK. The riveting sequel in the Noah Wolf Thriller series.

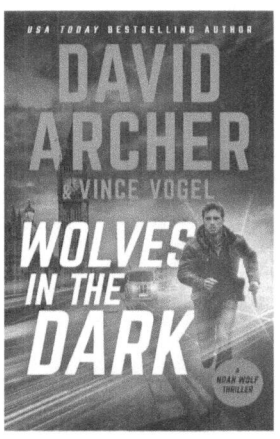

Scan the QR code below to purchase WOLVES IN THE DARK.
Or go to: righthouse.com/wolves-in-the-dark

DON'T MISS ANYTHING!

If you want to stay up to date on all new releases in this series, with this author, or with any of our new deals, you can do so by joining our newsletters below.

In addition, you will immediately gain access to our entire *Right House VIP Library*, which currently includes *THE WAY OF THE WOLF*—a prequel in the Noah Wolf series.

righthouse.com/email

(Easy to unsubscribe. No spam. Ever.)

ALSO BY DAVID ARCHER

Up to date books can be found at:

www.righthouse.com/david-archer

ROGUE THRILLERS

Gates of Hell (Book 1)

Hell's Fury (Book 2)

PETER BLACK THRILLERS

Burden of the Assassin (Book 1)

The Man Without A Face (Book 2)

Unpunished Deeds (Book 3)

Hunter Killer (Book 4)

Silent Shadows (Book 5)

The Last Run (Book 6)

Dark Corners (Book 7)

Ghost Operative (Book 8)

A Fire Burning (Book 9)

ALEX MASON THRILLERS

Origins (Prequel - Free)

Odin (Book 1)

Ice Cold Spy (Book 2)

Mason's Law (Book 3)

Assets and Liabilities (Book 4)

Russian Roulette (Book 5)

Executive Order (Book 6)

Dead Man Talking (Book 7)

All The King's Men (Book 8)

Flashpoint (Book 9)

Brotherhood of the Goat (Book 10)

Dead Hot (Book 11)

Blood on Megiddo (Book 12)

Son of Hell (Book 13)

Merchant of Death (Book 14)

NOAH WOLF THRILLERS

Way of the Wolf (Prequel - Free)

Code Name Camelot (Book 1)

Lone Wolf (Book 2)

In Sheep's Clothing (Book 3)

Hit for Hire (Book 4)

The Wolf's Bite (Book 5)

Black Sheep (Book 6)

Balance of Power (Book 7)

Time to Hunt (Book 8)

Red Square (Book 9)

Highest Order (Book 10)

Edge of Anarchy (Book 11)

Unknown Evil (Book 12)

Black Harvest (Book 13)

World Order (Book 14)

Caged Animal (Book 15)

Deep Allegiance (Book 16)

Pack Leader (Book 17)

High Treason (Book 18)

A Wolf Among Men (Book 19)

Rogue Intelligence (Book 20)

Alpha (Book 21)

Rogue Wolf (Book 22)

Shadows of Allegiance (Book 23)

In the Grip of Darkness (Book 24)

Wolves in the Dark (Book 25)

SAM PRICHARD MYSTERIES

Fallback (Prequel - Free)

The Grave Man (Book 1)

Death Sung Softly (Book 2)

Love and War (Book 3)

Framed (Book 4)

The Kill List (Book 5)

Drifter: Part One (Book 6)

Drifter: Part Two (Book 7)

Drifter: Part Three (Book 8)

The Last Song (Book 9)

Ghost (Book 10)

Hidden Agenda (Book 11)

SAM AND INDIE MYSTERIES

Aces and Eights (Book 1)

Fact or Fiction (Book 2)

Close to Home (Book 3)

Brave New World (Book 4)

Innocent Conspiracy (Book 5)

Unfinished Business (Book 6)

Live Bait (Book 7)

Alter Ego (Book 8)

More Than It Seems (Book 9)

Moving On (Book 10)

Worst Nightmare (Book 11)

Chasing Ghosts (Book 12)

Serial Superstition (Book 13)

CHANCE REDDICK THRILLERS

Innocent Injustice (Book 1)

Angel of Justice (Book 2)

High Stakes Hunting (Book 3)

Personal Asset (Book 4)

CASSIE MCGRAW MYSTERIES

What Lies Beneath (Book 1)

Can't Fight Fate (Book 2)

One Last Game (Book 3)

Never Really Gone (Book 4)

ABOUT US

Right House is an independent publisher created by authors for readers. We specialize in Action, Thriller, Mystery, and Crime novels.

If you enjoyed this novel, then there is a good chance you will like what else we have to offer! Please stay up to date by using any of the links below.

Join our mailing lists to stay up to date -->
righthouse.com/email
Visit our website --> righthouse.com
Contact us --> contact@righthouse.com

facebook.com/righthousebooks
x.com/righthousebooks
instagram.com/righthousebooks

www.ingramcontent.com/pod-product-compliance
Lightning Source LLC
Chambersburg PA
CBHW020510260626
47156CB00006B/1949